A DREAM OF A
WOMAN

Stories

Casey Plett

ARSENAL PULP PRESS
VANCOUVER

A DREAM OF A WOMAN
Copyright © 2021 by Casey Plett

ARSENAL PULP PRESS
Suite 202 – 211 East Georgia St.
Vancouver, BC V6A 1Z6
Canada
arsenalpulp.com

The publisher gratefully acknowledges the support of the Canada Council for the Arts and the British Columbia Arts Council for its publishing program, and the Government of Canada, and the Government of British Columbia (through the Book Publishing Tax Credit Program), for its publishing activities.

Arsenal Pulp Press acknowledges the xʷməθkʷəy̓əm (Musqueam), Sḵwx̱wú7mesh (Squamish), and səl̓ilwəta?ɬ (Tsleil-Waututh) Nations, custodians of the traditional, ancestral, and unceded territories where our office is located. We pay respect to their histories, traditions, and continuous living cultures and commit to accountability, respectful relations, and friendship.

This is a work of fiction. Any resemblance of characters to persons either living or deceased is purely coincidental.

"Couldn't Hear You Talk Anymore" first appeared in the *Offing*, Trans Issue 2015, November 23, 2015.
"Floodway" first appeared in *Your Impossible Voice*, Issue 23, Fall 2020.
"Hazel & Christopher" first appeared in the December 6 instalment of the Short Story Advent Calendar 2019 (ed. Michael Hingston).

Cover and text design by Jazmin Welch
Cover art by Carly Bodnar and Sybil Lamb
Edited by Shirarose Wilensky
Proofread by Alison Strobel

Printed and bound in Canada

Library and Archives Canada Cataloguing in Publication:
Title: A dream of a woman : stories / Casey Plett.
Names: Plett, Casey, author.
Identifiers: Canadiana (print) 20210217553 | Canadiana (ebook) 20210217596 | ISBN 9781551528564 (softcover) | ISBN 9781551528571 (HTML)
Classification: LCC PS8631.L48 D74 2021 | DDC C813/.6—dc23

For Sarah B.
(Miss you, always)

And for Juanita
(Sorry about the rough parts.)

"Why do they say ghosts are cold?
Mine are warm, a breath dampening your cheek,
a voice when you thought you were alone."
—JULIE BUNTIN, *Marlena*

"Temporarily could last a long time."
—ALISON STINE, *Road Out of Winter*

Contents

HAZEL & CHRISTOPHER

1

When Hazel grew up and moved out of the prairies, she would learn from movies and the news that small towns were supposed to be poor and dying. But Hazel never thought of her unhappy childhood as horrific, and Christopher's family was not only happy but rich. They lived in a cul-de-sac next to a canola field in a house with a wide yard surrounded by poplars; they were always renovating their basement. If you had pressed Hazel as a child, she maybe could've admitted she was jealous. In a glossily submerged way, maybe. Mostly, in that time she just loved being Christopher's best friend.

When they first touched each other they were eight, sleeping in an old inner room without windows in the basement. They were hyper and laughing hard, and then her eyes were close to the freckles on his shoulders.

They talked about gayness exactly once, just after Hazel and her mom moved across the province. They were on the phone and about to start high school. Hazel was in a stage of proto-transness, a stage in which she was terrified of herself and had no idea why.

She brought it up this way: "What do you think about gay people? Are they okay, or should they be killed? I don't know."

"They should probably be killed," Christopher said.

"Okay."

They talked on the phone a lot after Hazel moved away. She'd always wondered if Christopher remembered that. It would've been unusual for two boys. ("Boys.") Her mom let her call him for twenty minutes on the weekend. Long distance. Hazel would say, "But you talk to your boyfriend every night for hours!" And Hazel's mom, forever calm, would respond, "This'll make more sense to you as an adult."

It did make sense to Hazel now, if not in the way her mother probably imagined.

Christopher was always happy to talk. He didn't have the same emotional needs as Hazel back then, and even as a young teenager, Hazel recognized that. But he always made time for her. He did.

Hazel last saw Christopher when she was twenty. Home from out west, knowing her boy days were numbered, as were the reasons to come back to this part of the world. She and her mom were at her aunt's for Christmas, and Hazel walked from the other end of town in the snow, the creak of her boots the only sound in the pale afternoon sunset.

She walked in the door of Christopher's house and no one was on the first floor. She went down to the basement, noticed a bedroom off to the side with power tools everywhere and half-installed hardwood floors. In the rec room, Christopher and a couple other guys were watching *The Departed* with a two-four of Bud. (There was a particular kind of American, Hazel had learned since, who was bummed to know that Canadians drank Bud.) One of the guys said he wanted more beer but hated the girl who worked at the vendor.

Hazel had felt herself teetering on an edge then, between a fear of how volatile it might be to continue knowing these boys and a distant sadness at the knowledge that she might never see these stupid fuckers again.

Funnily enough, there *had* been a trans guy in town, her age, who'd come out around a year prior. He'd announced himself, then right away skipped off to the city. Hazel brought up his name like a test, like hazarding an exhibition round.

"So you guys hear about ...?"

"Oh God, the *dyke*!"

And everyone laughed.

"I have no problem with gay people," Christopher said. "But gender reassignment ..." A visible shiver came over him, something real and revulsive. He shook his head like he'd stomped on something crawly and was trying to forget about it.

When the two-four ran out, they all went to a party where the kitchen counters were so covered with bottles you couldn't see the laminate. A snarling boy said, "Who the fuck is that?" when Hazel arrived and Christopher said, "It's cool. He's from here," and the boy backed off and Hazel glowed as if she'd received wings. They all did shots, then played a drinking game, then drank rum out of Solo cups, then shotgunned beers in the garage with their coats on, and when Hazel stumbled into a wall, the boys laughed and said incredulously, "Are you *drunk*?!" It was seven p.m. and the moon was shining behind a blanket of clouds and after that they went to the bar.

Weeks later Hazel got on a plane and flew back west, and then she transitioned, then dropped out of school, and then fell away from all she'd ever known. And as the following decade churned, in tiny rooms in roiling bright cities, the thought of Christopher would flit down onto her, like a moonbeam startling her awake.

❧

Ten years later, she crash-landed back home—untriumphantly bunking with her mother in the city, the prairie winter beginning its months-long descent into lightlessness. And, among other things, she began to search for him.

She didn't have any friends left in Pilot Mound. Her aunt wouldn't talk to her, and her mother didn't know anything. Hazel couldn't even fucking find anything about Christopher on social media. Last she'd heard, years ago, he'd moved to the city, too. Even his parents she couldn't track down.

Idly and with pleasure, she set up her OkCupid preferences for him—boys of a certain age and height range. She looked for boys with red hair and dustings of freckles around their collarbones. She checked this every week or so. Whenever she heard of anyone with the name Chris, she would ask, "No chance you mean Christopher Penner, do you?"

Hazel really didn't expect anything to come of this. Her searches were like periodically buying a lottery ticket: a nice, dependable, dopamine-filled surge where the come-up of hope somehow always eclipsed the comedown of disappointment.

She wasn't doing much with her days besides going to AA and volunteering with a nascent sex workers' rights organization, of whose members Hazel was somehow the only one who'd ever touched boy parts for money. The nights she was home, she made dinner for her mom, though usually Hazel's mom was at her boyfriend's place or at work, and usually that suited Hazel just fine.

She had no idea what to do with her existence—if she had a future, or if she wanted one. In the absence of the alcohol she'd flooded herself with for half her life, her tired, newly sober body had handed her a sense of alertness she hadn't felt since she was a teenager. At the same time, she also felt herself turning into a slug as that body barely moved. Many days, she never left the house. She slept and watched Netflix and cooked.

Hazel figured, sooner or later, one of three things would happen:

1. Welfare would dump her.
2. She'd fall off the wagon.
3. Her mom would move in with her boyfriend, who, no matter how well he got along with Hazel, would be unlikely to, in tandem, take in a thirty-year-old transsexual ex-hooker in recovery.

Or maybe all of those things would happen at once. Regardless, she didn't imagine this quiet un-life would last forever. So, in the meantime, she hoarded her cash, went to AA and the nascent sex work-ers' rights organization, and shut off her brain. And one of few bright spots in imagining her future was when she indulged this loving spot in her past and scanned the internet in search of Christopher.

∽

Well, Hazel did do one other unusual thing in this period. She went on a date.

Marina from the nascent sex workers' rights organization—Marina who was not a sex worker but who was a grad student—introduced them. Marina knew the guy through a lefty something-or-other. Hazel had seen him around at a couple things. He was cute. Tall, blond hair, glasses. Good politics, ungregarious. Hazel was into all of this.

"You're getting dressed up?" asked her mom that evening.

Hazel was in the bathroom with the door open, in a flowery blue dress, applying eyeliner.

"I'm going on a date," said Hazel.

"A date," said her mom slowly. "Where?"

"Baked Expectations."

"No kidding," said her mom. "Your dad and I went there once. Long time ago."

"I haven't been on a date in years. A real date, anyway. I don't remember the last time that happened." Hazel said this awkwardly, still relearning how to talk to her mother, as an adult, a woman, a person commiserating.

Her mother softened at this. "No, huh?"

"Nope."

"It'd be nice if you met someone," her mom said quietly.

Hazel turned to look at her. *What a normal conversation,* she thought. *What a normal conversation for a daughter and a mother to be having.* Her mother shut the door behind her, and Hazel stared at the towel hanging on a hook, her feet shifting in the fluff of the rug.

The guy had a steaming tea in front of him when she sat down, and he invited her to get a coffee or something.

That was the most disappointing part. *Not even dinner?* Hazel thought.

He didn't get her, but he was smart, turned out to run an after-school arts program, and by the end of the night she'd started to like him. "I did a workshop in the country," he said. "Seventh-day Adventists, right? And they asked me if I was an atheist, and I said yes.

They had this look of shock on their faces. Then they said to me—I swear—they said, 'Do you live in Osborne Village?'"

Hazel laughed.

It was eleven o'clock when he revealed he had a wife. And a kid at home. They were opening up their relationship after thirteen years. "She's cool with us being here," he stressed, as if this would soothe her. When he drove her home, he joked about making out in the car and she got out the second he parked.

Then a Facebook message half an hour later: *I wish I had kissed you. I just wasn't sure if you wanted to. I'm not always totally sensitive to*—blah blah blah blah blah blah blah blah blah blah blah blah blah blah blah blah blah blah blah blah blah blah blah blah blah blah blah blah blah blah blah blah blah blah blah blah blah blah blah blah blah blah blah blah blah blah blah blah blah blah blah blah blah blah blah blah blah blah blah blah blah blah blah blah blah blah blah blah blah blah blah blah blah blah blah blah blah blah blah blah blah blah blah blah blah blah blah blah blah blah blah blah blah blah blah blah blah.

⌒

"How was your date?" her mom asked the next evening.

Hazel savoured the excited look on her mother's face, letting its image settle and take root in her mind.

"He had a wife and kids."

"Ew!" her mom said instantly.

"I know."

"Ugh! I. Well. You deserve better. I suppose that's all I'll say. You deserve better than someone expecting you to—slink around."

Hazel didn't tell her she wouldn't have had to slink around, that that was the thing that pissed her off, the burning phrase in her head: "She's cool with us being here." *I don't care how goddamn cool your wife is.*

So the wife gave the other woman her blessing now? That was supposed to change things? Why wouldn't Marina have mentioned this? (Would she have done so with a cis girl?) If this was how things were, was it really so weird she wanted to see what Christopher was up to these days?

⌇

Months later, after the new year, she was restless. Her mom was spending more time at her boyfriend's. She'd filled out some job applications for real, but her heart wasn't in it. Plus, firmly committing herself to alcoholism and sex work for much of her twenties hadn't done much for her resumé.

The nascent sex workers' rights organization was plugging along, though. It had grown to ten members and consisted of two factions: white academics/camgirls and twinky Metis social workers. The latter were starting to get their way after a disastrous public event led by the former.

Hazel didn't say much in the meetings. When she'd joined she'd hoped to just do boring legwork, but once it became clear the group was in its infancy—and the others discovered her to be not only the sole transsexual but also the sole person who'd sucked dick for money—suddenly everyone wanted her *opinion* on things, and a decade of Facebook and queer culture had made Hazel very tired of needing to have opinions.

So when Festival du Voyageur came along, Hazel went, and she went alone. She wanted to be in a crowd and watch people get stupid. She put on her old faux-fur coat and vamped up with thick makeup and a purple toque and caught the 29 up Route 70 and then the 10 over to Saint Boniface and began to feel alive and did not want to drink, not one iota. Hazel felt good about it. Those two things had been connected for a long time.

Drinking socially was never her problem anyway. Passing the LC after dark, being alone and sleepless ten blocks from the late-night vendor—that was hard. But now? Going to watch idiots instead of being the idiot? That was fun.

She had her last thirty dollars for the month in her pocket and paid fifteen to go in and watch Radio Radio thrill a crowd in a tent. Wandering outside in a chill of French and English and pretty young people in spacesuit coats, she saw a stand advertising *Giant Perogy Poutine with Bacon—$10* and barked, "Ha!" to no one. *Throw in some bannock to soak up the gravy and you'd have the peak Manitoba food,* she thought. Then she bought one.

Twenty minutes later, she was walking back from vomiting in the porta potties, but even that didn't feel horrible—who knew the last time she'd thrown up from something besides drinking? It felt innocent in its own way.

It was while drinking water in front of the main tent that she spotted red hair in a circle of snowsuits, and right then, Hazel knew.

She lingered on the periphery of the circle. The one talking was an alpha type with a ball cap who looked so much like Christopher's old buddy Matthew. The whole group, actually, looked like those guys from years ago.

Christopher glanced at her for a second's blankness, and then went back to listening to the ball cap.

Hazel thought, *He still looks so young. He looks so unbelievably young.*

Tall—a couple inches taller than Hazel. She'd forgotten. His hair grown just over his ears. Blue mitts, a grey toque sticking up like a chef's hat. And blue eyes with a ring of gold inside them. She was that close to him.

And he'd looked through her at first, as if she was any other girl. A specific kind of joy came to her in that, a joy she would always treasure in not being noticed.

The boys left to go back inside, and she said, "Christopher?"

He stopped, confused. "Yeah?"

"It's Hazel," she said.

"Hazel?"

At first he didn't get it, and she waited for him to at best laugh, or go lifeless. But then it was beautiful—old Hollywood in the finest way—and Hazel would never forget this scene for as long as she lived. A dawn of recognition travelled across Christopher's body. She said, "Hazel Cameron," and took off her toque and shook out her hair, letting it spill down her fake-fur coat, and then she added, "From Pilot Mound."

His face spread and cracked, like sunlight coming out of an egg.

"We used to know each other," she said, smiling. "A long time ago."

"HOLY SHIT! HAZEL!" And without another word (they came later: "You look amazing!" "I've thought about you for years!"), he hugged her. He hugged her and lifted her off the ground, her boots kicking and her nose buried in the back of his hair. It all really happened exactly like that.

On the first call (he called), she made it clear: "Do you want to go have dinner with me?"

"Yes," he said immediately. "Yes, I do."

"Like a date," Hazel said, unwilling to entertain any maybe fantasies anymore. "You realize this, right? I'm asking you to go on a date."

I sound like I'm his boss, she thought, leaning against the kitchen cabinets while her mom's dinner burned.

"Yes," he said again. "Yes. I want to go on a date with you, too."

⟋

They went to Paradise, that Italian place by Gordon Bell with the tinted windows. It was almost empty, with a sweet, apologetic, middle-aged waiter and menus with two-word items and no descriptions and prices that, if Christopher didn't offer to pay, were just low enough for Hazel to still make it to next month.

"Well, fuck, I dunno—you were in Toronto, then?" he said to her. Christopher was in a hoodie and khakis, and Hazel was in a pencil skirt.

"Montreal," she said. "Though I did live in Toronto a couple years. And Vancouver before that."

"I went with my parents to Montreal once," he remarked. "In high school. For a fencing competition."

"The fuck?" she said with a laugh. "A fencing competition?"

"I was on the fencing team in high school! I did it all four years. I"—he paused with a sense of grandeur—"was internationally competitive."

"Internationally competitive?"

"We went to Fargo once," he said.

"Wow."

"Montreal was better."

"Yeah."

"You still play hockey?" she said. (Christopher was always into sports, Hazel tagging along to his games. What kind of fucking boy in grade school goes to watch his friend's hockey games?)

"No. No, I haven't played anything since high school." He tugged at his hoodie. "I don't mind."

"No?"

"It gets—stupider, as you get older." He frowned. "Competition is more fun when you're a kid. It's literally the entire world, but, like, it still gets to be pointless."

He took a huge bite of his food. He ate by slowly gathering a large forkful on his plate, lowering his head, and then quickly and decisively stabbing the food into his mouth, like domination. "It gets ridiculous when adults make it mean something," he said. "You know?"

"I think so," said Hazel.

"I go to Jets games with my dad sometimes."

"I hate the Jets."

"Aw, c'mon, really?" He bit into a piece of garlic bread and Hazel followed suit, sawing into it with her knife like an animal.

"I fucking hate hockey," she said, scooping up butter.

"Nobody's perfect," he returned, unfazed. "How's your mom doing?"

"Fine. She's fucking some guy who owns an art gallery."

"Good for her," he said. "She still—aw, shit. What does your mom do again? I can't believe I don't remember this."

"Hospital tech. Sanitizes instruments. They ever cut you open at Health Sciences in the last five years, good chance my mom cleaned that scalpel."

"Well, good for her, eh?"

"She does okay. And the guy has family money, so. What about your folks?"

"Um. My mom's dead."

"*What?*" Hazel said. Christopher's parents had been very kind. And they'd always seemed so in love. There'd been a short period, as a kid, when Hazel had prayed seriously and nightly for her mother to have what they had.

Hazel reflected, in a nanosecond, that without realizing it she had always considered this a bulwark against death. As if somehow there might be an $x = x$ equation of happy straight marriages and long lives.

"Yeah," Christopher said. "She killed herself, actually."

"I'm so sorry." She broke the last piece of bread. "When was this?"

"Like two years ago."

Before she could stop herself, Hazel asked, "How's your dad?"

"Never been the same." Christopher delivered this information like he was in a meeting.

It was calm as outer space outside, cars half-concealed from sight by snowdrifts. Hazel could make out antennas, the tops of SUVs.

"I'm sorry," said Hazel. "I've lost a couple friends that way. I'm sorry."

"Yeah, well," he said, showing the first signs of discomfort. "Not exactly nice dinner conversation, I guess."

An old guy in a Michelin Man jacket walked in and shuffled over to a table.

"My mom's here now," Hazel said, offering this, knowing the difference between sympathy and self-concern. "In the city."

"So you don't have any connection to Pilot Mound anymore?" said Christopher.

The guy in the Michelin jacket slowly lowered himself into a seat, putting his hands on the table and closing his eyes. The waiter sauntered over, now with a lazy smile.

"None. No reason to visit anymore. Ever."

"Me either," Christopher said, sounding scared and unsure. "Damn, I guess I really don't. My dad moved here last year, too. Which is good. It's good he's near me."

They ate in silence, and then Hazel went to the bathroom. Next to the sink stood an ad for a dating show, a colourful list that said, "DOS AND DON'TS ON FIRST DATES." Her eyes rested on a DO:

Offer to go Dutch.
(Welcome to the 21st Century.)

She straightened her ponytail, smoothed her skirt, and went back downstairs. The old man now had a half carafe of wine and a basket of bread; he was staring ahead, inserting the food into his mouth.

"So what were you doing in Montreal?" asked Christopher.

"Becoming a girl and a drunk. I came back to quit at least one of those. Got any advice?" She'd planned this line out, to say at some point during the night, to gauge his reaction—and it sounded so silly coming out of her mouth, but Christopher laughed a true, unselfconscious laugh, and Hazel started to like him for real.

When he kissed her, hours later, on her doorstep, after paying for both of their meals, Hazel started to cry. She went up into her mom's bathroom, but instead of peeing, she sat on the toilet lid and cried. Hazel's mom heard her crying. She entered without knocking, and Hazel told her there was a boy. She said, "You remember Christopher Penner, right?" And her mom laughed a delirious, beautiful laugh and got down on her knees and hugged Hazel where she was sitting. "You two always did like each other so much." Hazel put her face in her mom's coat and let her mother touch her as she sat there, the carpet of the toilet lid cover rustling against her skirt.

∽

After Hazel fucked him for the first time, her legs wrapped around his body like a spider, she thought Christopher might cry. He had that look boys got after they came when the sex had really meant something to them. So many boys thought they were warriors after they had an orgasm. That, or they got sad. Or gave off waves of dissociation, and then weeks later admitted they were girls. (This had happened to Hazel not once, not twice, but *three* times.) But Christopher didn't cry—his eyes closed briefly, something grateful unlocked from within his body like he was with God, and it made Hazel feel beautiful.

2

Can I even begin to express how hard I began to re-believe in my life? How his bedroom is forever preserved in my memory as a centre of peace? Christopher had a big studio on Corydon with purple curtains and gentle traffic sounds and a neighbour who watched cable news that came through the walls as a burbling lull 24-7. For many months, when I stayed over at Christopher's house, he would get up, make coffee, and kiss me, still sleeping in the bed, before he went to work. I lived between that apartment and my mother's house, doing nothing.

He didn't seem to mind (something I would later realize I took for granted). Sounds so chaste, describing it now, though it wasn't. We fucked against buildings, and I went with him to parties. God, he liked to drink, almost as much as I had in the old days, but that part wasn't even hard. Once everybody knew I was sober, and wasn't trying to get me to drink, parties got fun! It was a kick to be around drunks and see so clearly now what was happening to them.

And sober sex. Do you know that had never happened before, either? It was through sex with him that I felt my body flower and come back to me. I felt my skin as a real part of the world. It was weird. Sex became not something that I tolerated, or even assented to, but a thing I *wanted* and *liked*. It felt like the same restless and tingling part of me that had stayed up late as a kid. A ghostly hand touching my insides, bringing something back to me about desire.

"You know, I only ever dated one other girl in my life," he said one night, after we'd made love. The moon was out, and it tinged his red hair a pale blue. A car's shadow from the street washed over the room.

"Really," I said.

"We dated for four years," he said, staring straight up from his pillow. "She had a kid, a little daughter."

I propped myself up on my elbow. "Why'd you break up?" I didn't mind hearing this stuff, and it wasn't unprecedented. We liked filling each other in on the vast blankness of what had happened during the past half of our lives.

"She fell out of love with me," he said.

"That's cold."

"No, it's fine," Christopher said. "I mean, it was awful, and it dragged out too long. But she didn't have the guts to leave me. And I wanted to believe she still loved me. It happens all the time."

"I see."

"Not that I'd know, I guess," he added. "The sample size is *n* equals one, as they say."

"Dating blows. You didn't miss much. How'd you meet?"

He hesitated. "Speed dating."

"*What?* That still exists?"

"It was in Fort Garry." He laughed. "It wasn't even at a bar or anything; it was so awkward. But we ended up liking each other. They give you a little piece of paper and they call you up if you marked each other as a match. We went on one date afterward, and then it was just normal."

"No shit."

"Did you ever date girls, too?" he asked. "I mean, after you—after you—"

It never failed to amaze me, in a fond, quiet way, how boys could touch and fuck a transsexual body, and then stammer their way through any implication of how that body got there. I don't know why I have a soft spot for that, but I do.

"I've never dated a woman," I said. "Except in high school, once. I hooked up with girls a few times and it was fun. I've never really dated men, either, to be honest. I haven't had many relationships as an adult, period." *Any relationships*, I didn't say.

We lay there in the moonlight. I'd never felt so calm. I felt like the first thirty years of my life were slipping into place and closing. We were very quiet for a while, but he wasn't sleeping.

"What I can tell you," I said, "is the first time I slept with a man. It was right after I moved to Toronto. I wasn't in a good place. I worked with this boy, and I lived in a shithole just east of downtown. Even today it's a rough corner. Anyway. This boy, Will, he asked if I wanted to hang out. Twice, I went over to his house and we watched TV, got drunk. We talked long into the night. Both times I expected—like, I thought: *He's hitting on me, right? This is how this works, this is how it ends up, right?* But then around one, two a.m., he'd say, all abrupt, that he had to get to sleep, had to get up early for work, see ya. I'd think, *I work at the same place, bitch!* But whatever. The third time I go over, Will says he's gonna make tacos and he's got a two-six of whisky. I brought a six-pack. And right away he says he broke up with his girl-friend the weekend before, so he's all emotional. I was like, *Ah, okay, here we go.* He put bacon in the tacos. I told him to eat some of the spare bacon and take a shot. We called them bacon chasers. I have a picture of me, still, that he took that night. I've got a flip phone and I'm wearing this ridiculous scarf. I look mad for some reason. But I was really happy.

"Anyway. Eventually, the whisky and the beer go and we are *fucked up*. And then I kiss him and he's surprised! I don't know. But he's into it, and we have sex, and let me tell you, baby, it was bad, like it was *nooooot* good. I'll spare the unsavoury details, but like, we were both too drunk to stand. And we were scared, and we didn't know what we were doing with each other's bodies."

Christopher sat up and put his arms around his knees, watching me talk to him.

"We blacked out and woke up the next day feeling terrible," I said. "He had to work, but it was my day off. I walked him to the subway and asked him to kiss me. He did, and then he left, and almost right away I had a text saying he just wanted to be friends."

"Motherfucker!" said Christopher.

"No, the sadness of that hadn't kicked in yet," I said. "I walked home, even though it took over an hour. And I felt so clearly that I had finally lost my virginity. It seems silly, right? It wasn't the first time I'd had sex as a woman. It wasn't the first time a lover had stuck something up me, either. It wasn't even the first time I'd touched boy penis. But fucking him and sleeping in his bed felt special, like something I would read about. And I guess maybe part of that feeling was heterosexist patriarchal whatever. But it occurred to me, as I was walking, hungover in the wind, feeling so in my body—that virginity is not the lie. *Singular* virginity, that's the lie. It made me think: Maybe virginity *is* real, and it can be lost, but it can also be given. Maybe there's something beautiful in the concept and not just ... ruinous. Maybe the truth is just that virginities are malleable, personal, and there are lots of them. And maybe you can even do them over again if you don't get it right the first time."

Christopher was quiet. I'd like to say he eventually said or murmured something before we fell asleep, but I just don't remember.

⌒

Once, when Christopher was drunk, he hit me in the balls. Well, he tapped me in the balls. It was supposed to be a joke, I guess. There was a split second where I didn't understand where the pain was coming from.

"*Haaaa*," he said. "You remember that? You remember that?"

I clocked him back before I even realized what I was doing, and then he was on the floor. He sobbed once, not from pain, I don't think.

He said he was sorry. He said he was drunk, and stupid, and that he was a bad and evil man he was bad he was bad he was bad he was evil.

Usually, when he was in blackout mode, I'd just guide him around like a cat. I remembered how pliable I used to be—at least, the shadowy mental cross-stitch I could summon from pinpricks of memories and what my friends told me later.

But this time I told him that he was good, that I loved him, and that I'd never leave him. I said, "You're a good man," over and over. I hoped it would sink in, even if he didn't remember.

In grade school, I used to hit him in the nuts all the time, unprompted, for fun, and he would go down just like that. Sometimes he'd get mad. Sometimes he'd laugh. No one thought it was weird. Boys. When I said I was an unhappy child, I meant that I was also an angry child.

⌒

Later that summer, a job offer came in for him in Kingston. They offered him a lot of money. "I'm thinking of taking it," he said.

For me, it wasn't a question. "If you wanted me to come with you, I'd come with you."

He was silent. Then he changed the subject.

A couple hours passed that night in which I said goodbye to him in my head. I thought: *Okay.* I thought: *Never mind.* I thought: *This strange boy from my past sewed my heart back together. I will mourn, I will hold him until he leaves, and then I will move on.*

As we were getting ready for bed, he turned to me with screaming eyes and said, "Are you coming with me? Are we doing this? Are we really doing this?" He was shaking as I kissed him.

⌒◠

So we left the city and I moved east, again. We settled into the second floor of an old house with a balcony, a house with no screaming outside, no one beating on doors, no sounds of male rage through the walls. Ontario Works got me a job in a rental management office and I closed my eyes the one time they evicted two hookers.

We lived there for a year. I'm thankful for all of this. If your early thirties can be a rebirth, after rebirth had, supposedly, already been part of your life (I bought into the transition-as-second-puberty stuff hard), then any period of your life can bring renewal. Can't it? I believe in that.

One day, I had this clear feeling. We went to this diner that had just opened. They used all local ingredients, claimed we really didn't have to tip, said they were proud to pay their workers an actual living wage. I had a sandwich with soft, thick bread, a kind of cheese I'd never heard of, and fresh greens, and coffee that was somehow so fucking good I didn't even put cream in it. I'd paid for meals that nice before, but this was the first time I did it without any regret or anxiety. That was the special thing. And we drove home (he drove home), and I thought, *I made it.*

3

And so then. The morning when it happened. You and I had been together eighteen months. We woke up in terrible heat. You went to open the windows and the air outside was wavy; our room was shimmering and gauzy in the light. Kids outside were running through the back lane, burning in the sun.

I put my head in your neck when you lay back down.

"Hazel," you said.

"Christopher." I folded my legs over yours. Your phone rang. I saw it was your dad. You said you didn't want to speak with him.

I only found out later that you told me second. I was always grateful for that. I was grateful you didn't tell me first.

When you did tell me, I hated you instantly. Because I knew my hurt would need immediate sealing. That I would need to fold my pain, stow it somewhere to shrivel and grow pale. This is the order these things go. Someday, a girl might do the same thing to you.

You told me how you knew from when we were little, how you admired me from afar, how you thought, when we got together, that maybe you didn't want to be a girl, that maybe just being with a trans girl would soothe this part of your mind. Do you know what it's like to so completely understand the force about to blow up your life?— well. I barely remember what you said after that. You were vacating your guts, and I was listening and nodding, but I could only think, *I don't want you to transition. I don't want you to be a girl. You were the sweetest boy to me, and I loved you, and I still love you, but now I have to help you. I have to guide you through clothes and bras, and I have to watch your eyes grow heavy. To see you grow out your hair—oh God, you're going to dye it, aren't you? Of course you are. You'll dye it something besides that pretty, pretty red. That pretty red hair.*

It only took me two weeks to break up with you. Isn't that awful? I couldn't—I don't know. I couldn't do it. You didn't know what was coming and I did. I know you wanted to try, but I promise you, we wouldn't have made it.

For the first few months, I'd get off work and I'd feel it in my body. I mean a heavy shroud would emerge from my arms and vibrate through my skin. I mean it was a physical feeling. If I hadn't known that feeling, been able to name it, known exactly why it was happening and that eventually it would end, I probably would have ended up dead. You probably don't want to hear that. But, well, I'm not dead.

I didn't stay sober long after I left you. I knew that was only a matter of time, too. I don't feel awful that I started drinking again. I was sober for long enough, and if alcoholics are always alcoholics, then can't that logic apply to sobriety, too? I can feel sobriety still there, those years of clarity and re-sprung desire still alive and sleeping in my bones. Like a lover forgiving me more than she should, waiting to come back when I'm ready.

I've seen your pictures. You look beautiful now. I guess you always were—well, I mean. You know what I mean, don't you?

You're applying for arts grants somewhere out east, I think. Like, east-east. From what I heard, you're living in an abandoned factory by the sea that's been turned into beautiful apartments. Your career has turned into the good-paying part of the gig economy, and your girl-friend's name is Mauve. How can I honestly start to tell you how happy I am for you? And how much I want him back? I'd never admit this to anyone, least of all you. Do you know what it means to be turned into the kind of person you hate against your will? God forgive me. God, please give me the strength, the kindness, the wisdom to cover this in my soul and keep it there. I would never tell you or another breathing creature how resentful I really feel.

OBSOLUTION

David met Iris in the middle of that one summer—he was freshly twenty-one and giving school another go. He'd discovered trivia nights, bought a blue-and-white hoodie, got a part-time data entry job in the federal building downtown. He slept in on days with no class, shuffling to the bus in pyjama bottoms at four o'clock against traffic. Went back home at nine-thirty as the sun washed over the river. On class days, he'd amble up to get lunch at Rocco's (everyone made fun of Rocco's, but their slices were *so fucking big*), grab a beer, and start the reading. Bars weren't a place for reading when David was a kid, but now? Here? It seemed they were.

He shared an apartment in Southeast with his best friend Ray, and his other best friend Leah was crashing on their couch. Not that those two were around much—Ray's lady tended to beckon, as did Leah's boys from OkCupid. But when they *were* around, they all stayed up late and played Smash and talked about every fucking thing in the world: teachers from high school, the election, how Portland was changing, political correctness, sex, feminism, *The Dark Knight*, the deleterious effect the Oscars most assuredly had on art. David would say things like, "Do you dare me to drink a gallon of milk in an hour?" And Ray would say, "Yeah, why not?" and Leah would say, "That's the stupidest fucking idea you've ever had," and then Ray an hour later: "Dude, you could use that as a movie sound effect for vomiting. That was amazing."

Ray and Leah had dated in high school and now were fun, piss-taking exes. Their landlord had sold the complex, but somehow the rent had only gone up a smidge. Obama had clinched the nomination, and one way or another, the Bush presidency was coming to a close. The winter of clouds and rain had finally given way to sun in June. It was a Pacific Northwest no-bugs-no-humidity-PBR-and-two-buck-Chuck summer, and it felt to David like a life.

Ray talked more on the nights when Leah was gone, because Ray was smarter than David. Ray studied sociology at Reed, and that's how David met Iris.

∽

It was a party down the street, a backyard barbecue in a house painted pink, Reedies still in town for the summer. Ray'd gone home for a week and Leah was on a date with a guy David only knew from online as *omg_kittensss.* Ray'd had to sell David on the party: "Go! Go. They always like seeing you." David could be timid at these things when Ray wasn't around.

They were innocent kids, the Reedies at that house. Girls who talked to their moms twice a day and would think nothing of asking them hard questions about sex. Boys newly enamoured with bumming smokes from strangers, boys who visited the county voting office on primary day because they'd lost their mail-in ballot and proclaimed upon return, "It was a microcosm of America."

At sunset they made a fire, and one girl said they should all roast marshmallows, and a boy said, "Did you know you can roast sour candy?!" and then half the party was off to the store. When they got back, a girl sat beside David, tapped out a smoke, and then cursed.

36

The girl was tall, wore a soft green sweater, had wavy black hair and ruddy skin. She had white glasses and a gigantic purse with a zipper.

"I left my fuckin' lighter at the Plaid. Let me tell you about ten-minutes-ago Iris, she's a real asshole."

"Do you buy cartons?" said one of the boys, giving her a light. "They're cheap at this place on Foster."

"No," she exhaled. "Buying a carton would mean I'm addicted." She was absolutely serious, zero irony, and this made it the funniest fucking thing David had ever heard. He snorted loud and Iris turned to face him. "I don't think I know you."

David was hunched over in his blue-and-white hoodie, his mussed dishwater-blond hair. He had a quiet, polite-boy mode when he met new people.

Where did you grow up? "Brookline, Massachusetts." Adding not unkindly in response to David's confused face, "It's a bougie suburb of Boston."

What was that like? "Lot of basements." (David thought that was hilarious, too.)

What are you studying? "Political science. Don't ask me what my thesis is. I've got no fucking clue."

What are you doing this summer? "Working at a pie shop. This town's a trip, you know? We put out a help wanted sign yesterday, and we got two hundred fucking resumés."

What brought you out here? "I'd never lived anywhere else. It was my version of running away."

And then, as the fire died and the party filtered into the house, Iris said, "I'm making an exit. And then I'm making some mac and cheese. Come with me?" The question mark barely there. Not "Do you want to come with me?" *Come with me.*

"We could go to my place?" he blurted. "I have a box there."

"No," Iris said. "We have to go to the store. I need Stouffer's brand. It's bougie, I know."

"Sure." Then he sighed. "Okay, look. What does 'bougie' mean?" and Iris kindly explained that, too.

∾

They did end up back at David's place, and they ate on the back porch, facing the street. Iris took off her sweater. On her right forearm was—

"You have a Johnny Rotten tattoo!"

"My one moment of rebellion." Iris blew on her food. "When I was eighteen. I had my moment; that was it. Reality is I'm a mama's girl. It's the worst. Shit, we didn't get wine. Do you want to get a bottle of wine after this?"

"I do," said David, but he didn't move. He sat, grinning at Iris like a dumbass, waiting for her to lean in and kiss him, and soon enough, she did.

∾

"What about you?" she said the next morning as David loaded the coffee maker. "Where's home?"

"Boring," David said dismissively.

"Whatever!"

David chuckled. "Gets 'em every time. I'm just being a jerk— Boring, Oregon."

"Now you get to enlighten me."

"It's like Gresham's Gresham."

"Aha, roger that, cap'n." You did not have to live in Portland very long to understand Gresham as an outsizedly maligned suburb. "Small-town boy, huh?"

"I was born in Seattle. I lived there when I was little. Downtown. But Boring's home now. My mom's there."

"Suburbia." Iris sighed. "What's your mom like, kid?"

David winked at her. "You got all day? No, my mom's awesome. I'm lucky. She's a tough ol' broad. I look up to her, honestly."

"What makes you call her a"—Iris paused, then enunciated—"tough old broad"?

"In a good way!" David stressed. "So, when I was five, she decided to apply to med school? That summer, my dad walked out."

"Shit."

"Yeah," David said, hopping up to sit on the counter. "And like, they were pretty broke already. We didn't have much to lean on. But she did it. And she's a doctor now. And check it out, I'm alive!" David laughed, a tall, soft summer figure in a T-shirt and shorts, swinging his legs. "And I still like hanging out with her. So she must've done something right."

"Strong woman," Iris said, impressed. "Sounds like you made out okay, kid."

"I think so." The coffee maker finished. "Do you want cream?"

Iris waved her hand. "I got it." And she took it from the fridge, then retrieved mugs like she lived there, and David started to love her.

It wasn't slow. That same night, they hung out at her place, watching *Cinema Paradiso* on Iris's insistence and making out through most of it ("Look at us, we're so cultured," she whispered as she gripped David's hair). After that, the questions were *Whose place tonight? Should I pick anything up?*

Ray got along with Iris fabulously, and they even went on double dates with Ray's girlfriend, which all four agreed felt very adult. Even Leah begrudgingly liked her. Leah'd always hated David's girlfriends, but she and Iris became smoking buddies at parties, and Iris hooked her up with a room on Woodstock. They all went to a lot of parties, Iris hauling leftover pie from work.

David learned Iris used to nanny, but it'd been hell with school, and she didn't need the money *that* badly. David learned she could get angry sometimes, about the strangest things. "I can't stand girls who wear those *fucking rubber boots.*" The multicoloured boots, the boots with polka dots. "You are a *grown woman*," she said. "*Act like it.*"

They fucked, a lot. Never in kinky-fun gonzo ways, just steadily in a bed, often early in the evening. David got lost in her body, her acres of hair, a hill of her above him. He wrapped her in his long arms every time and closed his eyes, ending with torsos fused, heads resting on upper backs. David liked to think about this the mornings after, him staring up at her, wrapping himself around her body before he closed his eyes and came. And he liked to think about being on the couch beforehand, when they'd stop making out and get up, like, *Okay, who are we kidding, let's go do this*, and lead each other into the bedroom with filled bellies and staticky heads.

No memory would he ever recall of the sex that first night, though. Maybe he'd been too nervous or drunk. David was never much of a serious drinker, but boy, did he drink with Iris.

࿔

"We went through five *bottles of wine last night?"* Iris's voice came from the kitchen.

"I guess we did." David yawned, emerging from the bedroom to see Iris looking down, standing over the recycling in a thin brown sleep shirt. "Holy shit."

"Because we had the two with dinner," she continued. "And then we went to the Plaid and got two more. And then we found that red in the cabinet."

"Well, we started at six," he said timidly, fastening his robe.

David was that kind of boy whose default attempt at comfort was a squeaky-voiced *it's-not-that-bad* routine. He would've cooed in an earthquake. It was just how he'd always been. "And we went to bed at one?" he said. "That's not too bad."

"It's still five bottles of wine," she snapped. "Jesus, Iris." She opened her dishwasher for mugs as the coffee burbled.

"Consider it a life well lived?"

"I *am* committed to decadence." David's eye caught on the bottles in the recycling. Lined up so neatly. He heard the sound of the fridge door. "But tonight, we're eating kale! Only kale. Nothing but kale."

It was later that night, when Iris was cooking, drinking sparkling water, and insisting on no help—"No way. You sit tight; Mama's making a spread"—that David knew he had to tell her. He was sitting at the kitchen table in huge black jeans. Iris was all arms at the stove when his eyes fell to the curve of her stomach and he thought, *Fuck*.

He didn't say it right then, though. David was not someone who could have consequential conversations unplanned. Capital-T Talks had to be internally scheduled and required anxious preparation. David did not understand chatting about feelings off the cuff. How could you take care to express your feelings truthfully if you didn't think about them first?

So next evening, on his back porch, David said, "I need to tell you something."

"What's up?"

David shut his eyes. "I'll understand if this is a deal-breaker, and I'm sorry I didn't tell you earlier."

"Jesus, what's going on? I'm assuming you didn't kill someone."

(Before this, it was Ray and Leah and his mom who knew. No one else. His friends had been chill, his mom less so. It'd been years ago, too. The summer he turned eighteen.)

"I have," David started. "I have," he tried again. "I have some issues with my gender."

The slightest emptiness of silence. Then: "Oh, babe. I don't think that's a deal-breaker. I'm glad you told me. What do you mean?"

"Sometimes," he began, "I wish I could be seen as a woman? Like. I want to—God this is so hard, I'm sorry. Sometimes I feel like maybe now and then I sort of want to be. A woman? And I wear girl's clothes sometimes. Half of my—holy Jesus, here we go. Okay, half of my underwear drawer is girl's underwear. Actually." He chose this point to shut up.

Iris studied him. She was waiting for him to go on.

"I'm sorry," he said.

And then Iris kissed him! "Oh, honey!" she said. "I mean, fuck, sure, I wasn't expecting this. But. Please. I still love you. I still want to be with you. Tell me what this means. I want to help. Like, does this mean you like boys, too?"

David's mind shot off through the trees, hearing Iris's voice through fog. "No," he finally said. "I've only been attracted to women.

I love women. And that's another thing," he said nervously. "Most people like me are definitely attracted to men. From what I can tell."

"Do you want to take hormones?" *She knows about hormones?!* "Do you want the surgery—"

"No, I don't think so," he said hastily. "That's such a huge question. I don't know if I want to *do* anything. Some people need it. You know? They're called 'true transsexuals.' They get sex changes and they *need* to and they know so clearly. There's this test called the Benjamin Scale—true transsexuals score a six, and I got between a two and a three? So I don't think I need surgery, but I also know I'm not, like, a regular boy either?" David was calmer now. "Took me years to figure that out."

Iris kissed him. Kissed him again. Refilled his wineglass. "Drink this, my dear. Hey, I love you. I love you! And that doesn't scare me off. And I know you're not sure, but if you ever wanted to change your body, or even get surgery, you could do that, and I'd still be here. Promise. No, look at me! *Look at me.* I don't care, okay? I promise!"

∽

Still, David was not quite sure. Days later, he wore panties to bed. When Iris discovered them, he said weakly, "Sure you want to do this?"

Iris rolled onto his body and ground against him. "Look at me, I'm just running away, aren't I?"

The next morning, Iris had just left when Ray came by the apartment.

Ray: "Hey fagbag! How's it going?"

David: "I'm happier than I've ever been in my entire life. Ever."

And David's mom, she loved Iris, too. He brought her home a few weeks in. Connie picked them up at the end of the Blue Line, honking in glee with her arm out the window—"So you nabbed my son, huh?"—laughing her head off as they got in the car and notably marking the first time David saw Iris even a little bit disarmed.

On the drive to Boring, they chit-chatted about David's data entry job, who Obama might pick for VP, Iris's hometown and how she liked the Northwest and blah blah blah. But at home, when Iris went to the bathroom, Connie turned to David with wet eyes and said, "She's so *nice*," a thing that Connie had never said about any human he had brought home. It made his heart move into his throat.

Bluster and dewy eyes aside, though, Connie was kinda having a rough time of it. It made David sad. Divorce. Again. Poor Mom. A man leaving again, this time David's stepdad, a stern but loving architect. They'd met when David was nine and Connie was drowning in med school applications.

David liked to tell the story of Connie straightforward and twinkle-eyed, a plucky tale of a single mom and son, straight out of a PG movie or middle-grade children's book. Truth was, when David's dad left, Connie didn't exactly pick herself up off the floor right away. Truth was those were rough years. Moving every few months, heat shut off in winter, stealing food from corner stores. Days she didn't get out of bed. That kind of thing.

Yet, then: the stern but loving architect and, soon after, a med school app that came back yes. Connie'd grown up in a big screaming family in a tiny house in LA before coming to Seattle, and then suddenly she was living in the Portland exurbs with her kid and new husband, going to OHSU. Turbocharged upward mobility, manna from heaven; she finished med school as David finished middle school.

And now. Here Connie was again, alone. Financially secure, at least. But alone. David's heart really did ache for his mom on this. He could hear it in her voice in her phone calls that had become just a little upped in frequency ("Hey kiddo, how ya doing? Well, I'm just driving home from the clinic ..."). He could hear it in her voice at the end of those calls, when David would say he should probably go, he and Iris were about to make dinner, nice to talk to you, I'll call you next week ... and Connie's cackle and good nature and *I-love-you-goodbye* were all just a little bit dimmer.

But bringing Iris home was a good time. They had wine after dinner and watched *A Fish Called Wanda*. (David's suggestion; Connie loved that movie.) They slept in David's old room. When he got up in the night to pee, and then returned with his feet padding on the quiet carpet, he saw Iris's body silhouetted and slumbering in the shadows of his bed, and God, he wanted to sit down and cry right there.

⌒

Summer ended and they all went back to school. They watched the conventions and got rowdy at Sarah Palin, and Ray said, "What a cunt!" as David laughed and Iris shushed them and Leah gave Iris a silent high-five.

The economy crashed, but because everybody was getting humanities degrees, they had all significantly burnished their mental armour for avoiding post-grad life questions anyway. Besides, the job market in Portland had already been shitballs, so really, it was like the rest of the country was just catching up. Or something.

"Two hundred fucking resumés for a fucking pie store," Iris reminded everyone of summer's help wanted sign.

Leah belched from a Hamm's. "It says a lot," she observed, "that I work at a vintage toy store, and everyone wants my job. And I hate my job. And I'm grateful for my job. And I hate that I'm grateful for my job."

"That's just Portland, though!" said Ray.

"Yeah," muttered David, "well, maybe everyone will stop fucking moving here now."

"Nah, give it a few years. Eighty-second's gonna be the new hipster hot spot."

"Get that fag future out of your mouth!" said David.

"Language!" said Iris.

Jokes aside, Connie did call David once melting down ("I can't sell the house! It's just my income now! What if I get laid off!"), prompting even gentle, it's-not-that-bad David to say with exasperation, "Jesus, Mom, you're a doctor now and I work for the government. We'd have to hit or fuck someone to lose our jobs!" Connie thought that was funny.

David meant it, though. He barely ever needed money from her. He was in school and had a secure gig; he wouldn't be a drain on her. And she did have career security. "We'll be all right," he stressed to her. They would, they would, they would.

David's classes? They were fine. He got mediocre grades because he did not work very hard. Luckily, his classes weren't very hard, either. This caused extreme consternation to Ray, whose lawyer parents were lone among their crowd for making clear a thing or two about grades. Ray's classes? Well, he was only at home when his girlfriend was busy, or he was sick of the library. He'd straggle out of his room to zombie-drink a glass of water and David would besiege him for a round of Smash, but it was always only one round. As David understood it, Ray's hell course was about railroads. Just railroads. In any case, it was kicking his ass. And Iris's classes? Oh boy. She was snowed under too, would call David as he bused back from work, eschewing pronouns to make her point: "Please. Come save. Just want blanket, wine, cute boy, and cigarette."

David didn't mind all this. Growing up, he'd never wanted for alone time. And it'd been strange, in the wake of the carnival-like summer, to reunite with solitude and find it blissful. He returned to plodding into trivia nights, smoking peacefully over pasta dinners and weirdo beers. Once, in a rare manic jailbreak as the election heated up, Ray ditched studying and dragged David and Leah out to a debate watch at a brew pub, and David put on a purple dress and the three of them got hammered with a crowd booming, "DRINK!" every time McCain prefaced his thundering with "My friends!"

And yet: the nights always ended with Iris, even if one of them was already asleep, and the other slid into bed past midnight. He'd awake with his arms around the soft furnace of her. Mornings they'd shower together and make out, and his clean body would get hard every time, though they never fucked in there.

Then, one night. David and Iris in David's bed. Watching a movie, waiting for a pizza. Iris was kissing him and put her hand on his dick, nestled under his grey panties. David was usually a good sport when he wasn't feeling it, but that night he was so tired. And besides, he'd overdressed earlier for a strangely warm day and he'd felt so sweaty and oogy for hours and he just wanted to eat the stupid pizza and go to sleep.

Iris began to jerk him off and David said, "No," without thinking about it. How could he say something like that?

"No," he said again. He felt—*gross*. He just felt *gross*. That, he couldn't say.

Iris got him hard and rolled on top of him.

"No," he said feebly, one more time, though his body had other ideas. So, David gave up and got a condom. *Okay, sure*, et cetera. Iris shuddered as he swelled—and then a chemical animal surged inside him, and he grabbed her hips and slammed into her. It was like they just had to start fucking for his body to remind David that David *did* like sex, okay, right, it actually *did* feel good. You know?

He came, the pizza arrived, and Iris paid for it in a robe. They ate and finished the movie and went to bed.

Next morning, they showered, as they did. But this particular time, as David stooped forward over himself to wash out his shampoo, Iris paused.

"Tilt your head back," she said.

"What?"

"Tilt your head back, David," she enunciated softly. "It makes washing your hair easier."

David turned around, away from the faucet, unstooped his head toward the water, and he felt his hair fall toward the floor.

Was David gonna transition? Who fucking knew? Not him. It was a scary thought. For years, he'd spent nights on the internet, discovering how one went about this. And every night, he'd gone to bed blocking out more fears than he'd started with. The spectres of poverty and rejection and violence alone were enough to instill an understanding in his body: You only do this if you're 300 percent sure. This wasn't just what doctors said; it was what the transgendered people themselves said. Why go through such a hellscape otherwise? David admired those who'd made the jump; to him, the true transsexuals were some of the bravest people he'd ever seen. But it destroyed his heart to read these stories. He would start out idly searching online forums for nice places to buy clothes in his size, and soon enough, he'd be reading about a woman in the emergency room, a woman fired and evicted, a woman whose kids refused to speak to her, wouldn't even *look* at her. Why the fuck would you go through all that if you didn't absolutely *have* to?

And it was clear to David he didn't have to. Being with Iris, in the *way he was with Iris*, it all felt luckier than he'd ever hoped for. He did go to a support group once ... Everyone was sad or exhausted or angry. Urban exhaustion, itself, scared David (returned childhood memories he preferred to forget), and anger was not an emotion he understood. A woman complained of a doctor's mistreatment—foot-dragging on getting her hormones—and David piped up with advice on how to talk to doctors better—his mom was one; he knew. They stared at him like static. So solely, they all seemed: sad, exhausted, angry. David's id screamed at him on the bus ride home: *This is the life I'd have? No thanks!*

Plus, he wore his dresses a few times around Iris and she said nothing. He really was lucky with her. He had time to figure this out. Maybe later, he could take, like, a small dose of hormones? Nothing drastic. If his skin could feel less heavy, if it could feel softer and less gross to the touch, sometimes it felt like that would be enough to solve his internal screaming. He had to research this more, he supposed. But he had time; he was in no rush. He was so young! He knew. He was so young.

"I wish there were more men in the world like you, not less," was a thing Leah'd said when he'd first come out to her. In the three years since, he'd carried that phrase around with him like an heirloom. A reminder of responsibility. This was the other thing: men were shitheads; he knew that. The obligation to stick around and be a less shitty shithead? It weighed on him.

Leah was the first one David had come out to, over AIM. The very first thing she had said was this: "As much as I used to joke (okay, dream) about you being gay, this isn't a surprise. You've always loved women. I don't mean in a creepy way. I mean you appreciate things about women in a way most men just don't." It had removed the first demon in David's head, to hear this. Months later, Leah'd taught him how to do makeup, sitting on his toilet in an apartment above Hawthorne. "It's an art, not a science," she'd said. "Here, you want to do foundation first. No, lip liner works like this. Here, it's okay. I'll show you."

So in the end, David could only think of it all: *God, I'm so lucky.* There was a weekend in October when Iris's parents visited. They'd all gone to Pambiche, that Cuban place in Northeast with apartments above that were painted green, pink, and yellow. They sat on the patio and Iris's mother pointed at a bay window hovering above them. "Can you imagine getting a little place there?"

"Dreamy," said Iris.

"It's probably not that easy," her mother said to David with lit-up eyes. "We're so silly, being from the East Coast. We think it's so easy to live anywhere else. Where we live, you know, there's all these young people who just think they'll show up in the city, and all of a sudden"—she gestured with good nature—"find the perfect place!"

"Not how it works, is it?" David smiled.

"Oh Lord, no!" said Iris's dad, a genial guy in an oxford shirt. "Nowadays ..."

"Good food!" her mother said. "David, how's your food?"

He nodded with his mouth full. "David picked this place," remarked Iris. "Good job, babe."

"Can you pick our breakfast for us, too?" her mother teased.

"Oh!" said the genial dad. "Because we made the wrong choice this morning, didn't we?"

"That restaurant was awful. I thought I'd puke."

"Where'd you—"

"I suppose it doesn't really matter," said Iris's mother. "David, where are we going after this? Cocktails?"

A life opened up like a sky in front of David that evening on the Pambiche patio. He saw a future of himself with long, flowing hair, his skin wraithlike and light to the touch, going to dinner with Iris and her parents in different cities. He and Iris could visit them in Boston, and they could visit wherever she got a university job while David taught high school, and they could do this for the rest of their lives. It wasn't hyperbole, David knew, to think this way. It was so possible.

Later, after cocktails, when he and Iris were at the bus stop, he was bent over himself in his suit jacket and khakis. "I need to get out of these clothes," he said nervously.

"But you look so handsome," said Iris.

That morning, Iris'd told him to dress nice, and he'd said, "Like a suit? I don't like wearing suits."

"Well, it's my parents."

"It's okay. I don't care about doing a show for them."

"Well, I do." So he'd put this on, and she'd kissed him and said, "You look hot."

After David had come out to Iris, he'd thought (naively, in retrospect) that the hard part was over. That she would understand, for example, that though he could *deal* with wearing clothes like suit jackets, that did not mean he was eager to do so. She knew he had gender issues. Couldn't Iris understand that? Why couldn't Iris understand that?!

Then it hit him the next day as he brooded on this: *Just like a fucking dude. Sure, everyone should just naaaaàaturally understand you. Dumbass.*

It became a rock rattling around in his head, a rock he was determined to shake out. Because (checkmate, David) he could've just said plainly, "Thank you, sweetie, and I know you're being nice, but I don't like being called handsome." He could've said, "I can compromise: I won't wear a dress, but I can't wear a suit." But he didn't say either of those things.

Next time, then. He really did love her. The next morning, David woke at Iris's house and she had already left. He stayed in bed feeling his skin on her sheets for a long time. Alone in her clean, airy room, stretched out under her heavy blankets, the sound of a lawn mower outside. And there, still, was the life awaiting him on the patio below the bay window.

That Thanksgiving, though, he shook a different rattling rock out of his head: he didn't go down to LA with his mom.

It stemmed from the year before, when Connie had picked him up at five a.m. as the neighbourhood luxuriated in darkness. David ambled out in a pea coat, and they chatted down I-5 and stopped at the IHOP in Springfield for breakfast. Waiting for their food, David had stared outside, where teenagers in a blue Chevrolet Celebrity were trying to park in a tight spot. They were screaming, like they'd been awake all night. A short girl with fire-red hair was yelling at the boy driving. But David could tell, it wasn't in anger.

"For tomorrow, at Grandma's ..." David began.

"Yes?"

Be present and look her in the eye! "Do you think it would be okay if I wore a dress?"

Connie's expression was inscrutable, and she said nothing. Then her head slowly swivelled from side to side. It was rare for her to say nothing—she'd grown to be a chatterbox with her kid, and besides that, she believed in talking stuff out. She'd gone through a parenting book period in med school. One was called *Kids Are Worth It! Giving Your Child the Gift of Inner Discipline.*

But now, Connie said nothing but the head swivel. At least the first time David had come out to her, back when he was eighteen, she'd talked. She'd said, "So that's pretty disappointing. Just as a mother, that's a disappointing thing to hear. That stuff's the fringe of society. You know that, right?"

Like, sure, that conversation hadn't gone quite as David hoped. But at least she'd talked.

Connie changed the subject, their pancakes arrived, and the dress in David's bag stayed there. He had not brought up gender stuff in the year since. He was in no rush to do so again, really—but he didn't want to go to Thanksgiving this year.

"I have to study," he told Connie blankly.

"Well, okay," she replied, in an uncharacteristically dead voice. "Okay. So. I'll miss you."

You shithead needy dude, he thought as he closed his phone. *It's not like you had to wear a suit or anything!*

And Iris kissed him and said, "I'm proud of you."

David was quiet.

"And some day," Iris continued, very quietly, very seriously, "we will go down there together, and you will wear whatever you want, and they will love you like I love you."

David stayed quiet.

Finally, he said, "Can we bake pies or something faggy like that?"

"Language! And heck yeah we can."

Although because Iris was the one actually buried under her studies, the day before Thanksgiving found David pie-making solo. He got up and made coffee, he and Iris showered, and then Iris took off for the library and Ray for his fam. "You should call your mom tomorrow," Ray said on his way out the door. "I think she'd like that." And then he left, leaving David in his robe alone.

He turned on the heat and set his laptop to play Bach's *Cello Suites*. He made a vegan pumpkin pie and a cream pie on a cookie crust held together with mashed banana, and then prepared a regular crust for a cherry pie to be finished the next day. He moved around the kitchen feeling the fluff of the robe shift on his skin, his bare feet slapping against the beige-tiled linoleum.

It was nice he had that quiet day to himself. Because actual Thanksgiving the next day at Leah's place? Freakazoid Town. David got up after Iris left to study for the morning (that *school*—seriously, how did Reedies sleep?). He made the cherry pie and stuck it in the oven, took a shower, and changed into a black dress, did his makeup, took the pie out and wrapped it, and then sank feckless hours into cleaning the living room. Iris came back and he apologized for his messy apartment and Iris waved the apology away. They loaded the pies into shopping bags and walked over to Leah's in the rain, getting fucking soaked. The second they got inside, Leah shrieked with a beer in her hand, "*David!* It's time to play Who's the President!"

"You start!"

Iris rolled her eyes and took the pies to the kitchen.

"Okay, here we go. Who's the president?"

"Fuck, fuck." David pretended to think. "Oh, I've got it! *Not George Bush in fifty-four more fucking days!*"

The room roared. Leah explained that on election night they had invented the best game at a house party way up in North Portland, David and Leah then yelling, "Hey everyone, who's the president?" out the windows on the car ride home, the entire city loud and alight. They didn't pass a single quiet block, not one.

"Where's the beer?"

"The fridge, you faggot! Where do you think it is?"

"Watch it, I'll jizz on you!" David laughed and flipped her off.

Leah spun around to the horrified guy watching. "It's cool," she said. "He's my best friend."

David forgot their kind of talk could shock people. But that's just how David and his friends talked! Plus, with Leah, like, she was Native, and David sometimes said similar words to her in kind. David and Leah had both told each other very earnestly that it was totally whatever, these words used in jest by friends were equally meaning- less. They weren't uptight or politically correct, and these words did not hurt them, did not hurt them at all.

Everyone was drunk by dinnertime. Leah's sweet-as-hell boyfriend had made a true fucking feast that everyone gobbled in twenty min- utes, the crowd then demolishing David's pies as he revelled in one bearded guy hoovering up the cherry. One of the older girls was exas- perated about a hookup, a guy so deep into Democratic canvassing he had a poster of Dennis Kucinich on his ceiling. David thought it had to be a joke and the girl said, "OH BOY, DO I WISH." Leah said it was time for Leah's Peppermint Patties, and the dudes asked, just what were Leah's Peppermint Patties? And Leah yelled, "Stop asking questions, you pussies! Just get on your knees!" They did. In David's mind, the dudes would've done anything Leah said. In this instance, what Leah did was stand over you with a bottle of peppermint schnapps in her left hand and a bottle of chocolate syrup in her right. She poured them into your mouth, and you had to shake your head to mix them, then swallow. They were fun. The peppermint schnapps was soon gone, and so was the beer. Iris led the charge with David to go for more. When they came back, there was puke in both sinks and the couch was somehow broken in the middle. A weary Leah said, "I'd rather drink these outside," which they did under a tarp the house had put up for smoking, as rain breezed over them, gentle Portland rain. "I like you, Iris," Leah said goofily. "Thanks for taking care of my boy." Everyone loved Iris. Everyone who loved David loved Iris.

PERFECT PLACES

Nicole being Nicole, she'd figured it'd be hard to attract men in this town. This small city of factory hands and casino dealers and nurses who commuted across the border. But it wasn't difficult for Nicole to attract men; it was difficult to attract men she liked.

There were a lot of older guys around here, and from their Tinder profiles to their bar stools, they all loved Nicole. They marvelled at how warm the weather was lately; they gushed about their ex-wives and their kids and the great jobs they once had. Men close to Nicole's own age of thirty-two? Not interested. Sure, they liked Nicole, yes. They'd joke with her, gossip, talk shit in line at Food Basics. High-five her when she crushed it at karaoke, wave hello when she came through the bar. And if a guy was giving her a legit hard time, that guy went out on his ass. (That'd only happened once, yet Nicole had never forgotten it—the bartender headlocking the guy out the door and yelling, "You come back here, your face is pavement, bud!")

She was friendly. She made easy friends. But mutual attraction? Mutual interest? She'd tried to be game, but it just wasn't happening.

Now, Nicole got her D. That wasn't a concern. Grindr, hooray, she got her D. And she had gone on plenty of dates since moving here. It was just that those dates were all born of forced hopefulness. Every time she said yes, she'd go, *I don't think I'm actually going to like this person.* And so far she hadn't been wrong. She'd gone out with corporate-ladder narcissists, list-checking curious cases, and, of course, the occasional straight couple whose interest vanished when Nicole divulged she was packing a boring old pussy. (Yes, Nicole was out on her profile, but her cunt did *not* qualify as pre-date conversation; she had *some* standards of propriety.) Before these forced-hopefulness dates, when she'd get mopey, Nicole would tell herself: Chin up, chin up! Surely the guy in question could surprise her, surely *she* knew how impossible it felt to accurately represent herself on a dating app, right? Ergo, didn't that mean she, too, could just as easily find her assumptions upset? So far: not really. She hadn't gone on a date with a single person here who filled her with genuine hope or excitement. Until that winter, a slushy January, when she received the message from Anthony: *I loved* Young Adult. *It's fantastic.*

He was just a few inches shorter than her, with a kind face and scruffy dirty-blond hair, black glasses, and what looked like permanent dark stubble. His profile was about boring shit like restaurants and *Game of Thrones*. Nicole liked him immediately, and she messaged back right away:

Charlize amiright?

Seriously! I would watch her do anything. I would watch a movie that's just her eating a sandwich. I would watch a movie of her sleeping.

lol creepy

Haha I guess that's not a savvy first impression from me huh. I'm Anthony but everyone calls me Ant. Weird I know but who gets to choose what people call you lol. You're really pretty ☺

Soon, he invited her over for dinner, and when Nicole said, "Why don't we do a bar?" Ant suggested Buddies without hesitation. He was really excited to meet her. Eight-thirty on Sunday if that wasn't too late?

⌒

That Sunday Nicole napped in the afternoon, and then woke at six to winter darkness, the lights from the Chrysler factory across the way shining into her room.

She lifted her computer onto the bed and opened herself to touch her cunt. She jerked off before dates for the same reasons anyone did, she supposed. Also, she'd learned, often the hard way, that sometimes she came off too eager.

Nicole watched straight porn while rubbing it out. Boring ol' exhaustingly misogynistic straight porn. Who gets to choose what does it for you? Gay porn had never done much for her, tranny porn could be fun but was too close to home, and queer porn, well, she'd tried.

She took a shower, soaping up her stinking pussy with Vagisil and delicately washing it clean. She shaved her legs and arms, her face, those crop circles around her nipples that had survived a decade-plus blast of estrogen. She got out and did her hair.

Her outfit? Nicole didn't do loud (she'd tried that), and she didn't do cute (she'd tried that). She liked black and dark blue with quiet patterns. Today, it was a navy blue dress with pinstripes and a silver half-slip underneath. Black tights and black boots. And when she did her face she put on black mascara but no lipstick or eyeliner. Some time ago, Nicole'd tried this combo and decided she passed better that way. Who knew how true this actually was, but. That was how Nicole did her makeup now.

"Fuck! Fuck! Fuck youuuuuu!" That was her neighbour next door. Nicole jolted and listened. Silence.

Her neighbour yelled like that often, and he always sounded mad and violent. Nicole could never hear the sounds of another person. It always sounded like he was alone.

She'd called the landlord after this first happened. He'd said, "You feel unsafe? Call the cops." Nicole didn't want to do that. Later, she'd asked her other neighbour on the floor, "Do you ever hear screaming from number two?" and the neighbour'd said, "No, no, not ever."

"Fuck! Fuuuuuuck!" Nicole preferred to leave when this happened. So, lucky her, she was already going.

She looked in the mirror at a tall, fat woman wearing mascara and a navy blue dress. She had never gotten over this experience of mirrors. The gap between her internal sense of self and the figure calmly looking back at her—it had grown over the years, not narrowed. She wouldn't call it dysphoria exactly (that had waned; it truly had). It was more unfamiliarity, a disidentification that some days felt more powerful than all those depressed teen years spent in the bathroom, squishing her face, pulling at her eyes, pressing her breasts together in strange fascination of the alien body in the glass.

Now, Nicole felt herself to be gazing at, well, not an alien. Just a stranger.

Then she laughed at herself. *Look in the mirror and see a stranger.* She really had become a boring old straight woman. Scram! Go gush about Charlize Theron, you hag! And she walked into the chilly night with a giggle. If her life had come to this, it wasn't a bad life, was it? No, no, not a bad life at all. She put her wipers on high, turned on some old pop-punk, and drove down Tecumseh pogoing in her seat, singing and hitting the steering wheel in the pissing January rain. She had a good job and her own apartment, and she went on dates and lived in a silly-ass little town where most people seemed to like her. It wasn't a bad life at all.

She got there early and got a booth. Her sister had texted—she was down to a few packs of ramen and needed a few hundred to get her to next month; if Nicole had anything to spare, she'd really appreciate it ...

And so Nicole was staring at her phone, tired as a scarecrow, when Ant rolled up with a highball and said, "I just had the wildest Uber driver of my whole life!" He launched into the story like Nicole was already an old friend. The cab driver was from BC. He had gone to jail for something or other, lived with his daughter who'd moved here for a guy, and now was sick of driving. Wanted to get into the restaurant business. "I told him I was a cook and the rest of the ride he's like, 'Tell me how you start. I think I'd be good at it!'" Ant laughed, but it was without a trace of unkindness. "Some fuckin' people."

He had bright black eyes that were deep and curious. His stubble was shaved, but he still had beard shadow. He spoke slowly and earnestly, as if he was worried you wouldn't catch everything. He wore a plaid button-up shirt under a hoodie (this town).

Within minutes, Nicole knew she wouldn't fall for Ant, but she also knew something else: she liked him. She *liked* him. She knew that. She let him talk. He'd been out west, working construction and restaurant gigs, lived in Banff for a while. "It's like Disneyland for rich people." He worked in this restaurant on Pillette. "I used to bartend on the West Side. It's crazy, man. I can't even go into Billie's anymore. I'll be doing shots 'til four in the morning." He said he usually didn't like going to bars. "I just know too many people."

"Sorry!" Nicole said. "We didn't have to meet in a bar. I'm not even a big drinker. I just—I'd rather meet people in public."

"A safety thing, totally," Ant enthused. "I was too forward about dinner at my place. Sorry."

"That's okay. Next time?"

"Yes, please!" he said, as cheerful as he'd said everything else.

After a couple hours, the bartender came over. "We're closing early."

Nicole and Ant had been the only ones since they came in.

"That's why I chose here," Ant said shyly, pulling on his coat. "I can't run into anyone."

"Let's go to the DH?"

She liked him too much to fuck him tonight, and a flushed wave of relief and delight washed over her as she understood this. They'd have this nice chaste first date, and then go over to his place for the second. This wasn't how things usually went for Nicole, and it was something that felt lovely and new. It really had been a long time since she'd met someone she liked.

Five minutes at the DH and Ant wasn't wrong. Two dudes sallied up looking straight out of *Letterkenny* central casting: "Ant! Buddy!" Nicole sat politely through one drink, and then turned to Ant.

"I've got work in the morning. But dinner next week? Friday? Maybe?"

"Absolutely!" Ant said, looking sad but saying nothing more.

Nicole drove home shrieking. Honest-to-God shrieking! How fucking long had it been?! She liked a guy for real, and the guy wanted to see her again. It had been. Such. A long. Time. Since both. Of those things. Had happened. She picked up Burger King on the drive home and ate it in bed watching Netflix, and then glugged NyQuil and hibernated. The next morning, she got ready in a sand-brained haze but was on *top* of shit the second she rolled in to work. Crushed it. It was a good life. It was a good life.

∽

Next Friday. She got home and showered. Soaped and scrubbed her smelly holes. Texted Ant if she should bring anything? (*No, just you!* ☺) Texted her sister that she couldn't lend her more money this week, not after what she sent on Monday, but she got paid in a few days and she'd help then, sorry ...

Maniacal laughter and the sound of a TV were coming from her neighbour's place. Sometimes that guy was in a good mood. He was always friendly when Nicole ran into him in the hall, including the one time he was clearly drunk (it was in the morning, but the guy was a shift worker—the only thing she knew about him, really). Nicole could swear she'd never heard anyone else's voice in that apartment. The maniacal laughter continued, clear over the top of actors' voices, which were muted and inorganic.

She drove down Tecumseh in misting rain. Ant lived on the West Side in a brick fourplex. The driveway was empty, and the air stank, and Ant's stubbled face lit up as he opened the door, like he hadn't been sure Nicole would in fact be standing there.

She climbed the stairs after him, and Ant used the banister to hoist himself up quickly, taking stairs three at a time. Nicole's eyes rested on the back of his jeans, his nimble grey-socked feet.

"You see the Red Wings?" he said as Nicole gave him her coat on the landing. "Eight to three. It was awesome. Wait—do you like sports? You probably don't like sports, do you?"

Nicole gazed at him for a second too long. "Not really."

"I'm sorry. I didn't mean to assume—"

"Ha! No. No, honey, I don't like sports. You can assume. In fact, how about we say that whatever you want to assume about me, you're probably right. Okay?"

"O-okay." Ant bustled to the kitchen, a nervous boy, a hoodie scuttling in front of the fridge. "Do you want something to drink?"

"What do you have?"

"Beer, wine, vodka."

"Do you have seltzer?"

"Vodka seltzer coming up."

Nicole sat on his couch, which was black and shiny and faded all at once. A flat-screen TV was bolted to the wall. A grey cat sniffed her feet. "Hey kitty. Hey honeybean. Hiiii."

"That's Sasha."

"Hi Sasha. Aren't you just *adorable? Oh no, you look so angry, don't you?*"

Sasha haughtily stepped back and glared at Nicole, then jumped on her lap and settled in, purring.

"Oh, she likes you!" Ant tramped back with their drinks. "She doesn't like anybody."

Nicole cheersed with a wan smile. "I ain't anybody."

"That's not true."

"It's a joke, friend."

She laughed, genuinely relaxed, feeling this indescribable emotion in intense, increasing rays. It wasn't love, and it wasn't perfect. It was just a deep, stable, good feeling. A feeling that said: *This guy actually likes me. And jeez, do I like him.* The nervousness coming off Ant, such clear, sweet concern that he needed to win Nicole over. She was overcome with a desire to soothe him, like *Shhh, shhh, honey, it's okay.*

Nicole petted his cat, ignored her vibrating phone, and listened to Ant talk more about his life and what it was like growing up in this town. "It was rougher," he said. "It's more peaceful now. I grew up on the West Side." Nicole threw her arm up on his couch, stretched out while he went back and forth from the kitchen, eventually returning with spaghetti bolognese.

They kissed once he cleared the plates. When he unzipped her dress she gasped, "Your bedroom. Take me there, please."

It was plain: mattress and box spring, nightstand, hardwood floors, art prints of maximalist, line-heavy drawings on the walls. Heavy green curtains. They made out and groped, Ant in his jeans, Nicole a little buzzed, with her tits out in her silver half-slip. There was something strangely innocent about it, something she cherished and didn't mind.

He stopped. "So I have something to tell you about what I like."

"Okay," she said dreamily.

"I like getting spanked?"

"Do you?" she said with a lazy smile. It'd been tame, what they'd done so far, but she had noticed little twitches that added up to this making sense. Tugs or grasps where his flesh would yield just a little sharply.

Nicole was an honest-to-God switch. And this info about Ant began to click deliciously into place. "Do you like getting spanked hard?" she said.

"Yes," he said instantly.

"Do you want me to spank you now?" she said, her voice dripping.

"Yes—*Ohh!*" She hit him and felt every pore of him vibrate in her arms.

"Take your pants off," she said. They were gone. His cock was curved around itself in his underwear, and she bent him over her knees and whaled on his tight little ass. He yelled and breathed at the same time, and she felt his dick pulse on her leg. Nicole felt like she could pick him up and set him down and do whatever she wanted with him.

"Do you want to take your underwear off?" she said quietly.

"Yes."

"Do you want me to touch your cock?"

"Yes."

Then he hesitated. "I've got something else to tell you."

"That's fine."

He hesitated again.

"Out with it."

His face reddened. "I get really hot from calling my partners Mommy."

Nicole's feeling of control strengthened as his warm body lay atop hers. "I like that," she said. "Call me Mommy."

"Are you sure?"

"Yes," she said without missing a beat.

Then she hit him *hard*, and wind flew out of him. "Oh yes, Mommy! Thank you, Mommy!" His cock a rod on her leg.

"Take your underwear off."

"Yes, Mommy."

A scratchy tickle took shape in the back of Nicole's brain, a small sinking corner in a room that said, *You don't like doing this*. She ignored it. She stroked him. He asked if he could eat her out. She said yes. He asked if she could call him a little boy. She said yes. She opened herself for him.

"Oh, that's good, my little boy," she said with her hands in his hair, her half-slip up around her waist. "Real good—*Oh!*"

Nicole loved getting head. She could let her pussy get eaten all fucking day. He ate her pussy like a good little boy, far beyond the point when most of her hookups got tired and gave up. Eventually, hot as shit for his cock and hot with control, feeling like he'd fuck her in the middle of the street if she told him to, she gasped, "Fuck me. Come on, little boy, give your cock to Mommy."

He lifted up from her cunt, sucking in air, and then froze again.

Oh boy. "What?" she said.

"There's one other thing." He looked frightened.

"Out with it."

"Oh God." Ant's face contorted.

"Honey"—Nicole breathed—"I won't judge you. And you know that."

"I have a diaper fetish."

Nicole entered a room in her mind. She turned around inside the room and closed the door. "Do you want to wear a diaper in bed with me?"

"Yes."

"Do you have one now you want to wear?"

"Yes."

Silence. "How does it, uh ..." She fumbled for words. "How does it work?"

The fear on Ant's face vanished momentarily, replaced by exhaustion and thoughtfulness. "There really isn't a way it—works. I just like wearing it. It's a special one they make for adults. Adult baby fetish is what some people call it. Some people like to be in cribs, play with blocks? That's not my thing. It's cool, obviously, but it's not my thing. For me, it's mostly about the diaper. And—"

His shyness returned.

"—And what we've been doing."

Nicole nodded. She gathered Ant in her arms and said, "Why don't you get your diaper, little boy?"

"Are you sure?" Ant looked her in the eye. "We don't have to."

"I'm sure. Get it for me."

"I can't believe this is happening." He disappeared into the bathroom.

A tiredness settled onto Nicole. A ripple that went down through her arms, clunked through her body all the way to the bottom. But it wasn't hopelessness or despair or anything like that. It was finality, resignation. She waited on the bed, topless in her silver half-slip in the lamplight.

He returned wearing the diaper. It was big and kelly green. It was kind of beautifully made. There was an unobtrusive opening in the middle. It crinkled like it was made out of paper.

She rode him in his bed, and he stayed hard the whole time. She kept him gathered in her arms. He vibrated like a top. He was so warm. It was like his body might start smoking. Nicole'd never seen someone so hot for what was happening.

It made her love him, just a little.

Eventually, he came in her. She stroked his hair as he panted. "Shhhh," she said. "Shhhh, that's good, little boy." She kissed him on the crown of his head. She folded her arms around him. They lay there, breathing with their eyes closed.

Then he got up. "Do you want another drink?"

"Sure."

He left and she heard him take off his diaper. The tired feeling returned. Nicole gazed at the rumpled bed, the wrinkles in the sheets where they'd made love. She stood up and looked in his closet. Nothing interesting.

She knelt by her bag and pulled out the full slip she liked to sleep in.

Ant tramped back in with her drink, topless in his jeans. "Oh!" he said. "Do you want to sleep here tonight?"

She accepted the drink. "That'd be nice," she said quietly. "Thank you. I'm so tired."

Nicole was passed out in minutes. She woke in the morning to the sound of rain. Ant's curtains let in no light from outside. She dressed slowly, accepted his coffee, and petted Sasha before she skedaddled.

She came over again a week later and they fucked *hard*, Ant screaming with Nicole's hand over his mouth. And both before and after they fucked, he said he loved how tall she was, how small he felt with her, that "You're so hot, Mommy," that he loved being her little boy. He asked repeatedly if she wanted more drinks, and she unerringly said yes, and she lost touch with herself and the pulse of her wanting, which for Nicole was not common, and she woke the next day with a blue-moon hangover, excusing her way downstairs, leaning out of her car to puke on Crawford on the drive home, the guys in the body shop across the way hooting as the rain turned her hair into strings.

The next evening, she curled over herself on the couch in her apartment, her thumbs over her phone. Nicole's face scrunched up in a tearless sob. She hated every inch of what she was about to do. She hated it, hated herself, hated every part of her own brain.

She typed, *I'm sorry*, and then kept her thumbs hovering over the screen.

What was shooting through Nicole's mind wasn't the gross stuff she'd heard all her life: "You're a *man*?! I'm not fucking *gay*!" et cetera. No, it was the unemotional responses. "Sorry, I'm not comfortable with that." "Don't think that's what I'm into. Apologies." On their own, sure, whatever, but the cascading, enveloping totality of them, metastasizing in the screen of her ego over the years to scratch down and down into the numb hurt of undesirability she thought she'd accepted, to fully examine its subterranean psychic consequences and line it up with the rejection she was about to hand to Ant now, it would be—what would it even be? She finished and sent the message, and then turned off her phone and threw it on the couch. "FUCK! FUCK! FUUUUUUUCK!" Her neighbour from next door.

Nicole sat with a closed fist to her mouth. A hate rose in her. She put on shoes and went down the stairs to the Double-Q one building over, ordered dinner and one beer, and sat at the plastic laminate bar nursing that one beer for hours, staring at the TV. It was true: she didn't like sports. Every bar in this town had on sports, just sports, just sports.

When she finally went home, all was quiet and her hate was sub-dued, sleeping, restfully waiting its turn. She turned on her phone, which had one message. Ant said he understood, that he hoped she knew she'd always have a friend in him, *see you around, bella!* It was so sweet. Really, he was a sweet boy.

She thought, *I didn't want to know what this felt like.* She disrobed. *I really didn't.* Slid open the curtains to her bed. *There's only so much you can do with empathy.* Put on the slip she liked to sleep in. *Enough.*

OBSOLUTION

It was more discovery than epiphany: David wasn't into Iris anymore.

He still loved her. But.

Yeah.

Just a few weeks after Thanksgiving, a mid-December night, that discovery: Iris had rented a movie, was gonna make tacos, but David felt restless and stifled. He begged off: "I might need a night to myself?"

"Sure, you're allowed to abandon me for once," Iris joked, and a cavern opened in David's guts. *Just once?* He knew then it was over.

(In his short life, David had comforted many women untying messy relationships. With crappy men, nice men, horrifying men. Many of these women hadn't been happy for a long time. Hadn't been happy since month four, month five, as they put it. They wished they'd broken it off sooner. David wasn't going to be like them. Fuck that.)

After sunset, he went downtown. He put on a black dress and grey overcoat and stared into the bus window's warped light. When he got off, it was cold but not raining and David liked this. He liked the dry, androgynous wrap that winter gave his body. He left his headphones quiet to keep an ear out for strangers and drifted north. He saw teenagers gaping under the wire-bristle sculpture across from Powell's, lit in milky sepia. One of them, the tallest boy, was reaching up to the bottom curve of the sculpture, straining to touch it.

He saw the Red Light and thought, *I could get some new skirts!* He owned a few, but they were so Pacific Northwest frumpy—long, multicoloured, wrinkly. David hated wearing them, actually, and some days this made him think, *Maybe it was a phase and it's over*, but today wasn't one of those days. *Maybe I'll finally find something Iris likes*, he thought before catching himself. *Right*.

Moot point, though. Nothing good in his size, a lady giving stink eye, and soon, he walked out, hands in his overcoat, wisps of snow falling that caused every car to halve its speed. He walked into a sex shop (no one looked at him funny in sex shops) and admired a blood-red high heel. A current flickered down his body as he took the vinyl in his hands. A size 9, whatever, but on the bottom a sticker—*available up to size 15?*!

A sign said shoes were twenty percent off next week, Monday to Friday. It was Sunday.

Then a voice shouted, "Hey!"—David nearly bobble-flung the shoe into the ceiling—"Sale's already on!"

"Seriously?" He turned.

The girl behind the counter had a goofy smile. "Yeah," she said. "I just decided."

David gave silent thanks for this, this kindness that both was and wasn't about money. She rang him up and said, "My girlfriends and I, we always say: 'New pair of shoes?' And we run around the house naked. Haha! Lie down on the bed and kick our heels. We call it a shoegasm." The word "fetish" flashed lightning behind David's eyes. Then he went home, and he turned on the heat, and he got naked and put on the heels and sat on his bed, staring at the wall.

∽

The next day he called his mom. They had to talk Christmas. First one without the architect in a long time. But David confided, too: it might be finito for him and Iris.

"Oh, no!" she cried. "Davey!"

Then she became all business; Connie was thoughtful that way. "So what's that about?"

"I don't know, Mom," David said nervously. "I like hanging out with her, but lately when we're together, I'm thinking how I'd rather be with my friends. Or just go out by myself. Alone! I think of spending nights with her and it makes me anxious. That's bad, isn't it?"

"Sure not a good thing," she agreed. "Let's think about this. Do you have reasons you want to stay with her?"

"She's good to me."

"I think so, too."

"She loves me."

"That's important. Do you love her?"

"Yes."

"Okay, so we know love's not the issue. Tell me what else."

There was a long silence. David could see his mother standing in her living room, looking at the boulevard that led into town.

"God," Connie eventually said, "this is only funny because I'm your mother—but sometimes I forget you're so young." Then she hastened to add, "I'm not trying to sound snotty. But you don't have commitments, you know? You don't have kids, you're not married, you don't live together. You don't own anything together. Like a house."

"You've seen the news, Mom. Who's going to own a house anymore?"

"Don't remind me. Anyway, you get what I mean." It wasn't even a joke that made sense. She'd refinanced the house, bought out the architect.

"So all that matters is my feelings?" David said.

Connie breathed, her resignation clear through the phone's speaker. Connie really did like Iris. Everyone who loved David liked Iris. "I'm saying," she continued, "if there are no practical matters? That makes it easier whatever you do, love bug."

"What about her feelings?"

"Can't control those, can you?"

"I guess not," David said slowly. "Guess not. Hey! Here's something," he added suddenly. "I don't feel like myself around her. Like when she and I are together, it's like I'm *performing* her boyfriend. Or something."

The truth of this surprised David.

"Well, you can't ignore that," Connie said glumly.

David opened the fridge. Iris had left a half bottle of pinot gris. He poured some into the stemware Iris had bought him months back. ("We are *not* drinking wine out of pint glasses. We are *not* eighteen anymore.")

"Know what makes me feel rotten about this?" he said. "Tell me I'm overthinking, but it's the only advice you ever gave me about dating. In middle school, I told you I had a crush on a girl. You said, 'Don't ever get involved with a woman who only likes the start.'"

"Ha! No kidding." Connie chuckled, like David had pulled out a dress she used to wear, a fragment that had belonged to one of Connie's older selves. "Did I say that?"

∽

A rolling blankness of despair lived in David most days. A long wave of clouds and water that blocked out colour, shadow, life, vitality. He was familiar with anxiety and dread, but the gradientless grade of this emptiness. It was different. And it came around more and more often. He spent more time in bed, more time detached from his own movement, his own feet on the floor.

In his adolescence, David was no dummy. He was sad, but he'd understood: hormones! Teenage things all teenagers experience. Teenagers with all the love and security in the world felt sad. But this demon-tinged blankness was not sadness, and increasingly, it came when he thought about his future. David wasn't feeling suicidal, but the idea of living past, say, his twenties? Out of the question. Couldn't grok it.

Unnerving, that. David thought he had things pretty good, you know?

In truth, this blankness had lived in David for years. Dozing perhaps, tossing in bed and hitting the snooze button, only recently hungry, up and at 'em.

His articulation of this fact, internalizing in the noon bedside quiet of his apartment that warmed-over adolescent moodiness was not, in fact, his problem: it was frightening, achingly gradual, a celestially slow and skyless dawn.

∽

David dumped Iris on her porch as she ashed in a beer can, staring away from him in a T-shirt with the sleeves cut off, oblivious to the cold.

"I'm impressed with your performance, sir," she finally said. "Because it seems like just yesterday we were fine."

He left her there, her arms outstretched. "Babe, no! Come on," she said. *Come to me.* "Tell me what's going on. We'll work this out. Let's just talk about it!"

Nope. "I have to go," David said with a warm smile, because even now, he couldn't help his reflexive comforting it's-not-that-bad bullshit.

I feel like I cheated on her. His hands pulled on his face as he walked home. But no! No. He didn't have regrets. He wouldn't string it out just to dump her later anyway, when she'd assuredly have been even more furious as she eventually cottoned on to his play-acting. (Or would she have cottoned? Anyway.)

The wispy snowflakes became a sudden hard snowfall, parked cars fast turning into mounds of feathers. *Are you fucking kidding me?* he thought. *I get the message, God! I'm an asshole, sure!* The anomalous snowdump fell through the night, a whole foot. A forty-year record, said the radio the next morning. When David got up, it was layered everywhere and getting mulched by cars and still falling. He watched a Subaru start across the road and spin its wheels trying to get into the street. He did not rise to help.

There was a house party that afternoon for his English class, but he figured that was probably cancelled. He opened his laptop and saw the email from the women hosting—

Wait, holy shit, it wasn't cancelled! *If you can slog through the snow, we'll be here!* said the subject line.

The house was thirty blocks away. He put on his black dress and left early; the buses were running at fractional speed, slush-churning tractors in Day-Glo tire chains. *Snowpocalypse* someone had written in the dust of a car window. At the party (*David! You came!*) he sat on a couch in a big living room with hardwood floors and so much natural light. It felt like a kinder version of those childhood apartments with his mother somehow. David sat quietly in his dress, listening to his classmates as the diffracted light moved through the room, clear and grey and open. The two women who lived in the house asked him if he'd thought about grad school (*Who knows?*), what he was doing for Christmas (*Boring!*). They liked guys wearing dresses, the women said. They thought he was so cool. Liberated. They were in their early thirties.

A younger boy walked by and said, "Hey David! Who's the president?" Everyone laughed. He was quiet that afternoon, but on the right day? David truly could be such a fuckin' clown.

∽

David's beseeching texts pulled Ray home that night. They played Smash and smoked a bowl and David explained about Iris as best he could. After, he said, "Did I do the right thing or the wrong thing?"

"The wrong thing," Ray said, without missing a beat. Then, at seeing David's frozen face, he chuckled. "Sorry, man. I think you threw away someone who really loved you."

A true fact that made everything small. Ray knew him better than anyone. Best friends since eighth grade and all that. Why *had* David broken up with Iris?! Why *had* he not tried to work it out? The only phrase churning up from his stomach, the only truth that survived any glare posed by these questions, which he did not put to Ray: *Because I wanted to.*

And Ray was a good pal; he didn't push it. They walked to the Plaid for chips and beer, did hyper Mitch Hedberg imitations walking back.

Except, later, David said, "Hey dude. About Iris."

"Hold up." Ray destroyed David with a Falcon Punch. "What about her?"

"A few times. She would ..."

David told Ray he would say no when he and Iris were in bed, and Iris would do things anyway. The language David used was *do things in bed I didn't always want to do*, and did not get more specific. He didn't talk about her pressing against David as he mumbled, *No, no*, about the time he'd fumbled with a condom and she'd said, *Put that away* and whisked it off as he said, *But, but, but*, didn't tell Ray about when David cried, *I can't!* as Iris jerked him off and she cried, *Yes, you can!* and lowered herself on top of him, didn't mention the first time, with the pizza, though the pizza always came to David's mind. It was a unique worm living in David, and eventually, David had stopped saying no and just accepted it. Until now, David had not told a soul, or let it poke into his consciousness. It wasn't like he ever had the stones to talk to her about it. Like couples were supposed to do. Talk about it.

"I mean, whatever," David said hesitantly. "I don't consider myself a sexual assault victim or anything. But she did sexual things with me without my approval. That ... seems like something to think about."

"Hm," grunted Ray.

He didn't cross paths with Iris again until months into the new year. She stayed on campus more, went to parties, but David kept his distance. (He'd ask Ray: "She still pissed at me?" Ray: "Yup!") He'd fallen in with a new crowd of Leah's anyway, centred on a small old house in Northeast. The house had a name and its name was Arnold and its walls were papered with art prints and jokes and photographs of loved people. The bathroom sported one of those signs over the shitter that´ said, PLEASE DO NOT THROW CIGARETTE BUTTS IN URINAL. IT MAKES THEM SOGGY AND HARD TO LIGHT. Thirtyish people drifted in and out of this crowd, but only four lived in the actual house, sweet considerate people all, expats from eastern Montana who'd gone to high school together. One, a moody girl who wore bandanas, had transitioned years back, and she told David, "Hey, if you wanna talk, you know. I can be nice." But all four were always nice. They hosted a Rock Band night every Tuesday, and David would hang there in a dress and heels and straightened hair. At one a.m., he'd change into pants and sneakers and take the last bus home. He would shower, and then stand in his room naked and put his head against the wall, and he wouldn't leave the house again until he had to, and once, he chain-smoked out the window until the sun came up. In late spring, Iris IM'd him. *Hey kid*.

They met at a neighbourhood bar. David got there early, and then Iris swept up to him in her white glasses. Her nails were silver. She said, "*Fuck*, it's good to see you. I'm starving. What's the food here?"

"I hope you like tater tots."

"This place would have fucking tater tots. This whole town is turning into a middle school." She hailed the bartender with her eyes on the menu. "Let me have a pint of PBR and the fries."

"Oh, you don't want to order the food."

Iris put the menu down. "What do you mean?" The bartender was a young guy with pretty eyes. "I'm hungry, of course I do."

"It's not good." The bartender pulled her beer and shook his head as if he, too, was just as disappointed. "Try C Bar across the street." He nodded to the door. "Their food's great."

"But I want to eat here!" Iris said, audibly bouncing between enraged and confused. "I want to drink with my friend, and I just need some calories. I literally don't care if you dump astronaut food on a plate. Can I not just order what's on your menu?"

"I'd rather you didn't!"

They went back and forth, and the bartender was pretty persistent, but it was hard to win an argument with Iris, and eventually, she had a plate of fries. She showered them in salt and ate one, and then looked from her food to David.

For half a second, her eyes narrowed in suspicion as she took him in.

"Your hair's getting really long," she said sourly.

David blinked and smiled. "It is. How are your fries?"

"Fucking incredible. Have some."

"What's up with that bartender?" David mixed ketchup and mustard on the side of the plate. "How do you just refuse to do your job?"

"Bet you they don't have a cook," she said. "So he had to make these. Notice how everything on the menu comes out of a microwave or a deep fryer? It's so the bartender can nip back there for a minute and they don't have to pay another guy. Meanwhile, all his customers are pissed no one's around to get them drinks."

"Then why have food at all?"

"To sell liquor. In Oregon bars, you don't need food for beer and wine, but you do for booze. Remember that one time at B-Side?"

"I was so wasted." David laughed. He had been very confused that he could not order a shot of rum. ("But this is a bar!" he'd said on his stool, like a child. "Babe," Iris had said.)

"You were ridiculous." Iris rolled her eyes. "But that's why B-Side doesn't have liquor or food. Which describes my own personal hell, obviously. This state, I tell ya."

"How do you know this?"

"I know every fact about alcohol regulations by jurisdiction. One day, I'll write an encyclopedic novel about it; just watch me. Did you know in Indiana you're only allowed to sell cold beer in a liquor store?

You can sell it warm in a gas station, but if you put it in a fridge, it's illegal."

"This is what you learn at fancy school, huh?" David said dryly.

"Oh, shut up, doctor's kid. I've seen your mom's house. How's she doing, by the way?"

"Great," David lied. A month ago, they'd had a fight when he came home in a dress. David had expected the fight. He hadn't expected Connie to say that what David did elsewhere was his business, but in her house, "There are rules, okay? It's not just whatever you feel like, okay? That's not how life *works, okay?*"

David noticed on Iris's shoulder: a black-inked circle with three wavering spokes curving out from it. "You got another tattoo!"

"Yeah." Iris didn't look up. "Last month. You wanna smoke after this? We have to go outside now."

"I know. What's your tattoo? Is it a symbol? What does it mean?"

"Nothing. I made up the design. I don't think tattoos should mean anything."

"What?"

"I've always thought so. Since I got Johnny," she tapped her forearm.

"You never said that to me."

"Huh," Iris said and forked up the last of her fries.

They didn't talk once about their ex status. It seemed Iris's outreach was more of a signal, communicating something like, "Hello, yes, I am now ready to be friends! Let us do that." It was sweet and undramatic. They walked home together, and Iris wrapped her arms around him outside his apartment. "It was so good to *see* you!" She staggered backwards toward the road, a finger pointed at him in joy. "Call me sometime!" David blew her a kiss as she disappeared around the corner. Inside, he turned on the heat, and Ray instantly pleaded with him to turn it down. He was about to graduate and his parents were ragging on him to get a job.

At the time, David didn't realize electric bills were a game to Ray, like beating a high score, numbers that meant whatever they felt like they meant. So David turned the heat back down and got his robe and said, "I had such a good time with Iris, man. It was really good to see her."

$\backsim$

The months went on. David got closer to the moody bandana'd trans woman from the Arnold house. At one party, as David blubbered about hormones ("Do I take them? What if I don't like them? What if they make me sick? What if I die? What if they make me depressed?"), she said, "Hey hon? What you want and what you need are the same thing."

David didn't believe this, but it did make him think.

That fall, he began dating this girl who lived in a creaking walk-up off Sandy, and when she told David the rent his mind blew up. "That's not what this kind of apartment is supposed to cost!" And a world he knew gave way to another. The girl was short and pierced everywhere, and when he brought up the whole gender-issues thing, she breathed in sharply and said, "I think androgyny is hot." Being honest, it was the kind of relationship he fell into? A thing that happened to him. The girlfriend connected him with a second job dishwashing, since data entry wouldn't carry him far once school ended.

The following spring, David graduated from PSU. Like a chump, he went to his commencement at the Rose Quarter, and when the crowd broke, he realized he hadn't made one real friend at that school, not one, and he threaded through the throng alone. He left the arena and stood on a corner in slacks and a sweater, waiting for Connie to pick him up. They went out for an awkward dinner together with his girlfriend at Sivalai, that Thai place on Stark where the food was perfect and bleary-eyed cheap, where the owner high-fived you walking in and hugged you going out.

∽

Then. One Saturday that July. David got cut from work early and emerged to stand in front of the restaurant in a black skirt with red ovals. It was uncommonly humid, air and windows waxy, sweat covering his back under his shirt. He felt the stink of himself rising into the street, but when he realized *My girlfriend thinks I'm off at midnight,* endorphins popped in him like oxygen. He texted Ray to see if he wanted to go dancing.

Recognizing this hooray-no-girlfriend-tonight feeling, he thought, *Fuck. Again? David, what is wrong with you?!*

Buzz in his bag. Probably her. He sat on a bench, pulled on his hair, opened his phone guiltily, and it was Iris: *Hey sweetiepants! I'm drunk near your restaurant, whatcha doing?*

The feeling of sweat and grossness flickered brighter exactly once in his body. Then he called her. "Hey drunkface!"

"Hello, sir, I am reporting for duty. Where are you?"

"Mississippi and Shaver. Where are *you*?"

"Oh, for—are you wearing a red skirt?"

He stood up and across the corner Iris waved, smoking in a green dress and Jackie O sunglasses. He hung up and Ray had texted him back: *Dude that's a bar, that costs money!*

David hugged Iris and said, "Do you want to go to eighties dance night at Lola's with me?"

"Fuck off, what? Okay, listen, you are the *only* person in this city who could drag me to something that ridiculous. That's how much I love you, okay?"

David posted up for a high-five. "No," Iris said. "And if you're taking me to this fucking dance-circus, let's get a drink first." She bumped her hip into David's ass. "I want to talk with you at least a *little*."

"Dancing isn't 'til nine. I know just the place."

They hopped on the MAX, and as the train was going over the river, some guys snickered and pointed. "Look at that freak wearing a fucking skirt." "Need your balls chopped off, dude?" David quietly stood up and motioned to Iris, and they moved to the other end of the car.

They got off at Glisan and walked to Tiger Bar. Iris ordered drinks and spring rolls, and then fell into a booth. "So you graduated, right?"

"In June," said David. "I'm new at this having-a-degree thing. Help. Teach me."

"I'm still at the bakery. I can't teach you shit. I'm moving to New York soon, though."

"New York? Who the fuck does that?" *No one's honest like an ex on good terms.* David had read that on the internet somewhere, and it resonated pleasantly with him.

"Mm-hmm," Iris said. "I've always wanted to end up there. And it's close to my parents, but not too close, you know?"

A kismet of dark light, a tiny circle, opened in David's belly.

"I'm thinking of moving, too," he blurted.

"Seriously?" She leaned her back against the wall and stretched her feet out along the booth seat. "I can't picture this town without you. It'd be like if they dug up the Willamette River. Or replaced Hawthorne with a dog racing track. It would irrevocably alter the landscape and not make any sense." She paused. "Clearly, this is on me and I shouldn't be determining your life choices."

David couldn't look her in the eye. He stared at the pool table. For the first time, he said the words: "I'm going to transition eventually. I don't know when. But it will happen."

Iris's breath went sharp. "Good for you."

"I can't do it here."

Iris didn't probe that statement further, and David loved her for that, felt right for talking spontaneously for once.

"Where would you go?" she said.

"I don't fuckin' know. Should I move to New York, too?"

"You could come with me."

She spoke so casually. Like proposing a restaurant option.

"For real?"

"I don't mean live with me! Sorry, honey," she added wryly. "I meant pool our resources. I don't know how I'm getting out there yet with my stuff. We could get a U-Haul. You have a driver's licence, right?"

"I do."

"Think on it." She could just fluidly chart out forward motion like this. Life paths were open things, and Iris picked and sampled and offered them at her choosing. "I have a room out there starting November 1. I was gonna go in October and look for a job."

And I could disappear, thought David.

This was how he'd first understood being trans as a teenager, that mashed-up kinetic version of knowledge from the old forums and GeoCities-adjacent websites. His overloaded circuitry could tease out only a few ethoses at a time from that online hairball of fervently good intentions and horror, but a more nuanced one was *Your old life won't exist.* The surgeries and hormones and voice training and document changes (and where you getting the money for those? Good question), they weren't just inarguably necessary on their own terms to survive a malevolent world. They were in service to an idea: that a successful transition was to slip inside the skin of a cisgender woman you conjured from the air. And the old you? He had to die.

This road map had frightened teenage David, to whom such recommendations felt like being told to float in the sky. Never mind willpower, the literal *ability* to pull it off seemed out of the question. He was too tall and broad-shouldered, too loud and silly, too shitty at keeping his own secrets, liked sex with women too much (another whole can of worms unto itself: this new you had to be straight).

So, beyond the planet-sized question of fear—to transition felt like he would lose something innate about himself. And ergo, this logic told him, there was another sign that he wasn't actually trans.

So.

In the subsequent years, he was warmed by radical blogs and the bandana'd trans woman who took umbrage with such an ethos, along with two guys in a gender studies class who quietly sat next to David for a while and eventually told him they were trans men. The men were a couple, and the men were kind. And David learned from all these people: That old mandated system? Which everyone had to play along with to get hormones until very recently, still did in most of the country? That old system was gatekeeping, transphobic, essentialist, et cetera, et cetera. It was classist and racist and founded on the idea that transness was inherently shameful and needed a specific corrective, and, by the way, for trans people to even be *friends* with each other was proof you were up to something weird. That old system said that not everyone who wanted to transition was meant to, and even if you did, that the goal of such a transition was cisness, to start out as one kind of cis person and end up another.

Truth was, as David slowly learned, the whole idea of "transition" itself was kinda fucked up in a certain way, you know? Some people just needed to take certain hormones to make life livable because their bodies happened to not produce those hormones. Truth was, you could be trans and not pass, and this might suck, but it didn't make you less trans or less of a woman. *What in the fucking fuck is gender, anyway?* said one of the trans men. You could be trans if it made you a homo, be trans without taking hormones, be trans and keep your old friends if they weren't dicks, be trans and keep your dick, be trans if you wanted to be *out* about it, for God's sake. You know what being stealth does to your soul? Do what you gotta do to survive, yes. Always. But. If stealth is an intrinsic, pure goal for its own sake, it'll kill you, friendo. So they all said. In one LiveJournal group, an intense *Buffy the Vampire Slayer* devotee illustrated her feelings thus, by caption-parodying that scene where Spike yells at Angel and Buffy: *You're not cis. You'll never be cis. You'll be trans 'til it kills you. You'll fight, and you'll shag, and you'll hate yourself 'til it makes you quiver, but you'll never be cis. Transgenderism isn't brains, children, it's blood! Blood screaming inside you to work its will!*

This post devolved into an intense debate in the comments about internalized self-hatred and the ethics of appropriate coping mechanisms thereof and led to an exodus of a dozen members along with a revamp of the group's rules page—but David liked the gist of it. That old world David had shivered at from afar, maybe it wouldn't be around forever. These were the ideas David discovered in his early twenties, and it made a future feel possible. If he wanted to be trans—whatever that meant?—David could maybe do it and keep his weird little Davidness.

But then David ran into a problem as he became more open on the street, slowly showed up to the dishwashing job in dresses, got the gawks and glares and dudes on the MAX asking, "Why are you wearing a fuckin' skirt?!" Gazing at the beginnings of an accepted fear that had previously seemed so mortifying. He would get home, thinking, *Fuck them. I can do this.* He would look up that clinic to get hormones and type out a list of possible names to show the LiveJournal group, and then.

Find his "courage."

Suddenly.

Waning.

Because holy jeez, the thought of telling his *mother he was a girl?* Risking that for good? That was just one light that winked out inside him. Coming out to his conservative data entry boss, coming home to Ray as he went through another puberty? Forever turning off the option of changing into boy clothes on late-night bus rides home?

The idea of keeping his current lucky little life, only girlified? Was that *really* possible?

Such an idea had been a balming thought, for a while, a mediating safety wire on which David could move across a canyon from "Fuck, how do I live as a boy when I wish I were a woman?" all the way over to "Fuck, I am a woman." But now, with its attendant realities fully bearing down on David, the thought of keeping his old life became slack and impossible. Because. Well.

Like—

Okay, put it this way. Let's say he got on hormones and picked a new name and kept at least the restaurant job and rolled the dice with his mom. Let's say he accepted his life would become less safe, but he could deal: he knew the stats; he was white and he wasn't a prostitute and the odds of random murder were in fact low, so buy some pepper spray and ride your bike more and get over yourself. Let's say he did all that and still came home to his awful apartment and played Smash. Two questions: a) Would Ray see him as a girl? And, more importantly, b) *Would he even see himself as a girl?*

Nope.

Five years ago, when David was eighteen, the stern but loving architect had learned of David's gender issues and sat him down in the living room. The architect had said, "Some people, they'll never be happy. Doesn't matter what they do. If they think they want to have a sex change surgery, lose weight, quit their job. Doesn't matter. They're still not happy. And what you're experiencing, David," he said, with hope and gentleness in his eyes, "is no different from what millions of young men over centuries have experienced. Searching for a solution, but it's a solution that doesn't come. The *only* thing available? Be happy with who you are. It's hard to learn. But transgendered: it's something I tolerate but would never respect or support. And if I didn't tell you this, it would mean I didn't love you."

It was the only time the architect ever told David he loved him. Connie had nodded at this solemnly.

David had no reason to disbelieve his stepfather then. Still didn't, honestly. It was all very reasonable. And in the subsequent five years, he would be in a skirt alone in his room, often stoned, sometimes drunk, sometimes both, and a whirl would appear in his body, and visions would come of his skin soft and glittering, covered in translucent layers, his hair falling everywhere, breasts under his clothes, without any doubt on earth in this spinning world that he was not a boy. No, no doubt at all. The only other times he felt that way were mornings in a lover's bed (never his own, never, ever his own), his eyes closed under the sheets, and he would shift his body in the bedding and imagine his lover and himself in this spinning, lucent sway. He would move to touch her—and in that fraction of time between beginning to move and actually touching her, that was when he most felt like a girl. The unreality he entered in those whisper-snapshots of seconds making a small and vibrant internal match to his drunk and high visions alone in his room, subsumed in his otherworldly, glowing, filtered, and frail version of himself.

This version of himself was the only one whose future felt unswallowed by rolling blankness, the only version that felt livable, and it *was* something new; this vision *was* of someone else. And at some point this vision began to beat out not just the reasoning of the architect that some people were never happy but also the reasoning of the blogs and his friends that his old life might coexist with the new.

In the end, he'd thought, awakening on a couch that spring at the Arnold house after a party, dreading work, groggily shifting his cold body under a ream of old blankets, *you don't just want to become a girl; you want to become a different person.* (Though then he spiralled again: *But doesn't everyone want to become a different person? Am I really a girl*— La lah la lah la lah.)

David had brooded on this a while now. Then, the other day, the bandana'd trans woman said, "Hey hon? You're probably a girl. I think you know that. That's not your problem anymore. However you get there? It's however you get there."

"What's Karaoke from Hell?" asked Iris, nodding to a flyer as she brought new drinks to the table.

"It's karaoke but with a band. Like an actual band. They have a drummer, guitar player, keyboards, everything."

"Oh my God, I have never desired anything less."

"You think that, but I come here for trivia and you get five extra points if you drink a Jersey Turnpike."

"Don't tell me what that is."

"A Jersey Turnpike is drinking the bar mat."

"I hate you so much."

"Hey, be nice to your U-Haul driver!"

They ate, left, bought a pint of rum, and walked to Lola's under the still sodium light. As they waited in line, they heard a guy say to a woman, "See, in the eighties, people *liked* this music. Everyone loves this stuff now, but it's at a distance. We all thought it was actually *good*."

Inside, in the bathroom, David changed into a fake velvet zip-up top. They ordered Cokes, and then poured in rum under the table, watched music videos projected on a floor-to-ceiling screen.

"I can't believe I'm about to dance to this," said Iris. She took a big drink, her eyes just above the rim of her cup.

"Um, *excuse* me, it's 'Maniac'!"

"You're lucky I have to be nice to you!" she hollered and rose from her seat, and they danced and Iris let loose a little as David shrieked and spun her, and between the two of them, they made a pretty big space in the crowd.

Soon, they were back at the table, panting. David's top had unzipped from the bottom and his scrabbling hands behind his back just made it worse. "Can you fix this for me?"

Iris clucked to herself, carefully refastened him. "You've got a lot to learn about being a woman, kid."

David swallowed. "I know."

Later, when Iris left to smoke, David filled a cup with water and wandered the edge of the dance floor as the crowd balled up more and more energy. A circle of people in a corner watched a breakdancer. David craned his neck to see better—

Oh my God.

The breakdancer was a guy from the old support group. From years ago. Well. "A guy." He was one of the few bio males around David's age, and at the support group he'd said, "I want sexual reassignment surgery. I don't know about anything else, but I know I want that." He and David became Facebook friends after, and they'd tried to message, but it didn't go anywhere, their exchanges awkward and flailing as a bad first date. The guy had no profile picture, a question mark above his name. He had, however, installed a widget that let you list multiple gender and sexuality options on your profile. His gender identity: *Psychologically androgynous.*

Tonight, he was wearing a button-up and khakis, flying around the floor like a bird, and when he stopped, the crowd blew up. The song had been "Lucky Star." He bowed, a lit-up body of sweat.

The guy saw David and froze. The crowd didn't notice. David nodded. The guy nodded back, but he looked scared. David knew he wasn't supposed to be there. He slipped back to the edge of the floor and scanned the room for Iris, but she wasn't there. From behind, he felt his skirt creep up his legs. He turned around and there was a woman with blonde hair, a tube top, and nice jeans, drawing back her hands. The woman giggled and said, "I just wanted to see."

David walked outside and found Iris with a chirpy old classmate fresh from a show at the Crystal. Iris saw David was ashen-faced in a way she couldn't understand, so she said, "Okay, honeybunch, you look ready to go home. You want to take a cab? Let's get a cab; we're adults. My treat—you got the rum." Soon, the city rushed above them on the 405, the skyline receded over the Ross Island Bridge, and darkness settled as they descended into the southeast quiet down McLoughlin. They talked little, not touching until they hugged in front of David's apartment. He'd figure this moving shit out, he said. He'd call her in the next week, he said. He felt good about it. Now. Determined. They *did* make pretty good exes. In the end.

COULDN'T HEAR YOU TALK ANYMORE

After Tiana recovered from surgery, she started hooking up with guys in Osborne Village. The guys never guessed what was up, though once, a mystified, coke-addled older man said, "Why are you so tight? Why are you so *tight*? Oh my God, are you a hermaphrodite?" She acted haughty: "God, no! Why would you say something like that?!" It worked. Most of them, though, she marvelled at their obliviousness. She wondered if it was bad lighting? Drunkenness. *Who knows?*

She passed nearly 100 percent of the time, but she didn't get it. Only once every five or six months would a stranger mispronoun Tiana or say something snide. But she didn't get it, and she wouldn't ever, and nothing short of a notarized letter from Janet Mock saying, "THIS IS HAPPENING" would make her realize this.

A lot of girls were coming out in her city, which she'd just returned to after years on the coast. Some of the girls were having a rough time, and some were having a rougher time. She found them at parties and on the street and on the internet. She put girls up at her place now and then. She invited people over a lot. She wanted to make her home a place girls could go; that was her hope. This is what she told herself was important.

She tried not to get too drunk around these girls when she met them at a party or bar.

She volunteered at the local gay centre. She tried to make a fuss about stuff now and then, but it was exhausting and she quit.

She tried to put together a nice adult life. Her hometown was cheap and she'd scored a manager retail job and the city had plays and movies and dances and sometimes Tiana went to them. And for every night she went out searching for boys, there were four nights where she stayed home and read. There was a diner around the corner where she was a regular, the kind of diner that gentrification just worked too slowly in this flyover town to either steamroll or slow-boil prices out of reason. She could afford to live on her own, an old place in West Broadway, and she could afford to do nice things like go to a homey diner on the regular. It was nice. She thought to herself, *God, this is nice*.

On Canada Day, she unlocked her bike and rode around the city with a flask of rye and it was kind of great. It was hot and everywhere there was gravel and dust and it was dirty and muggy and the wind that blew down was cool and swirled around her bike and clothes and the walls of old concrete. She biked through the most ancient district, where there were fans in every window of every building that wasn't empty. She biked west and there were men hanging out of every window in the back lanes. They hollered at her—but not in a nasty way. She waved as she biked and toasted them with her rye. By the time the sun set, she was pleasantly tipsy. She climbed the fire escape stairs opposite a nineteenth-century hotel discharging drunks. She watched them wheel around below her and wave, while above her the fireworks burst over the trees on the river. Tiana loved the shit out of days like this, she really, really did.

In the fall, she went back to the coast to visit the big cramped city where she'd come out, and where Tall Girls were more on the radar. Right away, she felt the repulsion on her like air, like bugs. She was swaying on the bus, enormous and looming, and a man reading a self-help book scanned her, and then pushed himself away to another spot. This large space opened up in front of her.

Just an hour later, Tiana was walking to her friend's house when a guy passed and said something about pussy, and she kept walking and he said, "Hey, c'mere, *c'mere!*" and she heard footsteps as she kept walking, she's sure that's what she heard, and she hoped they'd eventually end or wouldn't get louder, and she got inside and nothing happened. A couple of nights later, a guy followed her and tried to kiss her. She said, "No, no," very gently and softly; she detected no malice from him. She smiled and said no and pushed him away. As she did, his dick came out. He never managed to kiss her, though.

Back home, she thought about quitting her job, which she completely hated. Her co-workers were boring and her boss was an asshole. Maybe she should just apply for welfare? She knew girls on welfare. But then she'd have to give up her apartment. Plus, she'd have no money for booze. She could maybe get another job? Maybe. The last time Tiana'd tried to find something better, it was one of those once-every-five-months-not-passing times and the guy's voice went up an octave in the interview when he realized. He didn't say anything outright. His eyes just bounced for a second after the voice thing, and the rest of the interview was short. It was an office gig for a company that made canes. She wore this flattering skirt suit—she thought it was flattering. She was super qualified, too. She didn't get the job. Tiana's friends told her there were other jobs in this city that would take her. She didn't look for another job.

Now and then, her mom called. She and her mom grew up together in the country three hours away, two klicks south of the Trans-Canada and far down a gravel road. Her mom was retired now, on a teacher's pension, and was always chirpy when she called. Her mom'd say really nice things like, "Hello, my darling daughter!"

Her darling daughter.

Tiana knew how lucky she was. It hadn't always been this way; she really did know how lucky she was. There was a short but formative time when all she had wanted was her mother back, and now she had her mother back. She knew how lucky she was. When they hung up, she felt worthless and ungrateful, and she got drunk, always, and she didn't know why. She would sit straight up in bed, delivering shot after shot into her body, getting the kind of drunk where she didn't move; she just sat upright for more than an hour, lifting the bottle and hardly even feeling hammered (or any better). More a settled, stomach-folding cloud of anaesthetic haze. She would become part of the bed, the bottle on the floor, taking pull after pull after pull without moving, feeling nothing.

But tonight, now, in winter, Tiana'd had a normal evening and it was nice. She tottered around in front of the mirror before heading to bed. She'd just brushed her teeth, and after she took off her makeup, her eyes followed a divot from her collarbone. It was just shallow and curved enough to hold the spill from a shot glass, a finger, a baby mouse. There were quiet, regular moments like these when she found parts of her body beautiful. She put her hand over the divot, then over her chest.

Somewhere in her room was a picture of a young girl. It was from a long time ago, when Heath Ledger was fresh from his first round of Oscar bait and Kathleen Hanna was still sweaty from her last Michfest. The picture came from a fretty, alarmed article about trans children. Which sucked, but. The picture was lovely. The girl was wearing a dress, had a flower in her hair, and was—kind of amazingly for the time, she thinks—holding a baseball bat, ready to swing.

Like Tiana'd seen her mother do when she was a kid, she had carefully cut out the picture from the magazine and put it on her wall. And then a week later, she put it in a box because she'd had a visitor and her guts squirmed at the prospect of explaining why she had a strange little girl's picture on her wall. She knew she still had the picture somewhere—she'd kept it for years. She looked through her closet but couldn't find it.

She sat in a chair by her bed and thought. Kid might be graduating high school now. Maybe already had.

She leaned forward in the chair. She thought of a generation of girls who might grow up strong and unbothered and untouched, healthy, beautiful, learned, and full of love, who could fall into adulthood knowing girlhood, girlhood in full, having the chance at normal kinds of pain, who would grow and grow and grow and grow and grow and grow and grow and grow and become oceans, gentle armies, thick with passed-down wisdom and love. She believed and took heart from that. She did.

She picked up her bottle. She was about to go to bed but then saw a friend's message filling the room with light, so as she did, as she had always done, she picked up her phone and opened the message up.

OBSOLUTION

"I always knew I was shitty to you," said David. "I know it doesn't matter much now, but I'm sorry."

Iris exhaled in a stream that dissipated into the cricket-filled North Dakota night. David scuffed his shoes in front of the Amtrak station. Beyond them, a red lineup of brake lights waited to turn into a little downtown.

"We were in college, kid," she said. "And you were going through a lot."

"Thanks," he said. "Thanks, that's sweet of you."

Iris shrugged. She had a boy waiting for her in New York. He sounded nice. David wanted to meet him. He could go to their dinner parties, and meet them for lunch now and then, and maybe tag along when her mom showed up to visit?

Okay, let's not get hasty, kid.

They re-boarded, dumped their coats in the nest of their seats where they'd spent the last thirty hours, and Iris picked up this weirdo card game of hers. They went to the service car as the train moved through nighttime fields toward Minnesota.

Iris gazed out the window. "This is where my dad grew up."

"For real?"

"Literally no, but in the grand scheme of things, yes. He's from Beatrice, Nebraska. Five hundred miles south and east. Trust me, it doesn't look any different."

"Was he a farmer or something?"

Iris unbanded the cards, multicoloured, with images David didn't catch. She began to shuffle. "His parents were. They died early. I've only been there twice."

"Didn't you say he was a—shit, what's the word? Mennonite?"

"He grew up that way. He's not anymore. Obviously."

"Yeah," David said. "Was about to say I must have missed the hat and beard."

"That's Amish. Mennonites are different. The Amish split from the Mennonite Church in the seventeenth century. Some of the hard-core Menno sects wear plain dress, but my dad's family didn't grow up that way. It's complicated."

"Menno? You call them Mennos?" David laughed; Iris did not look amused. "Sorry. You never talk about that," he observed. "I feel like I know a million and one things about your mom, but nothing about your pops."

Iris did love to talk about her mom. Oldest of seven kids, grew up taking care of her sibs in New York State's North Country. All-American, a cheerleader. Split town after high school, cannonballed through women's studies at BU, was already tenure-track when Iris came along. "My aunts tell me money changed her, that she was different growing up," Iris said to David once. "My aunts also love to complain." David and Iris both carried iron admiration for their made-good mothers, for what they'd achieved and survived, believing they shared a similar special experience.

"My dad's just a quiet guy," said Iris. "He can be mean sometimes, about the strangest things. But he never talks about his upbringing or the church or whatever. Most of what I know's from what Mom told me about him. Most of what I know about Mennos is from books. He went east and cut a lot of ties once he graduated."

"But you visited this Nebraska place with him?"

An exhausted Amtrak guy swept past and opened the doors, the train's rattle filling the car, then silence again. Iris dealt the cards. "Twice. First to visit my grandparents, second to see his older brother. His brother wasn't a good dude. Probably still isn't. But my dad, he told me to call my grandparents 'Oma' and 'Opa.' That was important to him. And supposedly, we have our own language? I think it's called Plautdietsch? ... Low German! That's it in English. I heard my grandparents speak it to each other. It was beautiful. It's sort of like regular German but doesn't really sound like it. It was so musical, and gentle, and funny, I've never forgotten its sound. My dad prodded me to talk about school, then my grandma said something in that language to my grandpa and they laughed. They had the most peaceful laughter. There was nothing mean in it. But they're dead now, and my dad didn't learn. Anyway. Funny we're playing this game, actually; it's the one card game he was allowed growing up."

"Yeah, what the fuck am I holding in my hand anyway?"

"It's called Dutch Blitz. You'll love it. You get to shout and hit the table." David examined the images on the cards again. They looked like old-timey farm implements? There was a bucket and a cart. "Regular playing cards had implications of *gaaaambling*." Iris made a spooky motion with her hands. "So that was a no go, but this was okay."

"That's wild."

"It is. It all pops up with my dad more than I used to realize. It backgrounds his choices? Like: My mom and I go to Mass when we visit her family, and to her it's like, 'Who gives a shit? It's tradition, it's important to them, no big deal.' But he stays at home. Or like: He's suspicious of earnest people. Idealists. I get that from him. But he doesn't talk about it. The things I don't know."

As Iris explained the rules of the game, David thought back to when he'd suggested breathlessly that what if instead of driving a U-Haul they took the *train*—no, hear him out, the tickets would be super cheap with a companion fare sale, and they could check so many boxes on Amtrak, it was like half a U-Haul anyway, which it turns out would be sooo expensive to rent, plus with the price of gas and hotels? Come on, Iris, I know it'll be uncomfortable, but don't you want new furniture anyway, *please?* And to his surprise, Iris didn't fight. True, her initial reaction was "Oh my God, who are you? Simon and fucking Garfunkel?!" But after making some irritable noises she said, "What the hell. My father's ancestors would approve."

∽

David wouldn't have gone if it weren't for her. After that night at Lola's, the crystal-morning-doom thought of *I'm going to do what?!* kept him in bed for hours. Like: moving to New York to become transgendered— what the fuck?! It wasn't like he had anything to catch him out there, you know? This was where the architect had probably been truly right: Some people were never happy. Moving to a different city did not solve your fucking problems! For God's sake, he lived in Portland, Oregon, in the year of our Lord 2010; the mayor was a fag who'd admitted to boning an eighteen-year-old intern and HE WAS STILL THE MAYOR. If you can't figure shit out here, where else, David? Run away to New York? What—you think you're in the movies?

But to Iris it was a done deal. Her texts progressed smoothly in the following days: *Hey babe, you booked that U-Haul yet? Hey babe, let's*

*do a going-away party together. Hey babe, got the train tickets! You owe me
dollars. Hey babe, I know a couch you could sublet for a month or so. You
remember Ridwan from Reed? They're in the city now.*

And David couldn't say no. Some people made clear outlines of
their lives and laid out a plan and executed that plan. Some people
were that strong—that wasn't David, but it was Iris. So David had
nervously said to his friends, "Iris thinks I should come along to New
York with her." And Ray said, "That's amazing, broseph! Brosephina.
Do it!" He chanted sports-stadium style: "Do it! Do it! Da-vid,
Da-vid!" And Leah said, "I can't lie, I don't want you to go for my own
selfish reasons, because I love you and I want you here with me. But
maybe you need to go. Maybe you really should." And the bandana'd
trans woman said, "I know folks you should look up." Connie didn't
take it well, had tried to talk him out of it—"You don't know what's
gonna happen out there! You're gonna throw away your future to go
be all la-di-da? You think you'll go far? Good luck to you!" Yet even
she, on the day he left, had cracked a smile. "I gotta admit. My kid in
New York. Who'd have ever thunk?"

David and Iris played cards in the lounge car for an hour, then
went back to their seats to find the aisle across from theirs empty.
They stretched out and slept peacefully until the dawn light of
Minneapolis—Iris up and out the door to smoke on the platform and
David yawning an hour later downstairs with his toothbrush as the
train moved along the Mississippi. They had a five-hour layover in
Chicago and Iris found a pub for a decent dinner and David called
Ray with a Looney Tunes gangster accent: "See heeah, Marooney!
You'll nevah guess wheah eye am!" and Iris rolled her eyes and said,
"That's the last time you do that, thank you."

They boarded another train that would land them in New York the next day, and Iris fell asleep, but David couldn't. He went to the service car and read nervously while a man across from him had an open bottle of Sailor Jerry on the table, to whom an exhausted Amtrak guy walked past and chuckled, "You're having a good night!"

David gazed at them in his grey sweatshirt, his unwashed trails of dirty-blond hair, his black Dickies, his fingernails painted gunmetal blue. He went unnoticed as they moved through industrial Indiana. Outside was all dark. The train service was called the Lake Shore Limited, and it advertised brightly, *See America's Third Coast*. They'd be out of the Great Lakes by sunrise.

David went back to his seat and tried to sleep. He asked a different exhausted Amtrak guy if they'd be turning the lights off anytime soon. "The lights are off," the guy said, without emotion, looking right through him.

⁓

"Wake up! Wake up, you weasel." Iris shook David's legs sticking out from the love seat.

"Weasel." He'd been more drunk-dozing than sleeping, and he was instantly awake. "Where'd *weasel* come from?"

"I don't fuckin' know. Get up. The boy's coming back with bagels. We're getting you a real-deal New York breakfast."

David stretched. "Thanks for putting me up."

"Your first night in town!" Iris said briskly. "Had to show you a good time."

"What was that bar called again?"

"Pianos." She dug in her bag. "Don't forget it, sweet cheeks. It's hoppin'."

"*Sweet cheeks*. Who are you?"

"A girl who can't find her fucking cigarettes, apparently."

"I have some." The locks turned and Iris's boyfriend entered with greasy sacks and a tray of coffees.

"Oh, thank heaven alive," said Iris. "Let's go smoke, eat, and be merry." The boy kissed Iris and knocked on her roommate's door; a hand emerged with money and a thank-you, and then took a sack and disappeared again.

The boy was indeed real sweet. Wore a motorbike jacket and played in a band. Said, "I like your nail polish, man," to David when he and Iris'd straggled up the escalator from the train at Penn, gross and sweaty.

They ate on the fire escape as Iris smoked, looking over Delancey. David was still in sensory-shock overload. He'd never been east of Texas before this. Had always thought himself a city person, too. But. You know. Jeez. He ate his bagel staring at the skyline, at the endless clouds that did not part from endless glass. Last night, Iris had pointed out a view of the Chrysler Building, and David had blurted, "That's a real thing?"

"Okay," David said after finishing his bagel. "Give me a sense. I know what I see on Craigslist, but how much do you and your roommate pay for this apartment?"

"Two thousand altogether."

"*Two thousand fucking dollars?*"

"I pay twelve hundred for my studio," said Iris's boy. "I live in Williamsburg, though."

"Welcome to the big city." Iris bagged up the trash and gave it to the boy.

"If you didn't score a job yet, how are you paying rent?"

"Called my mom whining." She said without missing a beat, without pretension. She made fake-crying sounds. "Mommy, mommy. Helllp."

"That so?" David said grimly.

His mother had worked very hard for that kind of future. In Connie's view, David had thrown this away.

"Do you want to come with me to Ridwan's?" he said, changing the subject. "I'm sure they'd like to see you."

"Oh honey, here's another lesson. You're on the ass end of the park and the F train comes like once a year. You visit someone in New York, it doesn't take an hour; it takes half your day. Sorry, sweet cheeks. Call me if something goes wrong, 'kay?"

Ridwan set the last of David's boxes down in the living room. It'd been a few years since they'd seen each other, but they'd been instantly warm. David had mostly known Ridwan as a quiet goth from a Toronto South Asian family who was always at parties but sat in the corner, usually under a fog of weed. Now, they were bouncy and chipper, with a fuzzy moustache and a buzz cut. Doing a master's at NYU, so David heard.

"The living room's big, so it's no trouble giving you the space," Ridwan said, standing among plants, posters from activist rallies, and two couches, one of which now faced the wall. "You could get a curtain and close it off for privacy. If you wanted. And it's five hundred a month, if that's okay?"

"Yeah," said David, entranced. "This is fine." He opened his bag.

"Cool." Ridwan pocketed the cash. "It's hard to find a place in this city, so you can stay as long as you need, 'til you find something permanent. But we'd probably—we'd like to have our whole living room back by at least spring. Will that be okay?"

"Promise," David said. "I'll be out of your hair by March 1. How about that?"

"Cool. I have to study, but I'll be in my room. The others will be home tonight and you can meet them. My girlfriend, too. We can all hang out, if you want! But, hey"—suddenly, their tone grew serious— "one other thing."

"Yes?" David said fearfully, sweaty in the overheated apartment, liquid riveting under his tank top, his matted, tangled hair.

Ridwan looked hesitant. "Iris told me you're thinking about hormones?" Then, seeing the shock on David's face, they said, "Sorry! I didn't even know if she was supposed to tell me, or if she was outing you. I didn't want to assume anything—"

"It's okay." David said. "Yeah, I am. I do. I need to. Get some info on that."

"There's a clinic everyone goes to. It's really low cost. I just started going there. Do you have insurance?"

"Not anymore."

"If you get it again, don't tell them."

They stood there in silence. A wave of ache and understanding passed between them.

"So," Ridwan said, making to go to their room. "I'll text you the number. Just call and they'll set you up with an appointment."

Their door shut, and then David's phone dinged. He sat on the couch, sweat sticky on his back, and stared at a spot on the wall over the radiator.

He understood then, with a calm undertow of darkness, that he could not have made this choice without leaving. Getting on hormones back home, that would have never worked. He wouldn't have done it. It just wouldn't have happened. He'd marched to this point with his eyes fixed to the ground and only now looked up at a horizon that, in most other circumstances, he would've turned back from long ago. He supposed there was a lesson in there somewhere. A drop of sweat ran down his back and he grabbed his phone.

Now, David was good at this. When a task before him was pressingly necessary, he went at it without dithering. He had another month's rent on him but not much else, which meant he needed a job. So the next day he was pounding on every restaurant and bar door both cold and off Craigslist, with a resumé lying about his experience to match. It took two weeks of dragging his ass all over, but at the end he got work, at an old-man locals joint clinging onto a razed-and-revamped block of the Upper West Side, a railroad flat of a bar run by a Dominican guy who was both a teetotaller and a good-time Charlie. It fast turned into a decent gig. David was okay at the bartending thing, too, it turned out.

Living in New York City? Yeah. It did overwhelm David at first. Not a week in, he was on a crowded train stopped between 18th and 23rd Streets when the lights went out and he thought he would legit lose it, have a screaming, messy breakdown right there with his face in someone's butt.

It took some months to acclimate. But acclimate he did. Sure, the sixty square feet he called his room was a little claustrophobic, and he didn't love sleeping on a couch, but he'd done that enough as a kid. His roommates weren't the neatest and the kitchen was a roach factory, but thanks to work (Lord, right away he was working *all the fucking time*), he only cooked at home so much.

He went to his appointment at the clinic and got his hormones, came home and drew the curtain by his couch, and held the bottles of E and spiro, one in each hand.

You threw yourself off this cliff a long time ago, kid.

He popped the pills and texted Leah. *I just ate some estrogen and I'm still a dude these pills are bullshit*

Leah: *The PMS Factory regrets the delay in your delivery, we are working quickly to address your order. PS ENJOY YOUR LAST SURVIVING DAYS OF SANITY WOMAN*

PPS Love you <3 I'm really proud of you <3 <3

He texted Iris: *I got those hormones today. Thanks again for setting me up with Ridwan. I really appreciate it*

Iris: *Of course! What you doing Friday? Let me buy you the world's stupidest cocktail.*

He saw Iris around every few weeks. He'd text her when he was passing by the Lower East Side, or she'd call demanding brunch. "You look good, mama!" she'd always say.

∾

How to even talk about how those early months went by? How gruelling was the adjustment to life on hormones with grinding workweeks and no time or energy—not just the wringer of bar work but also the basic physical demands of living here, of taking the stairs and riding trains and carrying groceries up four flights. Yet this was paradoxically not without positives: the obliterating tiredness that now lived in David's body became a passageway through which he learned about that body. His internal self was no longer solely some blank oval of maleness; it was like now, suddenly, he had flesh and muscles and he could feel them and it wasn't bad. His chest became tender, his skin softer. His mood swings were different, organic somehow, like they belonged to the rhythm of the earth. There had been an electric, feral frenzy inside him all his life that was now so clearly tamed, placid and lying on the couch, raising its hands as if to say, *Hey, I don't want any more trouble*, a frenzy that had run relay with the rolling blankness that, too, had all but vanished. This all set David's metaphorical jaw: *I'm never going back.*

The clarity that he had done the right thing. It was refreshing, you know?

The street harassment, though—oof. It was starting to get weird. David would just go out in boy clothes, no makeup, without his hair done, no big deal, and he would hear that he was a faggot. It was like suddenly they could tell, like they could smell it on him.

Also, he'd told Connie he'd gone on hormones and—fucking granddaddy of our patron saint of Mistake Town—had *that* been the wrong idea. He began to get texts and emails about how they were dangerous, and how no one knew what they did to your body, and how did David know he wasn't doing irreversible damage?! Because he didn't know! And it freaked David out, and he ignored a few calls from her, and that made Connie *really* mad, and now every time they spoke, they almost bit each other's heads off, and ...

Yeah. Anyway.

What else is there to say when you find yourself changing your life, really doing it, hopping into a small ravine where the floor gives way until there's nothing but air and velocity and electrical current, and suddenly you're in a different world? Was this all too big to think about? It was, but being trans had always been too big to think about.

It really had been a trick of the mind—that easygoing, let-life-go-by David was somehow now living on a distant friend's New York couch and eating estrogen. It was a mental sleight of hand, an escape through a wall; the bovine stasis that had characterized his adult life suddenly transfigured into bovine momentum.

He was drinking less, too, even with bar life. Funny that. He liked his staff beer after a shift, and he'd have wine with his roomies, but no longer did he have more than two or three drinks. Well, cool. Drunk David could stay on the West Coast; that was fine.

One day, he pulled on a T-shirt and, as he was yawning and loading the coffee maker, a roommate said, "I don't mean this in a body-shamey way, but I'm just going to assume from what I know about you that this is helpful for the outside world, and I'm sorry if it's not: You might want to get a bra?"

It was helpful.

Iris gave David a ton of old clothes, and his roommates did, too, and Ridwan knew a tall trans guy doing a purge of lady costume bits; thus, David became awash in plaid tops, shiny skirts, polyester dresses that on him were like shirts, but he made it work. He was so, so grateful.

For once, too, David had a plan. He wanted to be a teacher. He thought he'd be good at it. He figured after a couple years, he'd be enough of a girl to move on, apply for a teaching certificate, and get a job at some hippie-dippie school. Or maybe even a public school, who knew? Some places there were laws that protected them now! Sure, the internet and his friends were full of stories about how those laws were effective as dust, still. Point was. Who the hell knew about the future? Maybe David would even pass okay, who knew! A guy at Walgreens had called him ma'am the other day. There had always been guardian angels to help David like this. He did not know why he was so blessed with them.

And best of all: He'd at first figured he had to be closeted at work, right? Serving the public and all that. So he'd just need to find another job once that stopped being possible (he'd begun, in fact, to switch his bra for one of Ridwan's old binders in the subway bathroom before shifts. Weird life). But one day after New Year's, he overheard his boss talking to a regular: "Holy shit, I told you about my nephew, right? He's always been gay, and that's fine; I don't judge. But he came around for Christmas and he's a fucking *woman* now! And let me tell you, he's hot! Like. Shit! This fucking world's crazy. I guess it's called transgender? Fucking crazy, man. I'm proud of him. Her. Her! She's a woman! She's got boobs and everything! I'm proud of her, you know? Fuck, get your life!"

⌒

One morning in February, David woke before noon on a day off. He lay pleasantly under his blankets, listening to the drifting din of the street, a murmur between Ridwan and their girlfriend coming from their room.

It would get dark in six hours. *I should explore the city for once.* David hadn't done much of that yet.

He laboured over shaving, makeup, doing his hair just so. He was beginning to detest the androgynous wrap that winter gave his body. He wore a dress and purple sweater tights beneath his big grey overcoat and took the train to East Broadway, got food in Chinatown, wandered down to city hall, walked up the Brooklyn Bridge under a cloudy sky and then back over. Asked around where the Fulton Fish Market was ("It moved, kid!"). He got on the ferry for a view of the

Statue of Liberty and took pictures at the railing as they passed, hustled off on Staten Island, and then hustled back on. He sat and took in the sparkling harbour as they went by the statue again. He dug out his phone to take a picture to send to his mom—

Saw his last text from her: *When are you coming home?*

Closed the phone, put it back in his pocket.

His face scrunched and tiny gasps came out of his mouth.

He put his hands to his cheeks and cried, very silently, a wave of despair heaving in his whole body.

He cried very, very silently.

Some minutes later, the wave had passed through him, for now. A man across from him was drinking from a tallboy, lost in thought.

"Hey," David said. "Give you a dollar for a slug of that."

The guy reached into a paper bag and pulled out a fresh one. "Gimme three and you can have this."

David handed him money. "Thanks."

"No problem. Hey! My man. Your makeup's running."

◦⌒◦

David got off the ferry and tossed the can into the recycling with a lazy merriment in his system. The sun was almost completely down. He would wander up to Delancey, he decided, and then he'd get back on the train and go home.

He was walking up Nassau when the clouds emptied on him. "Fuck, not again!" he said to no one, but he was laughing. His silly ass never used an umbrella growing up, not in the daylong dribble rains of Pacific Northwest winters.

He looked for the nearest subway station. Fuck, this was Lower Manhattan—wasn't there a train like every other block?!

By the time she got down into a stairwell, her clothes were like towels in a bathtub. Jeez, she was really soaked.

She texted Iris: *I have turned into a water buffalo and am by your house. You're not at your house, are you?*

Right away: *Oh no! Yes I'm here, toasty warm. Come!*

While she was waiting for the train, a small group of young guys inexplicably dressed in knight's armour were joking around, and one of them eventually noticed her. "My damsel in distress!" he said. "Art thou in need of a towel? Nay, my weapons are no match!"

David giggled. They got on together, the boys still joking. David stood and listened and softly laughed. She had a real spot in her heart for dudes making stupid jokes.

Her stop came and she said, "This is me. Goodbye, boys."

"Wait," one said, as the train screeched. "Are you a guy?"

Her smile froze. "Huh?"

Betrayal rose off the boy like smoke. "Are. You. A. Dude?"

The doors opened. "Fuck you!" David yelled, and the entire car recoiled at the noise. She clambered onto the platform.

She shook her fist and bellowed, "You fuckin' heard me!"

Rage continued to sizzle and spark in her body after the doors closed. *I've never done something like that before*, she thought, heaving on the steps. She hadn't. Sure, David had been a guy-guy back in the day, an annoying profane dude of a dude, but she had always been gentle. Everyone had always said this about her. David had always been very gentle.

She didn't know where this anger had come from.

Later, she'd understand the alchemical processes that fear and life upheaval could enact, allowing an entry point into the elusive escape velocity that can allow personalities to change. For better and for worse, and sometimes for worse still.

But now, she was only scared of herself. And scared, too, of course, of the world around her.

$\backsim$

"Oh my God, you're a walking lake!" Iris ushered David in, put a mug of hot tea in her hand. "Okay. Let's see," she said, as David shivered and sipped and dripped on her hallway floor. Iris was wearing an over-sized sweatshirt and blue bangles on her wrists. Her same old white glasses. "I'll lend you some dry clothes. You go into the bathroom right now and take a hot shower. I'm getting pneumonia just looking at you. I have makeup remover in there; trust me, you'll need it. Are you hungry? I'm hungry. We could order in."

Fifteen minutes later, David was sitting on Iris's couch in a green sleep shirt and pyjama pants with feathers on them. Iris was in the kitchen. "I don't have much booze in the house. Just some shitty whisky that doofus-head left. I've been trying not to drink it, which means I drank everything else, so I guess you get to reap the rewards." David hadn't asked for alcohol. "You like Chinese food, right? I got a bunch of shit while you were in the shower."

"I do," David said quietly. "I do. Thank you again."

"You bet." She mixed whisky Cokes.

David stretched her feet out. "So, how you been?"

"Well, doofus-head left a month ago, so pretty shitty. I'm starting to get over it."

"I'm sorry," David said. She'd seen Iris post about this, had sent her consoling messages, had tried to hang out, but their schedules never clicked, and anyway, Iris had a lot of friends in this city for screaming and venting purposes. Iris had always made friends fast that way.

Iris shrugged. "You know what, we weren't right for each other. I knew it, too. He was nicer than he was boring, but he was boring. I probably didn't like him as much as I wanted to like him." She sat down with their drinks.

"Do you wonder about that?" David said. "How do you tell the difference?"

"Oh honey," she said, clearly annoyed, that way Iris could communicate, *How about this conversation is now over.*

The rain continued, white noise as they talked in Iris's cube of a living room. "Still nannying?" David said.

"Yeah. I started freelancing for this marketing company, too. I spend a lot of time on makeup blogs."

"Excuse me?"

She waved her hand. "You don't want to know. You know, there are quizzes out there that girls take? And they ask how long you spend on your face every morning, and the options go up to two hours, and I repeat, there are women taking these quizzes quite earnestly?"

"No," David said dryly, "I didn't know that, but I'm glad you get paid to know this."

"I don't even go into the office more than once a week," Iris said. "Do it from home. In my pyjamas. Then again, I nanny in my pyjamas, too. You're in my work clothes right now."

"I feel so honoured!"

"You'd be the only one. How's Ridwan?"

"Good. They fight with their girlfriend a lot; that's kind of a shame."

Iris tsked. "I never liked her."

"I dunno. I'll miss them both. I'm moving next week," said David. "Off the Jefferson L."

"That's real Bushwick, hon. But that's cool. How's Ray? You ever talk to him?"

"Um," David said. "That's not been so great."

Iris's face dropped. "Don't tell me."

David sucked in breath. "He wasn't answering my calls for a while. And then, like, we were joking on this thread and I messaged him to say look what's going on and he said he was just having a hard time talking to me because he'd known me for so long as a dude."

"That sucks," Iris said. "I'm sorry. You don't deserve that."

"Yeah," David said. "Well."

"I thought he'd be better."

"Me too," David said darkly.

"How's your mom?"

David did nothing but wince. A rare look of real pain came to Iris's face. "Oh muffin. No. What's going on?"

"Let's just say I won't be making an It Gets Better video anytime soon. But honest, I'm doing real good; everything's good. Work's great. I came out there."

"You're kidding!"

"Nope. My boss was just like, 'That's cool.' I guess he's got a trans niece? I'll take it, heh. I told them to keep calling me the same name and pronouns and everything, like I'm in no hurry. But I wear a dress there and nobody cares. Every now and then some drunk guy will say a thing and a regular will be like, 'Chill, that's just David.' Sometimes they call me 'David with the Tits.' Funny life," she said gamely.

"That's wild," Iris said seriously. "You don't always have an easy time of it out in the world. I've seen your bar, it's not exactly Queer City. Why do you think that's been so chill?"

David thought it over. "I think when you just do something, and own it, and take what's yours and act like it's natural, it's harder for someone to push back. Like, then you're not making it weird; *they're* making it weird. You know? You've flipped the tables on them. It's because my co-workers and my boss are good. I think that's all it comes down to."

"On a small scale," she said, "you can do anything you want so long as the others in the room back you up. Anything. I think I really believe that. Doesn't matter what the world's about."

"Huh."

The buzzer. "That was quick."

They ate their food watching *The Bachelor*. They laughed and gossiped and emptied the bottle of doofus's whisky and called Leah back home and yelled about missing each other, and then all three tried to prank call Ray, but he didn't pick up. At ten o'clock, the two of them sat cross-legged facing each other, playing Never Have I Ever. ("What the fuck do you mean you've never played this?" Iris said.) David won.

When they fell silent for the first time in hours, Iris closed her eyes and leaned forward, and when they kissed and brought their arms together, every old crackling sensation of Iris's body collided with every beautiful virgin feeling of David liking her own. A sweet scalding feeling of affection bubbled into David's heart, and it said: *I love you. Thank you.* Soon, they were on the bed, Iris straddling David and lifting off her shirt, fingering her bra, Iris chuckling to herself and fiddling undoing it. There she was, there she was. David arched her back as Iris ground into her and cupped her head, Iris's fingers splayed around the girl's face like Iris was trying to hold her insides in, like David might bubble over and spill and Iris had to keep the girl in her skin, that was how hard Iris held her. She cooed, "I like this new hybrid body, lover. I like," and that was a little weird, but okay. David gazed up at Iris as her dick slowly, slowly rose, Iris's heavy-lidded eyes almost closed, her hair spilling in the moonlight. Iris's body hadn't changed since they'd last been together. Iris leaned over and put her hands onto the girl's chest as she pushed herself down onto her. David stretched her body beneath her lover, wrapped her hands around the bed frame, felt the cool of the sheets on her skin. *Oh*—it was then she realized—*this is what it's actually like to be touched.* Iris had always liked to play music, before, but now there was only quiet and rain.

COULDN'T HEAR YOU TALK ANYMORE

I think a lot about the first time we met. You were wearing that tomato paisley dress. Your hair was pulled high and hanging like a hook behind your neck. You were sitting next to me in the bar, which was unusual right away. Other women usually weren't there alone.

I was coming out of my post-op-gone-wild period with guys in the Village, and you ordered a vodka and Diet 7 Up. I saw it in you right away; to know you was to know how you drank. I saw it in how you ordered and watched him pour and how your sips weren't sips or gulps.

I said I liked your dress. You said my eyeliner was nice.

I said, "Yes, hello, my name is Tiana and I get into a fight with my eyeliner every day and today I happened to be lucky." To which you said, without missing a beat, "It can smell fear."

I said you were funny.

You said, "*I'm* funny?"

Your laugh was heaving and full; it sounded like you were choking.

Do you remember any of this?

You were one of the first girls in a long time who I didn't guess was trans. You read me right away. Which. Whatever. Obviously.

Had you really never fucked someone the first day you met them? Before me? You alluded to it once; I found it strange. I know you were young, but you were also hot and funny and a drinker, and that's just not a celibacy combo. Maybe that's different for us? I dunno.

We straightened out the we're-transsexuals thing, got into the stuff we get into. Your sister couldn't deal, your mom was a sweetheart, everyone else semi-tolerated your existence except for a kind uncle who lived in the West End. You eventually found a job. You grew up in Winkler, but you weren't Menno—

—and I'm sorry, I wanted you to stop right away. I know that's a jerk thing, but I'd played too many rounds of Show Your Scars. I hated that shit so much. Plus, trans girls of your generation, they never start with the bad stuff, the stuff they really need to talk about. It comes out later. And you were so young and sweet—I felt hopeless thinking of the inevitable rest of it.

But then, then, you said the first you'd heard of trans anyone was Laura Jane Grace, and her coming out made you realize you were a girl, and you were on the Klinic waiting list a month later, and that wasn't even two years ago, and oh my God, it was so long ago that you saw that *Rolling Stone* cover with "Rock Star Who Became a Woman" or whatever—

Seeing you in front of me, with your dress and tied-up hair, saying those words. It was so surreal. You know when that article came out, there was like a solid week where every weirdo trans dyke was talking about kids like you? It's strange how much hope and love and expectation we put on you when, by default, we didn't know any of you yet. So, shortly after you mentioned Laura, I said, "Shhhhh" and put a finger on your lips and kissed you. That was the right thing to do, obviously. But I wasn't in lust, and I wasn't won over: I just couldn't hear you talk anymore.

Queers are the only group I know who dread their kids won't grow up traumatized enough. But we did have great hope and love for you all, too. For a very long time, I'd *thought* I wanted to work for

My Community and stuff, but in practice, I just showed up to the odd event and self-destructed. It was a little different by the time we met. By then, I was trying my best. I'm glad you showed up to the second Trans Lady Picnic we had.

I wasn't in the best shape when I met you, but I was really giving it a go. Trying to keep myself together. I was calmer. I was quieter. I felt better. Surgery helped. I was mostly just going to work and going home. I don't know if I appeared stable. But I felt it. I love what you always used to say: "Whoever said alcoholics can't be healthy without quitting just didn't love drinking enough to figure out a way." Ha.

The night before we met, I'd looked through my closet for a picture I cut out years ago from a magazine article about trans kids on blockers—but I couldn't find it (still can't). Then I had a long and awful message convo with an old friend, and then I had a bad dream. I dreamt my cousin had killed himself, and in a note, he said he idolized me. I'm used to nightmares, and I'm able to shake off bad dreams, but that one was still bothering me when you sat down next to me at the bar.

I think it was the first bad night of winter, too. I just remember when we opened the door to leave, it was like the city was flying sideways through clouds. Yet walking with you over the bridge and through the Exchange, passing between buildings, I felt unabandoned and beautiful, even though there was no one else around and the air was like needles.

It's funny how we began to chase boys together after that first time. We would complain about boys, mack on boys, and still, in the end, go home fuzzy and fuck. You know that made me feel cis? The us-going-home part. Of all the things, I guess that's weird. But I knew these two girls when I was younger who had that kind of relationship:

basically straight, not in love—but took a limitless amount of comfort in each other, and part of that comfort included sex. That's how I ended up feeling about you.

Later on that first night, you said you were this skinny because you realized if you could train your throat to talk like a girl, train your body to walk with its hips, train your face to stand electric shocks, it couldn't be too hard to train your stomach to like the feeling of hunger. Later on that month, you told me you were raped, that you'd tried to kill yourself four times, how you tried to do it. And even later in the month, you brought out the before pictures from a deactivated profile and said, "Look, look at that. Look at that stupid dude!"

Not much is different with me these days. I miss you. I'm glad we had the night we did before you went away. I find it so funny you're in *Ottawa*. No one goes to Ottawa. I always imagined you in a real city, one with suburbs and revitalized districts and a consistent stream of new restaurants. I imagined you sharing a three-bedroom apartment with rich girls who don't understand what you're from, who have old and new meanings for "cheap" and use the new one like no one had ever extracted anything from the world before.

This morning, I was trying to remember some hilarious thing you said to me at the Sherbrook once. I was telling a story at work and your words flipped out of focus and sort of static-buzzed away. My brain is like that lately, these blips of minutes here and there that just, like, go missing—I guess I'm getting older. I wish I could remember what you said! I do remember this other thing, one morning when we were both too hungover to breathe: you said, "Think of walking, as, like, sending weight falling in the right direction."

One night, we were watching an episode of something—I never told you this—and you had fallen asleep. It was late. I sat up to go to the bathroom and felt a calming rush of power and lucidity surging into me. That kind of feeling, late in the night, when you're getting less drunk but still definitely not sober. I looked at you breathing; you were asleep. I touched your cheek. Outside your window there were no stars, just a fuzzy glow of random light. I whispered with my fingers on your skin, "Let no one hurt this woman again." I prayed it to the Lord, too, which I hope you don't mind. It felt right to do, and it felt right to say. Your breath was even. I'm pretty sure you didn't wake up. And you were so warm (your body was always so unbelievably warm). There was laughing from the playground behind your building. I stood up and looked past the curtain, and there were two women and a man, fucked up on something. I don't know if it's fair to tell you all this. You don't know any of it happened.

I still live in West Broadway and I got the most gorgeous apartment last summer. You would love my building. My new place is on Good. It's huge, on the third floor, and it has a sunroom and a bathroom with hexagonal tiles. You would love it so much. My window's open, and it's snowing, but it's actually not cold at all. New flakes are coming down, pretty, American-style ones, fat and soft and quiet. It's starting to cover up the mulched snow out in the lane. I finally realized the other day what it reminds me of: the chocolate dirt that gummy worms stick out of in candy store displays. City snow. Everyone thinks it's gross, but I think city snow is beautiful. Like you know you live somewhere. This is an unusual night.

I'm in my bed and the room is rotating but very softly and slowly. Do you remember when you first ever started to drink, like your brain didn't know what was going on and the world Ferris-wheeled and it was like, "Oh my God, what is happening to me?!" But now, it's just so gentle and warm. It's lovely. I feel so fond right now, thinking of you.

I feel warm but not hot or sweaty. I'm in my nightgown; I got a new one, shimmering red and embroidered with black lace. I feel perfect. It's a good night. I'm glad I decided to write to you.

Last night, this girl posted that someone in a van had thrown a bottle at her on Sargent (that kind of thing's been happening more around here lately), and she was hurt and really freaked out and felt like she was going to do something bad.

Like usual, I started to reply in the comment box. Then I stopped. I shut the laptop. Put it under the bed. And something in my heart unknotted and pulled loose. I felt still and at peace. I haven't even opened it back up since then. It's the best thing. It's an incredible thing, to be free.

I think about you all the time. Someone put an armchair out by the Dumpster just a few minutes ago, and already, it looks like it's covered in feathers. Write me back, if you can. It's really looking so lovely out here.

OBSOLUTION

David's face ached. It was the day after she'd moved into her new place; she was at a party Ridwan had invited her to in Prospect Heights and she didn't recognize one person, and in fact, judging from Ridwan's texts, it was starting to sound like they might not actually come. Everybody was six inches shorter than her and many of them smelled good. David inched through the crowd like a monster. Her hair was in a ponytail and she wore a dress with yellow flowers. Athens Boys Choir was playing, and people were singing along. "I'm an F-A-G-E-T-T-E ..."

The trans man couple back in Portland had taken David to an Athens Boys Choir show years ago. David missed those two.

She'd come to the party after her shift. On the walk to the train, a hipster girl smoking under an awning spied David, turned to a baby-faced guy in a hoodie, and said, "I'm *so* over boys in dresses." On the walk from the train, some dudes elbowed each other and said, "It's a m*aaaa*n!"

None of this was remarkable. David was just tired.

She went into the kitchen for water. A small girl in a black polka-dot dress was there, leaning against the counter, drinking a glass of milk.

"Excuse me," David said brusquely, motioning to the sink.

"Sorry." The girl made way. "Hey! Don't you live with Ridwan?"

"Not anymore. I just moved."

"You're from Oregon, right?"

"Sadly."

The girl laughed. "Me too. Hi. That's all." She had razor-sharp black bangs, heavy eyeliner and lipstick, and her dress was shiny and crinkly. She was dolled up right on a line between girlfriend and porn star.

That was when David clocked her. *How can you be so beautiful?* she thought.

Fleetingly, she realized she also missed the Arnold house. *You don't have friends like you here, do you?*

Then: *Is this girl really like me?*

Then: "Sorry. What?"

"What's your name?" said the girl.

The girl looked sad as she said it, like she knew when these conversations were lost before they began. But then David said, "Vera." It had come to her last night. A stranger with that name had commented on a Facebook thread, and she went, *There it is*. And now it was just out of her mouth. It had just happened.

She added, "But everyone knows me as—"

"—I know," the girl interrupted. "It's okay. Vera's nice. I'm Zoe."

"Hi."

"Hi."

"Enjoying the party?"

"No," said Zoe. "I just live here."

"Do you know if Ridwan is coming? I'm starting to think they won't show."

"I wouldn't come if I didn't live here either."

Vera laughed. "I just wish they'd told me. If you're backing out, that's fine, but then *tell* me, you know?"

"They've got anxiety," Zoe said politely. "Sometimes it gets bad for them. I know that can be frustrating for a friend, but that won't change what they deal with."

For a second, Vera was annoyed. Her first thought was: *So?! They've got anxiety? I've got anxiety! Should I expect anyone to care about* me *every time I'm fucked up—*

Her next thought was: *Oh. Huh.*

"Fair enough." Vera rubbed her face. "I could be nicer about it."

Zoe raised her glass of milk. "Rarely hurts."

Then, suddenly, an arm went around Vera's neck and a voice yelled, "You *bitch*!" Vera screamed, and then saw it was Iris.

"Why didn't I know you'd be here?" Iris said.

"Shit, I'm sorry." Vera hugged her. "This is Iris," she deadpanned to Zoe. "Iris, Zoe."

"*Enchanté*," Iris said. "What are you two up to? I was gonna smoke." She waved to the fire escape. "Join me."

"*I like this new hybrid body,*" Iris whispered again that night into Vera's ear, leaning over and thrusting onto her. "I like."

"Thank you," Vera said automatically, like a robot. Moonlight from the window lit the bottom of Iris's face, the top half covered in shadow.

Iris tried to jerk Vera off, but "tried" was the operative word.

"Oh ..." Vera said. "That just happens a lot now. Hormones. They. They don't do nothing, you know."

"Yeah, I'm aware," Iris said crossly. "But this didn't happen the other night?"

She went down on Vera, or at least tried to, and Vera felt herself leave her body, detach in a way that suddenly reminded her of—

"Sorry," she said, scooting up. "I don't think. If we're gonna do this. You can't touch me there."

"Oh," Iris cooed, "I think we gave that up a long time ago."

"I'm serious."

Iris lifted her head. She was drunk. "You're really gonna ...?" She looked so very confused.

"No," Vera whispered. "I'm sorry."

They kept at it, but Iris seemed to not know what to do, like she was driving a car with the controls ripped out. She touched Vera's dick again.

"Please stop," said Vera.

Iris's hand withdrew. Vera fingered her, and Iris was into it, and she touched Vera's dick one more time.

"Please stop," said Vera gently.

"Shhhh," said Iris.

Vera firmly took Iris's hand away.

Soon they stopped touching each other, and soon they drifted off to sleep.

Vera thought nothing of it until she woke in the night to pee. She got back in bed, and then lay there awake as Iris slept beside her.

Vera.

Yeah, that was nice.

Some things.

Shit, she could finally change her ID then, couldn't she? Supposedly that was easy in this state. She rolled out of bed and grabbed Iris's laptop, tiptoed into the living room.

She opened the computer. Iris had been listening to Bright Eyes. She alt-tabbed to get to the internet and instead landed on a Word document, a full single-spaced page that was clearly about her. Vera caught the phrase "my hetero lover has become my homo lover." Immediately, she minimized the doc.

You have broken her privacy. A voice came to her. *So now you forget what you saw.*

And Vera did. Instead, she loaded up the old forums to find a thread on gender marker requirements for a New York driver's licence. Shit, you only needed a letter from a doctor for the marker, but the name change was a whole thing with courts, and that cost money, too. Fuuuuuck. There were a bunch of confusing-ass forms, but there was a legal project here to help people with them. If Vera could call their office first thing in the morning, she'd have hours to start getting this done before her shift uptown.

༺༅

Some nights later, she was sitting in her bedroom. It was one of those old illegal places in a factory, the bedrooms constructed wholesale out of drywall within a huge room, that in the previous century had made pianos or typewriters or something. The ceilings were so high, in fact, that Vera's room was far off the ground above the kitchen, as if on stilts. But the rent was pretty okay, considering. She really did want to save up, and then try for her teaching certificate. She'd just scored another gig at a gay bar in Williamsburg, too.

Iris popped up in her Gchat. *Hey lover, working tonight?*

Without thinking, Vera typed, *No, I'm home. How are you?*

Starving, but Thai is on the way. You should come over.

Vera stared at the screen for a long time. For a second, she went to a very dark place. And then she typed, *I'm sorry, but I don't think I will. Last time I was there I told you "no" a few times while we were in bed and then you kept doing those things. We can hang out, but I don't think I want to be physical anymore. I'm sorry, that's just how I feel. And that's why I don't want to come over tonight.*

Vera took a literal deep breath and pressed send and waited for Iris to type back, but instead, Iris logged off.

Vera sat in the quiet of her room alone.

She left and stood at the top of her stairs overlooking the kitchen. One of her roommates was making dinner. "Do you want company?" Vera said.

"Sure. That sounds nice."

"What are you making?"

"Curry. Want some?"

They ate together at the little table, the roommate scrolling on an iPhone. Suddenly, Vera said in a rush, "Something shitty happened tonight and I don't want to talk about it but I think it would help for me to be around people this evening. Though if you're busy, it's okay."

The roommate looked up and her resting grimace face softened. She put down her phone and motioned to it. "Sorry. I was listening. Don't ever get one of these fucking things; you'll never look at a human again. I'm sorry something shitty happened. Unfortunately, I have homework, but if it sounds helpful you can come over to my room and read or something like that. Does that sound like something you'd want to do?"

It did. Vera read on the roommate's bed until fatigue overcame her, and then she crawled into her room with melancholy gratitude. *I need people to care about me*, she thought. *I need people to hear me. I need someone I love to hear me.*

It struck Vera that the old her was never great about articulating her desires or needs. *That's something*, she thought.

The next morning, an email from Iris. *Sorry I couldn't talk last night. But you accused me of the worst thing I could think of ...*

It went on from there. Vera closed her computer and decided she would wait a day before responding. Vera was starting to feel pissed off at Iris. Vera was starting to feel angry about a lot of things, actually, Iris just being one of them. But with Iris, Vera focused on that term she'd used: "hybrid body." It made Vera feel cold, like a machine, a product. An invention.

And so the next day, Vera didn't respond. She didn't have to respond, she thought, not if she didn't want to. She didn't have to do anything concerning this woman she didn't want to! No!

A week later, Iris texted: *Hey mama I know shit's awkward as hell. Do you want to get lunch and talk about it? Just if you want.*

They met at a bistro off Union Square, Iris half an hour late thanks to a bus that was slower than if she'd walked. She blathered about her job and her whackadoodle artist uncle, until Vera, stony-faced, said, "We need to talk about stuff."

Immediately, Iris hunched over herself. "I know, I know." Her eyes were on her plate, set in deep embarrassment behind her white glasses. It made Vera feel wretched. Iris had always been so assured, so commanding, and to see an Iris that was not those things filled Vera's insides with ugly liquid. "I'm sorry," Iris said. "I'm sorry I did that to you. I don't even remember what happened, honestly. Which is frightening when I think about it. And probably means figuring out some drinking shit for me."

"Maybe that's not a bad idea," Vera whispered.

For better or for worse, by the time they stood up, Vera's anger had dimmed. She had always forgiven easy. Oh well, oh well, oh well.

Iris said, "I guess now I'm the bad guy between us," and Vera laughed, even though she didn't want to.

⌒

Months passed without them talking. Vera wondered if Iris was pissed at her again, or maybe too embarrassed to reach out, but Vera was starting not to care. Life was wearing at her. She and Connie were completely not speaking ("You are my son," Connie'd said resignedly last phone call. "You can do whatever you want, that's fine. You'll lead your life and it's yours. You get to do that. But I gave *birth* to you. You're my *son*. And there is *nothing* that *anyone* can do to make that change."). The shit Vera got on the street was getting worse, and she no longer could even pretend to change into a boy costume if she wanted. That was just gone now. The slog of work was long, long, and she went for a trach shave consult and—shit—it was not cheap. She'd started electro, which was nice but also jeez. Put it this way, Vera didn't have much of a pain tolerance. She made a couple new friends from work, but they always wanted to party and Vera didn't want that anymore. She'd spent good years frying brain cells as a closeted college student, y'know? She was ready for her adult life to start. She wanted her adult life to start.

The one bright spot was Zoe, actually. They'd been hitting it off nice. Zoe had her over a bunch and she taught Vera how to sew, and Vera cooked them elaborate, healthy meals, for which Zoe was very thankful ("I hate cooking," Zoe said. "Every time I remember you can mix peanut butter in oatmeal I kick myself for forgetting. That's the kind of cook I am."). They were even the same age, twenty-four, though Zoe was already a couple years into the lady pills. Vera'd never befriended other trans women besides the bandana'd lady back in

136

Portland, and even that friendship had been at somewhat of a remove. But Vera and Zoe got along perfect, and they didn't talk about trans stuff much either, really, and that was magic, a gift, an incredibly normal thing Vera had no idea how much she needed in a time when everything felt so crap.

One night during this period, a chilly May Wednesday, a party-hard co-worker pal from Long Island invited Vera to a rager out in the ass end of Brooklyn, and Vera went because fuck it, it'd been a long time, and she laughed when she walked into the party in the middle of the night, because it was in a house! When was the last time she'd even been in a fucking house! She had changed into a rainbow-coloured dress after her shift that was both form-fitting and flowy, and she felt silly and beautiful. She did shots with her pal, said hello to some dude in a top hat and a beard, and some tall boy with lime-green hair who was also her height (she so appreciated people her height ...). She smoked on the porch, told loud, intentionally unfunny jokes, shot-gunned a beer in the backyard because fuck it, and everything was hilarious, and everything was warm, and the boys here were like ... paying attention to her? And didn't seem to think she was disgusting or a joke? It was nice, it was. Lately, she'd begun to get scared of that, both because she'd noticed boys in a more sexual way lately, and because of those momentary moments of passing, where she at once luxuriated in the rare positive attention while still being always on guard. Vera'd said to her pal on the way over, "They know you're bringing a tranny to the party, right?" The pal made circles with her hands and said, "Girl, you're not the only one in New York City, okay? You're not in the boonies anymore; you're fine." Vera took real comfort in that. That was a nice thought. Humbling, even. Like. What did that one fridge magnet say? *Don't be humble—you're not that great.* Something like that. Vera was drunk. Like *drunk*-drunk. Vera hadn't been this drunk in a long time, but as this night wore on, she realized, oh shit, I'm *drunk*. She fell on her ass. She laughed. She bowed to a crowd that was dancing, everyone hooting. Outside, she shotgunned another beer and pumped her fist, and a guy said, "Not bad for a woman," and without missing a beat, Vera belched a mushroom cloud into the guy's face. She went back inside to dance and fell on her ass again and said to the hooting crowd, "Ladies and gentlemen, your host!" which didn't make any sense, but anyway. Then there was a large blank patch in her memory, which kicked in sometime much later, with Vera on her knees in an upstairs bedroom in front of a penis going in and out of her mouth. It belonged to the boy with lime-green hair. The thought she remembered was: *I don't like this. I hope we can stop soon. Maybe we can do something else.* Her body was moving mechanically, seemingly outside of her control. The boy wasn't forcing her per se; she was actively sucking while he was thrusting. But it was like she was watching herself in an old homemade movie. And then her gag reflex revolted, and then spray-puke was everywhere—on his dick, on the floor, on her rainbow-coloured dress. She remembered screaming. She remembered sobbing. She remembered trying to clean up the puke, but she was too drunk to do that with much efficacy and kept tripping over shit. Someone guided her to a bathroom. Someone said, "Oh, fucking gross!" Her pal from work emerged at some point, talked to her soothingly, said, "It's okay, girl, it's okay, we'll get you cleaned up, then we'll get you home." Vera was sobbing in the shower, leaning against the wall for balance. "Come on!" said the pal. "Real soon you'll be home. You're gonna be home so soon, just clean yourself up." Vera tried to throw her dress away when she got out. The pal, exasperated, found a huge T-shirt and sweatpants and wrestled Vera into them, somehow got a car called way the hell out there, packed Vera into it with her purse and coat, gave the driver Vera's address. Vera puked in the car, too, and the driver swore and demanded money and yelled to get the hell out. Vera wandered unfamiliar streets sobbing, with the moon out but no stars; you could never see any stars in this city, not a single one. A man, an old and visibly tired man, out smoking on his stoop, took note of the crying figure shuffling by in oversized sweatpants and said, "Hey, hey baby girl ... You need help getting where you're going, don't you?" Vera snorted and nodded miserably. She was a little more lucid now, enough to hear the man's directions to the nearest train. When, an hour later, she finally walked up the stairs of the Jefferson L, strangers keeping their disgusted distance, trickles of dawn were seeping through the city. She took a long, long, long hot shower and slept for six hours, and then got up for another shift. Her pal was there. "Girl, you were messed up last night." Vera nodded numbly. The pal gave Vera her dress, smelling good and clean. "I washed it for you." Vera thanked her, packed it away. The pal stared at her. "Girl, are you okay?" Vera said, "My ass hurts. Like a lot." It did, an intense ache, not in the sexual way. "Oh yeah," said the pal. "You fell down a lot. Like a lot." Vera thought, *I wasn't able to stand. When I did what I did. I couldn't even stand. He probably had to help me up the fucking stairs.* She didn't have a great rest of the spring.

∽

Or summer.

∽

Then. One bright morning in August. Vera woke up early on a day off feeling uncommonly energetic, sunlight shining through her window, laughter from the neighbourhood bubbling up from the street. Her roommates watching something funny in the kitchen.

Vera stretched and stared at the ceiling. She felt ready for an adventure, in a wholesome, Winnie-the-Pooh kind of way. *For fuck's sake,* she thought good-naturedly. *Maybe it's your turn for the olive branch.*

Iris was on Gchat. Vera typed, *Hey stranger, you don't want to hang out today do you?*

Instantly, Vera's phone rang. She typed *lol* into the chat and picked up. "So yes?"

"Holy shit with the timing, babycakes." Iris's voice. It *was* nice to hear Iris's voice. "I'm about to visit my uncle in New Hampshire. Do you want to come with me? I'm only going up for a night. We'll be back tomorrow."

Vera laughed. "You're kidding me. New Hampshire? What time tomorrow?"

"I don't know, probably like six."

Vera looked around her room, as if an older and wiser person might apparate there to shake their head and say, *Just do it. Been a while since you had fun in your life.*

"I might be able to switch shifts—New Hampshire? Oh my God, dude! And here I'd just been thinking, 'Gee, maybe Iris would like to get some fries, I could use some fries, let's get some fries.' *New Hampshire?* Are you even a real person?"

"I'm a spirit of wonders, babycakes. Come on, the government's about to default! Next week our credit cards will be a thousand percent! Live a little!"

Vera chuckled. She didn't read the news much anymore, but she had been following the whole debt-ceiling thing. Maybe the country was literally about to go bankrupt? Life was weird. "I think that logic means the opposite, buddy."

"Whatever. I'll even get your ticket, how about that? And don't you know where you live by now? Get fries at a deli and we'll eat on the way."

⌒

The bus plodded up the FDR as they settled in. "My mom's coming, too," Iris said. "We'll drive with her to the place."

"Cool," Vera said. She was thinking, *Where will we sleep?* and *Your mom? Won't she hate me? Does she even know who I am?!*

But. The way life had been going, it just felt too nice to let an old friend take the driver's seat. "Long as we're back tomorrow like you said," Vera said.

"No problem," Iris assured her. "And don't worry about my mom. She knows about you; it's all good."

"Is it?"

Iris laughed. "You know something? Before I met you, I thought all Davids were assholes, and then you came along and messed that up. Now you're not a David, so I guess it's true again. That's nice."

"Happy to be of service."

⌒

Iris's mom looked exactly the same. She said, "Vera! It's so nice to meet you," and shook her hand. She spoke to Vera like they'd never met. She and Iris chatted in the front seat on their way to Brookline. Iris's mom had to pick something up back at home.

Vera stared up at every building on the drive from Boston. She'd been expecting a smaller New York, maybe? But everything here looked so much older. It was like watching a movie or being in Europe or something.

When they pulled onto Iris's street, Vera gaped. Around them were huge, old houses that clearly had always sheltered a single family, that had existed for a hundred years, and they were beautiful houses, surrounded by beautiful trees, the opposite of sterility or cookie cutter suburb numbness. The street gave off this quiet, warm vibration, like it had always been full of humans like Iris's parents who were going up, up, up. In all of Vera's tumbles up and down the class ladder, she had not seen anything like it.

When Iris and her mom beckoned her in, Vera drifted through the front door like she was in a dream. She was a tower of a girl in black shorts and a pink T-shirt. The dog nipped her heels and Iris scooped him up. "I'll give you the tour."

In the living room, walls lined with books and lamps and no television. The walls painted a cream yellow. And upstairs, Iris's bedroom. A full bed with crisp sheets, eggshell-coloured curtains with air blowing lightly through them. Heavy patterned blankets. A rolltop desk in the corner. A wooden chair.

There was an alternate life where the two of them had been making love in this room for years.

When Vera was a kid, this storybook brand of life seemed distant and far away. Not impossible, as Vera'd been a hopeful kid, just— distant. When she was a teenager, and her mom was doing well, it seemed close enough, but the growing realization that she wanted to be a lady made such bounty seem impossible while also, well, wanting to live. And then, for those brief shining few months, when she and Iris were actually dating, Vera thought it was in her grasp, that she could have it all, that a beautiful new twenty-first-century dream was making lives possible that before were unthinkable.

She had forgotten about that dream. But here it was. Iris had grown up in this room with its airy curtains. If Vera had been a different person, just a little bit of a different person, she might have a key to this house already. Their mothers might already be friends. This house might be a getaway for Vera and Iris on weekends and the dog might recognize Vera on sight. Her old self could be walking up to the gate right now in tousled hair, panties beneath her big black jeans, waving to the neighbours and letting the dog out, waiting patiently with a scooper as the sun set behind the house across the way. There's Jim from next door. The dog barks. "Hello sir, welcome back. Where's Iris?" "Hello, Jim. She had to take the later bus. But she'll be here soon." "Come have a drink if you like." "Thanks, but I'm getting dinner ready." Good boy. (I wish there were more men in the world like you, not less.)

"Do you want to take a nap or something?" Iris said with concerned eyes. "You look really tired."

Vera gazed at Iris with a flash of tenderness. "No," she said. "Thank you. I'll be fine."

෴

New Hampshire was even more of a how-is-this-a-real-place moment for Vera. Postcard-quaint New England clapboard, et cetera. Iris's uncle was at an artist's retreat. His name was Charles, an incalculably funny gay man with a black moustache. He painted portraits. They were gorgeous. He had a little studio out here all to himself for a month. "We're not supposed to have overnight visitors," he said, "but phooey, you're family." He and his friends got along famously with Vera and

Iris and Iris's mom, staying up late in the main hall, shooting pool and playing Ping-Pong and plowing through bottles of wine. They smoked under the stars with a writer from South Dakota who said, "I've been here in winter and even the snow is nice. It's like snow on TV." Iris nonchalantly wrapped her hand around Vera's as the writer said this.

Iris's mom slept on a cot in the studio, with Vera and Iris beside her in a big sleeping bag. Her mom was snoring right away, and Vera and Iris talked into the night. As they grew silent, Iris grappled again for Vera's hand. The worm in Vera's insides flooded through her one more time. Vera squeezed her hand, released it, and turned away.

⁓

The next night after work, Vera deleted Iris's number, blocked her on Facebook, and changed her email address. It felt thrilling, limitless, like a midnight sea.

Then she messaged Zoe in a long furious string. *Hi I know it's super fucking late but any chance tomorrow you have an hour or two to hear me open all my guts up about a thing? No pressure. Uh, I mean hi how you doing. Fuck me. Uh, you're probably asleep which is why you're offline. Love you. Talk soon.* She sent Leah a similar message, though Leah always responded sporadically.

Vera paced around her room and grabbed her cigarettes and began to chain-smoke out the window. Her Gchat blooped. Zoe. *Oh of course. I just got up. You're probably going to sleep, aren't you.*

I should. I'm not in crisis I'm not even like sad or fucked up. I just think I really need to talk about it.

<3 I've been there. Are you free later today? I have to work but I want to listen to you and it sounds like maybe it's better if we do this when we're both rested and aren't pressed for time. Text me when you get up k?

Ok <3 Thank you

They met in the late afternoon, Zoe waving in a translucent yellow blouse over a camisole. They walked around Prospect Park twice, and Vera told her all about Iris.

"It's complicated," said Vera. "She's hurt me. A long time ago, I hurt her, too. Not that it's the same—I don't know. I owe her a lot. She helped me get on hormones. I wouldn't have come here without her. I *couldn't* have. You know?"

Zoe nodded. By then they'd sat at a picnic table with coffees. Zoe hadn't talked much, but she'd been listening deeply. "I do."

"I don't want to see her anymore. I don't want her in my life anymore. I don't know why, I don't know why yesterday made me feel so weird." (Though Vera knew exactly why: It was how she felt when Iris reached for her hand. It felt so silly. Iris'd clearly meant it as a gesture of friendly affection, yet Vera instantly felt as gross as when in bed Iris had—well, whatever.) "I just know I need it to be over. Is that fucked up? Is there something wrong with that?"

"No," Zoe said after a pause. "There's nothing wrong with that. I don't think you ever have to keep someone in your life you don't want to. I think the question is whether you owe her that conversation. It sounds like you've decided that you don't. That one's on you. But if you don't want her around, that's okay full stop, honey."

Vera sobbed a little bit. She wiped her eyes. "Sorry. I've always been a crier."

Zoe offered her hand, and Vera took it and squeezed.

"You're nice," said Vera, blinking tears in the sunlight. "You're nice to me. You're one of the nicest fucking people I've met in this city."

"The world isn't very nice to us," said Zoe quietly. "So we have to be."

"Thanks, Oprah." Vera paused. "Sorry."

"You're fine. Just. Some trans women are awful to each other. I wish more of us could be friends."

Vera nodded. "I made this friend in Portland? One of us. She helped me come out, too. She was like a sister. She helped me through so much bullshit. I haven't heard from her in months. She just stopped responding to me. She had her own shit, I know. Maybe I hounded her too much. I used to need this a lot more. To process stuff. Ask any of my friends from high school; they were all my fucking therapists. I guess that's what girlfriends are for. I never opened up to them, though ... Sorry, I'm rambling." She stared ahead moodily. "I talk about shit less now. What I'm doing with you today, it's unusual now. Lucky you."

"Sorry about your friend."

Vera breathed out. "I dunno if I need to talk more about"—the name suddenly took a strange shape in her mouth—"Iris. This weird thing just needs to end." She slapped her hands on the table. "Okay. Okay."

"How are you?" Vera said after a silence. "You've heard my bullshit all day."

Zoe grimaced. "Been better. I may have to leave town."

Vera's heart sank. "Oh no. What's going on?"

"I think my company's going under. I hear companies that don't exist don't need receptionists. It's not for sure yet, but."

"Fuck, I'm so sorry."

Zoe's eyes shifted. "Yeah. Maybe I could find something else, but. Our rent went up, too. You just. This city—you give so much and you get so little. I might go back home to Eugene. I don't know."

"Hey." Vera took out her ponytail and redid it tight. "I know you have a lot of friends. But you can always crash with me, okay? Or if you wanna try bartending. It sucks, but we could set you up."

Zoe laughed. "I'm too clumsy for that."

"Fuck do you mean?" Vera smirked. She mimicked opening a bottle. "Can you do this?" Did the same with pulling a pint. "Can you do this?"

"I worked at three cafés in high school and was gone each time within two months. If I broke only one thing a week, it was a miracle."

Vera lit a cigarette. "Yeah, but you're a woman now, which means you're better at everything."

"I was always a woman," Zoe said automatically.

Vera stopped, her smoke an inch from her lips. "Of course ..."

"All I'm saying," Vera resumed. "You change your mind, you know who to call."

"Thanks. If it's that or living with my mom, I might."

Vera exhaled. "What's your mom like, kid?"

"A mess. We didn't talk for a bit after. You know—" Zoe gestured to her body.

"Yeah."

"And we had trouble besides that stuff. But we've been talking more now. It's actually better? Maybe she finally grew up, who the hell knows."

"How long," Vera said carefully, "did you two go without speaking?"

"Six months? It sucked, but like I said, she and I have other bullshit besides transsexuality. She's not a bad person. I love her; she loves me. She's just a lot. She's just a mess, that's all."

"I see." It had been about that long since Vera'd talked to Connie. Vera was starting to not have a lot of hope there. On the one hand, it made her unspeakably despondent, in a way that took her guts out. On the other hand. Well. It didn't happen for everyone.

⌒

That night, Vera worked in Williamsburg and it was dead. She sent Leah a silly mock photo of herself sleeping on the bar. *I miss the hell out of you*, she said. *I'd really like to talk to you one of these days. Call me?*

Then two T-girls she knew rolled in, Lucy and Annie. There was no event or anything, no support group, no benefit. They were just ... hanging out.

Despite what Zoe said, it seemed like every week Vera met another one. She had begun the year knowing zero trans ladies here, and now they seemed everywhere. Some of these girls had lady'd up years ago and were just now emerging from stealth or isolation. Some had just come out of the closet and were emerging from, well, mostly isolation. And these girls were making trans stuff, like ... funny? They threw around the word "transsexual" in good fun, like it was slang, and not a relic of True Trans gatekeeper bullshit. And the world was so fucking small! One night, Vera heard about this comedian named Red Durkin (a trans comedian? Even just the phrase sounded wild) and watched all her videos, cracking up and mesmerized. And then the following week, Zoe dragged her to this show and Vera *met Red herself?!* Red did a hilarious bit impersonating a Chaz Bono wannabe, and then Vera smoked with her out back. Later that night, some dude screamed at her on the train that she was a faggot and this whole town was filled with fucking faggots, and Vera smiled like a jerk and pretended to laugh while praying, *Don't-hurt-me-don't-hurt-me*, and then she bolted out at the next stop while—it only occurred to her afterward—none of the other passengers had looked up. Her days so often felt like this, a mélange of excitement and embattlement.

She'd idly dropped in on a show off the Morgan stop the other day, and the opening band was this goth outfit, and Vera was rocking out when she realized the bassist was one of them. The girl was just hanging out, doing her thing, in heavy eyeliner and a black minidress. Nobody seemed to care. Vera weighed this right there watching that girl—how it shouldn't have shocked her, yet it shocked her. Something so blasé hadn't been normal for Vera until that moment, a truth that until she died she'd carry around with her in a way she could never express.

For good or ill, the littlest stuff in this stage of Vera's life kept turning up butterfly-effect meaningful. Example: The other day, she'd gone thrifting for a winter coat. Her old one was falling apart, and she wanted to get a new one cheap while it was warm. The weekend before, a man had said hello with a smile and she'd said hello back and his face had done a thing and as she'd passed by she heard "THAT'S A MAN!" She walked just a little faster and heard "THAT'S A MAN!" She turned around and the guy looked pretty angry and was pointing and shouting, "THAT'S A MAN!" And then she turned the next corner and threaded herself through a crowd. It occurred to her she was wearing a fire-engine red hoodie, and this made her stand out in a crush of people. So when Vera went thrifting for a coat, she selected one that was black, and the next time she thought about dyeing her hair, she coloured it midnight blue, and her wardrobe gradually cycled into blacks and whites and dark blues and silvers, and that became how Vera set out visible to the world in the mid-morning of her womanhood, how she would look for a long time, and how everyone from this period would remember her.

Lucy and Annie posted up on stools. "Yeah ..." Vera deadpanned, gesturing to the empty tables, "gonna be a while before I can serve you. We're pretty slammed."

"Oh, fuck off." Lucy laughed and bought a round. "How you been?"

Vera wiped the bar. "Eh. You ever have an ex in your life too long? I'm dealing with that."

Both women nodded.

"Did you get laid at least?" Lucy said in her English lilt.

Vera winced. "No, actually that's part of the—she wasn't good to me. Anyway, that cord is cut. It's done."

"Was she cis?" said Lucy.

"Yes—"

"Well, hurrah!" she said. "Vera, can I buy you a shot? Cheers to less terrible cis exes in your life!"

They did a shot and Vera grimaced. "Enough of my bullshit. How are you guys?"

"I have the opposite problem," Annie said, her Afro'd hair gleaming in the bar light.

"Not enough exes in your life?" Vera snarked.

Annie shook her head and looked into her whisky. "I think I fucked it up with this girl I was seeing."

"I'm sorry," Vera said. "Do you want to talk about it?"

"No," Annie looked embarrassed. "Then again, not talking about it's sort of been my problem."

"Is your girl also cis?" said Lucy.

"No."

"Right, best get her back then. What's her number? I'll call her for you."

Annie laughed. Vera said, "Who is she? We know her?"

"Maybe? Lizzy, Lizzy Inada?"

"Oh, I think so!" said Vera. "Punk girl, funny ...?"

"That's her."

"What happened?"

Annie paused, looking up, visibly recalling a memory. Then her expression faltered. "I think I actually don't wanna talk about it. But hey, maybe this is a nice story: When she and I first met? I didn't realize she was coming on to me. I didn't realize trans women hooking up with each other was, like, a *possibility*. We were chatting outside the bar and I just thought, *That's nice. I don't have many trans lady friends. And for once she's not white. That's even nicer.* And then she was like, 'Can I kiss you?' And right there. In two seconds. The world was different."

Vera had listened raptly. "That's lovely."

Annie smiled into her glass. "We had some good times."

Vera was cashing out a bill at the other end of the bar when she heard Lucy, angry. "What the *fuck*!"

"You okay?" Vera called.

Lucy was staring at her phone. "What the fucking *fuck*! Have you heard of this show *Work It*?"

Annie's face slackened. "Oh. That. Yeah."

"What's this?" Vera said.

Lucy flipped her phone to Vera and Vera read out loud: "'This high-concept comedy centres on two unrepentant guy's guys who, unable to find work, dress as women to get jobs as pharmaceutical reps. Not only do they pull it off, but they might just learn to be better men in the process'—oh my God, that's the most ridiculous thing I've ever seen."

"Watch it win a million Emmys," Annie said darkly.

"Can you believe fucking *Entertainment Weekly* is calling this 'high-concept'?!" Lucy said. "I can't stand America. If I stay any longer I'll be an American. I have to leave."

Annie tapped her glass on the bar. "I mean, I hate to say it—not to give them any credit, because they won't have meant it this way—but it's not a dishonest idea about what gender is. A way to get something."

Vera's back had been turned and she stopped and turned around. "Excuse me?"

"Gender is transactional," Annie said. "It doesn't exist in a vacuum."

"Of course gender doesn't exist in a vacuum, but how is it transactional? We're making pretty bad transactions if that's the case. Worst capitalists ever?" It came out more meanly than Vera meant it.

"No, she's right Vera," said Lucy. "All right, listen, I am old, okay, and I'm pretty done with this shit, but I came out in 2001, right? That time, I was only gendered correctly by homeless people. I thought there was something nice about that at first. Liberal bullshit, whatever. Later I realized, in that period of my life, they were the only ones who needed something from me."

"Maybe I mean *communication*, too," Annie added. "It's not a social construct and it's not some innate magic thing. Gender's just a way of getting something across. It's a way of telling the world what you need. What you want. What you can't handle. And the world responds accordingly. The world may be fucked up about it, but that's what's happening."

Vera thought this was crap. "Okay, then if no one fucking recognizes we're women, why bother being women?"

"When a cis man chooses to wear a suit, he is communicating something to himself and to the world," said Lucy. "When you take your spiro, it's the same thing. Without gender, there is no way to want something from yourself or other people. Gender is language. That's all gender is."

"You sound like one of those bullshit professors that's never actually met a trans person," Vera said sourly. In the back of her head: *I never used to talk like this.*

"Look," Annie said. "We're all women. Of course. But if you had never met a woman, you wouldn't know you were one."

The bar had filled. A score of party gays needed Vera's attention. One wasn't shy. "*Excuse me!*"

"All you'd know is that something was wrong," Lucy added. She drained her beer. "In some fashion or another."

"You've given me a lot to think about," said Vera. (What if Iris had been a different person? That too.)

∽

That night, still no word from Leah. In a sudden bolt of viciousness, Vera deleted her number and blocked her, too. Then she riffled through her Facebook in a fugue and unfriended almost everyone from her old life. When she was finished, she crumpled into her chair as if she'd collapsed into a subway seat after a long day.

She messaged Zoe a single heart. *I'm so glad I have you to listen. It's been a while since that's happened. Don't forget, you need a couch or you wanna try the bar, give me a call. Thank you again. For everything.*

ROSE CITY, CITY OF ROSES

Sunday, May 17, 2020

Sue,

It's Nicole. I dreamed about you last night. What happened in the dream, I don't remember. There was you, a pool table, a sea of empty two-litre soda bottles, and a framed portrait of an old hookup of mine, a sweet guy with a scratchy beard and a diaper fetish who I wish I'd treated better. It was one of those random dreams that felt sensible and relaxing. And in it, you were alive as ever.

So when I woke up, and remembered you were gone, I felt real despair. I stayed in bed for some time. It's only been two months since you died, Sue, yet I hadn't thought about you for a few days there, until last night, when you were in my dream.

You died young, of a disease you had fought for a long time, in a moment when the world was falling apart around you. And the people who loved you, disparate and far-flung as they are, could not gather. I have my own superstitions about how this affects people who are gone, and I hope for your sake I'm wrong about them.

I suppose I hope you're laughing at me right now, thinking this makes any kind of difference.

I'm aware you know about grief and loss, that you learned this long ago, in middle school, when your boyfriend died in the towers. (Not that we ever talked about it ... Lloyd told me.) Sometimes I think it's one of the cruellest things, when someone grieving is surrounded only by those who didn't know the person who's gone.

Without anchors, grief dissolves in the brain like salt in water, invisible and unremovable, silent and interwoven. Example: I have a photo of you on my wall. It's clearly from high school. You're laughing in a crowded kitchen, but the house doesn't look familiar. Lloyd is the only other identifiable person in the picture, and he's looking at who-ever you're looking at, but that's all the clues. There's no one in my life right now who could help make this picture make sense, or who would bond with me over its guesswork. Regardless, anyone from those days would agree: this picture of you is *perfect*. Your laugh that was joy-filled and pissy and blade-sharp, unmimickable by anyone. I can imagine showing this picture now to the guys from back then, and to all of them, the sound of your laugh would be crystalline. But if I said any of this to a stranger, to even the kindest, most interested stranger, there's nothing I could truly get across. It would fall apart as I was speaking, in the way of memories after dreams.

I'm still in Canada. In a small city right across the border from Detroit. I forget if I was here last time we talked, but I've been here a few years. It's all right. It's the Rust Belt, but it's also easy to exist; that's the shortest way I can explain this town. I work for a publishing company in the artsy district. I sold my car and got a nice apartment that's quiet and safe. I like to bus to work in the mornings, and then walk home in the evenings. Evenings, for me, have always been harder than mornings. In normal times, that's not so bad—I'm an adult with a good job; I have the resources to pursue the quotidian ways one makes an evening easier in the twenty-first century. I do like my eve-ning walks. The riverfront is nice and the Detroit skyline is beautiful. Sometimes I stop in at Villains for a drink on the way. I feel whatever about drinking, but I like bars. I like to sit and read and nurse one and linger.

That's not happening right now with pandemic life, obviously. Right now, everything is so dark I can barely talk about it. If the future holds anything normal, I could see myself becoming a good-natured old hag with a permanent seat at the bar who no one ever sees tipsy. I like the karaoke at Villains on Sundays, too. And, I swear, that place is the only joint in this town that doesn't always have on just sports.

⌒

I found an old email from you last night, like from fucking 2004. I'd apologized for calling you at one-thirty in the morning. You said it was okay, you were sorry you missed the call, you were just watching TV, but you'd turned your phone on silent. I didn't have a cell yet and couldn't text.

My email was from around 2:00 a.m. Yours was from 3:34. I'd forgotten how late we stayed up when we were younger, how seriously afflicted you were with insomnia, how miserable and absent my body was of serotonin. I was exploding with sadness, and I didn't know why, and I didn't mind phoning you to talk about it, either. You were so kind about it, always. Thanks for that.

I know teenagers are often just that way. I suppose I think of it in retrospect with particular melancholy being trans. I dunno. You were once the recipient of hours of my bullshit, so. I wonder what you'd think of my life as it is today.

Did I ever tell you I messed around with girls a few times? I was a sexless ghost in high school, as you know, and the few people I even told I liked boys—it was more just 'cause that was *easier*, the quickest way to make sense of myself. Both for me and for those around me. Lots of straight people don't know this history (maybe you do? You've surprised me before), but there was a time when the idea of being a homo *after* your sex change just foreclosed any peeping pinhole of acceptance the outside world might deign to give a transsexual life.

I'm still single. Obviously, not much dating's going on at the moment. I've heard of people sitting masked at picnic tables—that's just too sad to me. These last couple months have been murder, but some things I won't do.

I flipped through this book in the store a while back, an essay collection by a woman writing about her life and the disconnects between her and the world. It reminded me of what you and I used to write in LiveJournals and all the rest. I thought, *If I'd seen this woman's writing semi-privately on a screen, it would have slaughtered me*. Yet the book in my hand left me cold. I think some words are only meant to be delivered in ephemeral pixels. We were sold that what's written on the internet was forever, but the fact is, so much of it was impermanent daydreams and abysses, gone the second you forgot how to look it up or the owner deleted it or unfriended you, or it lived on a remote subdivision that the Wayback Machine just wasn't meant to capture. You're one of those; you deleted your LiveJournal years ago, and I know I know I know, I did too, but I'm still here and you're not.

... Sorry.

You were maybe the only, and I mean the *only*, person who, from the beginning, ever made me feel something like normal.

Right before the world went to shit, a thing happened with this girl I know. I've wanted to tell someone about it for a while, and I think you're the only one who'd understand why it was important to me. You're the only one. I have to put this somewhere, and then hope you hear it, wherever you are.

So.

⌒

Many years ago, when I was twenty-one, I met this woman named Cleo. Her style was a careful, curated mix, a curation I now can only describe as a trans dyke who takes pains to pass, but she's still a dyke. She wore a long black hoodie with red trim and patches sewn on with dental floss. Bright red lipstick and a nose ring big enough to hurt somebody. She had black hair and green eyes.

This was during a time when I didn't know anyone like myself. We were on a bus going downtown. She had a water bottle in one hand and was whispering into her phone in the other. I was a row behind, where I could watch her. She got off in Old Town, and I got off, too, and followed after her and said, "Hey!"

Her shoulders tensed before she turned. She softened when she saw me.

"Sorry," I said. "Hi."

"Hi? Do I know you?"

"Maybe. Sorry, this is weird. Are we sisters?"

The internet taught me that move.

She finally smiled then. "I think we are." She shook my hand, and it sent a cool bolt through my arm. "My name's Cleo."

"I'm Nicole."

We stared at each other awkwardly. It's age-old. You meet someone whose mould of pariah weirdo looks something like yours, and you try to reach out, but you're on guard, because what if you hate each other, or what if she sucks—*plus*, what if somebody clocks the two of you together when on your own you would've gone undetected? That mode of thought was around more back then, partly because of gatekeeping bullshit and partly because of good reason.

Cleo said, "Do you want a drink?"

I sipped from her water bottle (vodka) and handed it back and she tipped it up. And her body visibly relaxed. Like I could see the electricity running through her veins.

Next thing I remember, we were walking over the Burnside Bridge. She asked, "How old are you?"

"Why do you care?"

"Because you're cute, that's why."

It was there, right there, that I knew I loved the sound of trans women's voices. I remember the exact cadence of how she said it. The memory of this sentence would have me clocking would-be stealthers for years, no bullshit. The slight elongation at the end, the pitch-dip in the middle of the sentence. Not that we all talk the way she did. But some of us do.

"Are you saying you want me older or younger?"

She laughed. "Okay, that's creepy. Let's talk about something else."

"I'm twenty-one exactly. How old are you?"

"Oh shit," she said. "Girl, older than you."

She led me to an old warehouse in the Central Eastside with OFFICE LIQUIDATORS painted on the front in three-foot letters. Cleo moved through an open door. "Follow me."

We walked through lit hallways. We heard the voices of people at work, faint and far away. Cleo turned up a flight of stairs, and suddenly, we were in a cavernous, slanted room. It was like an enormous lecture hall, but filled with desks and rolling chairs and filing cabinets instead of seats.

"Check it out!" She scrambled up toward the back. Her hoodie was falling off her shoulders, and the light made a huge shadow of her on the wall. We were at the top and panting. "Turn around," she said.

There was a huge window on the other side of the room taking up the upper half of the wall, looking onto the interstate. It was near sunset, and the concrete was blasted with light. You couldn't see the skyline on the river's other side.

"This is pretty," I said, awed.

"*You're* pretty," she said. She said it with sass. She said it without looking at me. Then she said, "Do you want to make out?" That was another first for me: the idea that you'd ask. We kissed slow, delicately, and I felt for the first time the largeness of another human's body as beautiful.

Later, in the dark, we walked through a cemetery swigging from her water bottle, and there was, of all things, a rolling office chair sitting in the middle of a path. She flopped into it and said, "Push me!" I pushed her down the walk until the chair spun out and she landed in the grass. I got in and she pushed me, hooting all the way out to the street.

We passed a woman in the cleanest, crispest shirt in an empty, bright shop. She was putting racks up on a wall and her front door was open. Cleo asked, "What are you doing?" and the woman in the crisp shirt said, "I'm putting in my store. I'm going to sell clothes!"

Cleo pushed me on 'til we stopped at a light, and I stood up and kicked the chair spinning into a doorway. "I'm drunk!" I said with surprise. A falter of sadness crossed Cleo's face. "Yeah," she said. "I have that effect on people."

She led me through a backyard filled with purple lights to a detached garage. Inside: a concrete floor and no insulation, a dresser and a space heater and a bed with a sleeping bag for a blanket. She turned on the heater and said, "Come here."

She fucked me with my legs straight up, gathered in one of her arms.

The next morning, she took me in the house to make breakfast. There was detritus on every surface of the kitchen and a bookshelf filled with gay shit and mass-market sci-fi. In the living room was a makeshift bench press, above which was a Sharpie'd sign: I AM A QUEER MUFF-DIVING SPARKLE GLITTER FAGGOT AND PROUD.

I leaned over to kiss her as she whisked eggs. She kissed me back, and then suddenly she had me by the hair and leaned me back over the stove with her hands in my crotch and, God, it was fucking hot, and I cried out, and then I apologized and she gave me a look that was very stern and said, "Loud sex is allowed in this house."

I had to work after we ate, and noon found me on a bus going into the far north of the city smelling like cum and grease, looking out the window onto what felt like a different Earth.

We hung out once more before she split town. She was already drunk and we went to the old nickel arcade. We had a hoot. She dominated at pinball. The next morning, she put on country tunes while we lay in bed. A man and a woman were singing together and it was beautiful. Punks who like country! There's a lot of them, huh? I have fond memories of that.

Cleo got up and told me to wait. She returned with breakfast in bed, and ugh, how fucking sweet is that, right? But—it freaked me out. I don't know. I was attracted to her, I liked hanging out and I liked the sex, but I didn't feel anything more. Which I wasn't able to say. You may remember I did not always understand how one responds to romantic intimacy.

I ate her toast and eggs, and then got up and was all "Well, I gotta work!" though my shift didn't start 'til one.

And as I was getting dressed, with the space heater roaring, Cleo said in a voice that broke out of a sob, "Could you ... Could you just come cuddle me for a bit?"

Cleo had radiated power and confidence until that point, power and confidence I had given to her without knowing. (Here's a secret: I used to fret my name was boring, but know why I like it now? No one overestimates a Nicole.) I took my clothes back off and got into bed and I felt her body unclench while mine left the room.

She said, "We're meant to be kept from each other, you know," her verve returned.

She bounced out of town a few weeks later. She was one of those punks who did that, drifted. How she stitched her life together, I don't know. But before I left that day, Cleo burned me that country album. I found out later it was Robert Plant and Alison Krauss doing covers, and I thought of Cleo every time I listened to it, though I wouldn't see her again for a dozen years.

You know the rest of what happened to me, or some of it, anyway. I fell in love with a boy, a young boy from Lake Oswego whose innocence and sweetness befitted his eighteen years. He'd just left his family and the Mormon Church, and we bonded for a long time over that. He more or less moved into my room while we were together. He was a magical boy. Good at fixing things. Twice, he bought me groceries while I was literally napping, exhausted from work. He was a nice boy. We had both been made for different lives, except I couldn't go back, and he could, and eventually, that's what he did.

I moved in with Lloyd after that. I had no idea what else to do. He posted that he was looking for a roommate, and I responded, and suddenly, I was living with him.

I called him, by the way, with the news about you. He always thought of you fondly, always, I want you to know.

One night, I went out for dinner with Lloyd and his girlfriend at Marie Callender's. I told them I'd been talking to this Canadian guy on the internet.

Lloyd said, "Wasn't your grandfather born in Canada or something? Can't you apply for citizenship with that?"

I said, "Yeah, New Brunswick, but I dunno."

Lloyd lost it. "How many people like you!"—he paused—"I mean, in your situation, would give an arm to just up and *go* to Canada?" Provinces had just begun to fund bottom surgery again, and Lloyd knew I wanted it. (Lloyd asked me about bottom surgery a lot.)

I didn't have a good answer. His girlfriend put a hand on his arm. "Sweetie, this is her home. Maybe it's not that simple."

That night, after jerking off before bed, I started crying. (Very tragic tranny.) I slumped against myself and I thought, *He's right. There's no shame in taking an exit that's good. When else will it happen?*

I might really believe that. Every now and then you get offered an exit, something you didn't plan for, something you don't deserve, and something you don't believe you can rely on. So you don't take it. Eventually, I realized: It doesn't matter. No one deserves anything, really. I was on a plane a year later.

I stayed in Edmonton with that boy from the internet for a long time. He worked camera at a news station, he was obsessed with urban planning; he had a thing for getting tied up and he thought that was extreme and I loved that about him. And his parents—ugh—they were beautiful souls, apostates from a little Mennonite town. They made room for me in their family without question, and they were so incredibly kind. Those were a good few years. I built a life in that city, and yes, I got my pussy. I could've stayed with that boy forever, but one winter evening, as wind rage-whistled outside, he looked at me in the yellow kitchen light and he said, "I've been seeing someone."

I looked for a job to get me out of town, anywhere away from him. The publishing company here had a paid internship, and I jumped on it, and then they kept me. I've been here a while. Cleo came back into my life last fall.

⌒

Cleo was part of this network I've only ever glimpsed through the internet, a network of trans women travelling and loving and fucking each other. She lived in LA, working as a midwife, but still, one day I'd see pictures of her picnicking in Chicago with other girls in sundresses, and then suddenly I would see pictures of her in Tennessee, the girls wearing leather shorts and glitter and holding chainsaws.

This isn't to say I wanted what I assumed these women had. I knew the life I wanted and the life I didn't. I mean to say it fascinated me, and that when Cleo messaged me last November, to say that she was here, she was stuck, and could she crash with me?—sure, it was a surprise, but it also made perfect sense. Like of course, after all this time, this was the context in which I'd see her again.

I'd been walking home by the river when she messaged. The air was brisk and cool. *There was bullshit with my passport*, Cleo explained. *They just let me through but my bus left hours ago.*

I told her I was close to the tunnel; I'd be on my way.

She said, *What's your compatibility with bars?*

This intentionality of communication, a very delicate and pointed openness. Queers like to talk shit about being terrible communicators, but I don't think that's always true. I'm trying to say I loved it when Cleo said this to me.

My compatibility with bars is great, I said. Then, remembering Cleo was Cleo, I added, *I won't drink that much though.*

Cleo replied, *Me neither, I'm sober. Where do I meet you?*

∾

She was already sitting in the dark light when I walked into Villains, a glass of fizzing liquid on the table and a picture of Agent Smith from *The Matrix* behind her. That's the shtick at Villains. The decor is all paintings of bad guys, from Darth Vader to Yosemite Sam to the old woman from *The Goonies*. I think it's cute.

Cleo wore a dress with green flowers and an unzipped grey wool jacket. She stood and spread her arms wide. "I made it to Canada!"

After we hugged, I got an OV and sat. "What are you doing here? Where were you going? Toronto ...?"

"Montreal. How are *you*? The years have been kind to you, lady. You look great."

"Uh-huh." What can I say? That compliment rolls off me. I added, "Hey, congratulations on your sobriety."

"Ha!" Cleo let out a sharp bark. "Sure, thanks."

It was as if we'd both somehow inadvertently insulted each other, then both decided to let it pass. As we sat in silence, this girl with red hair walked by and waved to me, a girl who's here all the time. Young kid. One night, she showed me a stripper's socials who she thought was just the coolest. She was matter-of-fact about it.

I don't mind the next generation. I'd be happy to put them all in charge and skip ours, to be honest.

Then Cleo spoke quietly. "I'm trying to move here."

Let me tell you, Sue: who the years had been kind to was her. Her eyes were more sunken, and her roots a subtle grey, but besides that, she looked no different—and I mean *no* different—than she had staring down at me in her bed twelve years ago, her forearm wrapped around my legs. If I hadn't known her, you could've told me she was any age between twenty-five and fifty and I would've believed you.

"What do you mean you're trying to move here?" I snapped.

"To Canada!" Cleo said. Then she saw my face and put a hand up. "Oh. No, I don't mean, like, *here*." She pointed a finger down at the ground. "Don't worry. I wouldn't do that to you. This girl I worked with lives up there. I'm just trying to leave the US. She knows doula people; I'm gonna talk with them."

"I see," I said disbelievingly.

"This is a long-term project," she added dryly. "I'd never hop the border and be like, 'Surprise!'"

"You have no idea," I said grimly, "how many people have asked me if they could do that."

"Anyone take you up on it?"

"No. Lotta joke marriage proposals, though."

Cleo gave a wry smile. "How does that make you feel?"

For a rare second, I felt my voice go hollow. "Terrible," I whispered. Cleo nodded.

I blinked and sipped my beer. "I don't mean to be uncharitable. I know America's fucking weird right now. It's harder to live without papers here—you should know that, by the way—but that's not what people are asking about. People say what they need to say."

A grin moved around Cleo's lips. "You can be *actually* uncharitable if you want."

That made me laugh. "I'd rather not, thanks. Hey, if you can get up here, *bienvenue*."

"Thanks. I got another bus for tomorrow. It's in the morning. Really glad you could put me up. You wanna walk and get food?"

"Lemme hit the ladies room."

The bathroom graffiti's another bizarro balm in this place. They never paint over it, either. Choice examples:

DON'T DO ANAL IF THEY WON'T EAT ASS

YOU'RE NOT HIS FUCKING MOTHER

TAKE BETTER CARE OF YOURSELF, MY FRIEND, followed by *OH HALLELUJAH OUR PROBLEMS ARE SOLVED WE HAVE BANANA BREAD* (?)

LEARN THE DIFFERENCE BETWEEN BAD DICK AND GOOD DICK, which someone had then crisply crossed out with one line of a black Sharpie—but only one line; it was all still legible.

The riverfront was dark now, wind gusting along the water. Cleo was startled by the skyline. "Oh shit, Detroit's there. Like it's *right* there."

"You didn't notice on the bus ...?"

"I was sleeping."

Cleo didn't walk so much as bounce, legs flying out in front of her. Her coat flapped in the breeze.

At home we ordered pho and sat in front of the TV. We idly talked more, but we also just ate and watched in silence. It felt nice, like how my sister and I used to spend evenings. I made up the couch for her to sleep. She burrowed into the pillows and pulled the blankets up and reached for her phone. Cleo looked young as she did this, younger than me for the first time since I'd met her. She looked so pretty and innocent, and it was then I understood that in a very particular way she had managed to preserve herself. It made my heart split open.

I made to say good night and go to bed. Then I stopped. "Okay, tell me," I said. "Do I *not* congratulate you on your sobriety?"

She looked up from her phone and flashed me a wolfish smile. "I don't trust anybody with it."

"No?"

"Nope."

I put my hand on my bedroom door. "Cool." *Go to sleep, loser.*

"You know what I hate most?"

I took my hand off the door. "Tell me."

She stayed in the same position but put her phone down. "I hate before-and-after pictures of drinking. It's like before-and-after weight-loss photos. I dunno how you feel about that, but I think it's just as fucked up."

I nodded.

"The before pictures are blurred, poor quality," she continued. "They're always supposed to be pathetic and sad. Whatever the before people are feeling? It must have been at once depressing and immaterial. And if they're smiling? Must just be masking the deep pain. The before person is supposed to be a different human, someone who no longer exists. And they are selling you that the life on the other side is going to be meaningful for the first time."

"Sounds like—" I started to say, but she cut me off.

"Transition photos." Her eyes danced, not looking at me. "Exactly."

⤮

Every now and then, I realize that it's been months since I've been touched. I can't tell you how dark it feels. When I can't be alone in my apartment anymore, I walk the riverside and the streets and the campus in my neighbourhood, and the quiet feels like it's going to kill me. Yes, sometimes there are people, and sometimes they're even with each other, and sometimes I can even see their faces—but that's worse, somehow. Because there's such an undeniable reason underlying the fact that I cannot get close to them. In the sickest, most awful way, it feels like being a teenager again. All these strangers, they have lives and they're going on without you and what you can do is nothing, nothing, nothing but walk alone and sit in your room. Supposedly, one day, life will be different, but how does that mean anything and how can you believe that? The strangers say they're feeling the same way. I know I should believe they are.

⤮

The next morning, I watched Cleo leave in the rain out my window. There was no rhythm to how Cleo walked, either. She would list to one direction, and then back with no pattern, throwing herself into forward motion.

Next evening was Sunday karaoke at Villains. This guy I know, Tommy, posted up next to my stool.

I once had a one-night stand with Tommy, after meeting him in this very bar. He took me to a house in Walkerville, a house he owned and lived in by himself. He was in his late thirties and worked in a factory. We tried to have sex, and we did for a bit, but he was hammered and couldn't keep it up with a condom. I told him he could fuck me bareback, but then we both passed out. That morning, I drifted in and out of sleep in his bed until noon. I saw the sunlight coming through his curtains. Eventually, he woke me in a timid voice. "Don't you think you should be getting up?" I gave him my number, and he drove me home.

Months later, I saw him at Villains again, this time with a woman. He introduced us. "This is my girlfriend." They had just met. She was friendly and tiny and skinny. She wore a tank top and big silver glasses, and she had long black hair.

Now, she was across the bar, putting in songs for karaoke. Tommy flagged the bartender and turned to me. "Did I see you leave with someone the other night?"

I blushed. "Yeah. Old friend. She left yesterday."

"Aw"—he grinned—"I thought maybe you two were—I dunno."

"No." I wonder sometimes: Did the script get flipped? Do they *want* us to be lesbians now? I changed the subject. "Are you singing?"

"I'm doing the Dead Milkmen. What'd you put in?"

"Oh, I wouldn't tell you!" I said. "It's bad luck to give away your tune."

⌒

Sometimes I watch TV and I want to throw it against the wall. Sometimes I read a book and I want to rip out every page. Sometimes I am in a restaurant, patiently waiting for my takeout, and I see a straight couple my age laughing as they get their bags and go home and I want to block the entrance right in front of them and claw my eyes out and say, "Tell me—how did it happen? Did you meet at a fucking art opening? After a whole dramatic year on Tinder? DID YOU MEET AT

FUCKING TIM HORTONS?! Are you going home to your fucking cat or your fish or your ADORABLE CHILD?!"

I have never been an aggressive person, as you know. And I would like to say I don't know where this urge to rage comes from. Except. Of course. I know exactly where it comes from. It shouldn't be so simple.

You were the angry one, during the time we were closest. Angry at your brothers, angry at your parents, angry at your cruel goof of an ex-boyfriend who all the drama kids thought was the sweetest (jerks). But, Sue, you were also angry at your friends. They had no interest in showing you they cared, at least not to the degree that you wanted. I wonder why you never got mad at me—if I was a random exception, or if I was the only one who you understood cared about you. I hope it's the latter.

I'm so, so sorry I didn't know how sick you were. I'm so fucking sad you're gone. I can't tell you how much I wish we'd had more time. Even though there was never romance between us, or any universe where that could've made sense, something inside me feels like we could've grown old with each other, pieced together something resembling companionship, some kind of life in a small house with separate bedrooms and a cluttered kitchen table. God, I'm so sorry. I know that must sound so weird, but it's true and I've only realized that just now. Here. After you're gone. I've just realized that now. I'm so sad, I feel like I can't even move.

∽

What happened when Cleo left that morning: We were up early, eating breakfast on the couch. Our conversation was very warm. And suddenly, she said, "I don't mean to be bold. But I always thought there was unfinished business. Between you and me."

I could've kissed her right then. I just didn't want to. That's the other thing. I have always paid attention to my wanting, listened to its pulse, understood where it was leading me. The moment she and I shared years ago was lovely, but my wanting said something different now. I told her all of this, in so many words, and she understood.

It was so tempting. I was so lonely, Sue. But I have always paid attention to the guide of my wanting. And in the months afterward, as I second-guessed myself about Cleo, I realized that loneliness didn't need to preclude fellowship, and, well, I had that. My friends from work, the D I got from the apps, those doofheads over at Villains who gave me high-fives and remembered me, who were always friendly, every single time.

I don't mean to say I was happy, or that I wasn't truly lonely, because I was. I mean to say I'd created a daily life that served as a bulwark against darkness and despair, and that's why I wanted to tell you all of this, Sue, because I was proud of that life in a way that you in particular (and maybe only you) could appreciate.

That's all gone now. These months have been so hard. And no one knows what happens next. Some say it'll be like this for another year, or more, or who knows, and hearing that feels like a vast blank screen blotting my vision into nothing. It's a true thing. But I'm not scared. A new fact about me that might truly surprise you is I've become good at waiting.

OBSOLUTION

When Vera was in high school, she'd awkwardly dated this quiet girl who loved Garbage. They were both fourteen. The girl wore black and sometimes yellow, like a bumblebee. She had the prettiest eyes.

After her, there was a nymphomaniac from Hood River to whom Vera lost her het virginity. Then a tall girl with black hair who inexplicably refused to hang with Vera outside school. Then a vegan during Vera's one year down at SOU in Ashland, a girl obsessed with emo music and M.F.K. Fisher. And later, a woman in her thirties with a moon face who ran a movie theatre.

Vera was the dumper in all cases. Vera didn't have a great rep back in the day, honestly. She fell out of love easily, and the idea of someone *needing* Vera had always been somewhat of a fright to her. The odd particulars of how boring childhood-divorce-crap-shrapnel had hit her, maybe? Who knew?

At the end of that first full year living in New York, Vera met this girl with freckles on New Year's at Macri Park. They hooked up a few times, then began to date, and Vera fell for her hard. The girl was distant and not very nice—they spent most of their time fucking or arguing, and the girl dumped her that summer. Vera was crushed, but this, too, was a new experience for her (in a time of never-ending new experiences). Like to be on this side of a breakup made her heart finally learn to use a certain muscle.

Vera moved out of Bushwick and into a three-bedroom situation in Kensington with two low-key queers who worked in social services. The rent was higher, but she'd learned to get as numb to that as her paycheques would allow.

She had a romance that fall with a girl named Robyn, a blonde-haired drunk of a grad student. They met at a dance party playing Rihanna. The song they danced to was "Diamonds." The relationship was hot and loving and they went out for months and Robyn held Vera through freezes and rages. She helped Vera process that night at the party with the green-haired boy, for one. "He wasn't good to me, was he?" Vera had whispered. "No, no, my love," Robyn said with Vera in her arms. "No, he wasn't." Helped her process stuff about Connie, for another. "That's the thing," Robyn had said softly. "After a certain age, bio family is chosen family, too. You choose to keep it up—or you don't. Both kinds can be unhealthy. Both kinds can be good. And you're never obligated to do a thing to someone who isn't good to you. Ever. It gets to be on your terms, I promise, Vera. You get to set terms, too, now."

For this Vera would forever be grateful. But the drinking. And it wasn't just the nights when Robyn was sobbing indecipherably and inconsolably but also nights when Robyn was calmly sipping from a bottle as they had deep, touching, gutturally meaningful exchanges, exchanges that broken trans women sometimes have that provide a long-standing armour, adamantine in both sadness and understanding—and the next morning, Robyn wouldn't remember a thing. This would make Vera feel impossibly lonely. It made her second-guess some things in a bad way. Like maybe Vera was imagining her own love, her own healing.

One night, after a double shift, Vera came home at five in the morning to find piss on the living room floor and a pot of boiling water on the kitchen stove as Robyn snored with a laptop open to Florence + the Machine videos. The next day, Vera said, "You either quit drinking or you don't come back here. Go home and make your choice." She was shaking when she said it, scared of the confidence in her voice, scared of the determination and power she held. Power that Vera did not know when she had acquired. And Robyn looked at her with an intense woundedness Vera had never seen, a stricken, betrayed look that for years would haunt Vera's dreams. But after that, they were done.

Vera applied to nursing school, and she got in. High school teacher—no, Vera decided she couldn't do that; that was an old fantasy. She couldn't handle being someone who was responsible for youth. When the nursing school acceptance came, she emailed Connie with the heaviest of hearts to say, "I thought you'd want to know this was happening. You still inspire me. I miss you." Connie, true to form, emailed back like they hadn't only been speaking sporadically for years: "That is wonderful! I'm so proud of you. I miss you too and love you."

Vera thought for a long afternoon after receiving that email. Her and Connie had been doing a little better lately, though Vera was still hurting from last winter when she'd tried to go to LA for Thanksgiving ("You'd have to dress proper," Connie'd said matter-of-factly. "Don't come otherwise. You can't expect them to just take it, okay? You've gotta be reasonable with this stuff.")

That had hurt. Still, now, Vera'd detected in Connie a resurging softness, a softness Vera had always known existed in her mother and had hoped would eventually resettle onto her. Finally, Vera responded with a very plain message: "You don't have to believe I'm a woman. But if you want to keep a relationship with me, you'll need to pretend that you do."

That evening, from Connie, one word: "Okay."

Vera put her head on her desk and breathed a long, shuddering sigh. She knew she was lucky. It didn't happen for everyone.

⌒

It was a year later, Vera popping up at her transfer stop in Long Island City to smoke on her way home. She was in no particular hurry, lazily enjoying herself. Across the way at a bus stop, she spied a woman in sunglasses digging into a takeout bag ...

"Holy shit," Vera whispered.

Vera knew right away she wasn't going to stop herself. "Yoohooooo!" Vera stood and waved.

Iris didn't notice.

Vera cupped her mouth. "HEY! IRIS!"

Iris looked around confused, and then suddenly her face had a Grand Canyon smile.

They went to a diner and had a big fucking dinner, both of them warm toward each other from the second they embraced. Iris was dating a new boy, still living in the same apartment, though it'd be demolished for condos soon and she'd have to move. She was full time at the marketing company and making major bank.

There was no discussion of Vera's ghosting, nor any flickering current of romance or attraction between them. That was all done; that was obvious. There was only warmth. Also, enough pauses in their conversation toward the end of the meal that it seemed clear that they weren't destined to be lifelong friends, that maybe this was truly the last time.

And then:

"I have to apologize to you for something," Iris said.

Vera's brain got whiplash. "Oh?" she said cautiously.

"There was this time back in Portland, when we were on the MAX. You were in a skirt. And these guys were laughing at you and saying horrible stuff. And you just stood up real quietly and said, like, 'Let's go over here,' and we went to the other end of the car. I've always felt so bad about that. I never said anything. I didn't stick up for you."

Vera stared at Iris. For a few beats she was silent.

"That's funny," Vera said darkly. "Because I don't remember that at all."

"No?" Iris said timidly.

"I believe you," Vera said. "I have no reason to think that didn't happen. It just would've happened so often. I'd have no reason for it to stick out in my memory." *I remember other things,* she thought. But then also, *What else don't I remember?*

They embraced and held each other for some time before parting ways in the Long Island City dusk. A week later, Vera flew to LA to visit her grandma, long suffering from Alzheimer's and not long for the world. She met Connie and an aunt at LAX, and the aunt drove them to the care home. Vera had missed out on the goodbyes to the family house, had missed a whole reordering and restructuring of the fam over the years.

They hugged Vera's grandma and chatted with her as she stared resolutely ahead. After an hour, Vera sat on her haunches and held the older woman's hand to say goodbye. Finally, her grandma spoke, very slowly, each word enunciated like a sentence:

"Who. Are. You."

"I'm Vera." Vera smiled. She'd rather not do this around the others, but ... "You knew me as David. David? Do you remember David?"

Her grandma stared straight ahead.

Connie took a place beside Vera, smiled too. "My daughter," Connie said. "Can you see? Do we look alike?"

Vera's grandma shook her head. She closed her eyes in front of the two figures squatting side by side in front of her.

On the car ride home, Vera mentioned she'd seen Iris the other day. Connie lit up. Vera texted Iris, *My mom says hello*, and Iris called an hour later as Vera paced on her aunt's porch. They talked for some time. "You'll always be my West Coaster!" Iris said. "Give Connie my best. Give her a big hug."

And that evening, when Vera felt the urge to spit and snarl about a thoughtless comment her aunt made, it occurred to Vera that she could be mean sometimes, about the strangest things. Vera realized her selfhood was sutured with these women from her life, that the only lie about the old him dying was that the skin of the person she'd stepped into wasn't a cis lady she'd conjured from the air but a blanket fashioned from a kaleidoscope of them, shards and spackles that lived in her like bacteria, like DNA, joyous and ailing, a double helix of protection and illness.

That was the last day Vera and Iris ever spoke.

Six years went by. A lot of time.

Still, Vera did think of her.

Vera was thirty-three now. These days, she was doing pretty good.

She'd reconnected with Leah, who'd said, "I'm sorry I didn't make you feel like you were important." To which Vera replied, "I'm sorry I disappeared without telling you I was upset." Leah worked accounting for some firm by Goose Hollow. They texted despondently about politics, cried darkly on the phone the night Trump won. They'd spend evenings on video calls trading YouTube links. There were certain words they didn't use for each other anymore, and they didn't talk about this.

Ray. He'd ended up a stats analyst in North Carolina. He was engaged. He'd been the one to reach out, and Vera forgave him, because what else was Vera going to do—hold a grudge? She had plans to drive out for the bachelor party.

And Zoe ... oh, Zoe. Zoe had always stayed in touch. She'd gone back to Eugene and stayed there, and when Vera went home to see her mom, Zoe would train up and visit. Connie and Zoe actually got along real nice. Once, they were all cruising down Division near Vera and Ray's old apartment, and Vera looked up at the hurtling lines of condos above her and said, "It's like they decided to put in a canyon."

Vera'd left New York and wound up in rural Minnesota, living in a back-to-the-land queer house and working as a nurse in an ER. It was stressful as fuck but secure, and the work suited her. It gave her and Connie a lot to talk about, too.

Vera had a girlfriend she referred to as "my sweetie," a tech tran going apeshit for the second Bernie campaign. The sweetie lived in Milwaukee. They'd met on HER. Vera had always only loved women. That never changed. Vera loved driving to the sweetie's place and back. The sunset-slope of trees and hills. Gentle commas in her quiet little life. She was still kind of a loner, to be honest, even though her relationship was good. Vera didn't really know what to do about that.

Now and then, she'd remember certain moments. Screaming at those dudes on the subway, or snapping surly insults at her friends. She'd remember: *In those years, I could get angry.* What had happened to that anger? Where did it lie, sleeping and lysogenic within her? Occasionally, Vera considered these lump-shaped memories of her rage, rare anomalous recollections that surfaced unpredictably, like outsized moons. She would remember, yes, that's how she'd felt. But she couldn't remember what that feeling had felt like. In an odd, melancholy way, it was almost like as she progressed through woman-hood, she'd reverted to elements of her gentle teenage boy self. This wasn't as contradictory to Vera as it would have seemed when she was younger. But it was strange.

Rural Minnesota. It was all right. She tended to pass now, so. She rarely got shit. It also didn't snow out here as much as she thought it would? The sweetie once made fun of her for this. "Winter is an obsolution! It's a relic of the twentieth century! Fake news!" Vera had rolled her eyes. "What the fuck is an obsolution?" The sweetie pulled out her phone and recited: "'An old media format that is no longer popular or easily accessible, such as floppy disks, VHS tapes, or stone tablets.' I like to think of it as when something no longer translates," the sweetie explained. "It means something so wholly different now." Interesting enough. Though: it definitely got colder than it did back home, but Vera was never, like, cold in the house? "It's the structures," the sweetie said absent-mindedly. "Where you grew up, you never get a real freeze. They didn't need to build stuff that strong."

Vera did like this girl. Long as she stuck around, Vera'd stick around, too. The sweetie had a power-femme thing going on, wore suit jackets and blouses with shiny slacks and lipstick. Paid out the ass for a studio in Milwaukee. A studio in Milwaukee! The real obsolution was a cheap apartment, Vera thought. Folks still used that phrase, but. It wasn't useful anymore. Vera said "folks" now instead of "people." Anyway, she and the sweetie did love each other, and Vera could see it working. She'd see. Things had worked out for Vera, really. Vera was the kind of transsexual things tended to work out for.

That all the women Vera'd dated over these years were trans like her—it wasn't exactly intentional. Yet, see, often in her daily life, certain women would touch Vera without asking and a wormy ripple would begin in her body. It didn't happen with her own kind; it didn't happen with men. In her job, women touched her a lot, and she'd learned to ride over those moments like speed bumps. It was what it was. Did it matter whether she blamed Iris for this? Vera thought no, what utility was there in that? But she did hope that if, one day, she did want to date a woman not like herself, Vera could overcome what lived in her body and open herself to let that happen. One day, maybe.

Funny thing was, she and Iris did still text now and then. Iris would say things like, *A trans woman at work sued our insurance to get electrolysis and won!* She and Vera would like each other's posts on Instagram. Once, Vera and the sweetie took an Amtrak to Philly and Vera sent Iris a picture of a man snoring in the lounge: *These things: Still ridiculous. News at 11.* What Vera hoped? She hoped Iris was happy. It seemed she now had a husband, who was by all indications sweet and kind. They'd been married some years now. They lived deep in Queens. Vera also hoped that Iris was good to him, and if so, that he knew nothing about Iris's past. Vera could never tell another breathing creature how replete her bones were, how full of undirected forgiveness.

ENOUGH TROUBLE

Therefore do not worry about tomorrow,
for tomorrow will worry about itself.
Each day has enough trouble of its own.
—MATTHEW 6:34
(New International Version)

1

Thank God it stopped raining. That's Gemma's first thought as the car enters town. It's a humid summer night. Gemma grew up here in this town of 8,000 people. She has not returned in years.

She's come to see a girl named Ava, a shy, tall beauty from St. Vital, who Gemma met when Ava was visiting the city in spring. Gemma has a good feeling about her.

Gemma has twenty-six dollars to her name. She is a professional drinker and a sloppy hooker, and she no longer has her room in the city, a big third floor on Langside. Her friends had offered her many favours, and as a result, Gemma now has very few friends. Gemma's future is a black box to be pondered only days at a time, but right now, she has a good feeling about Ava—a feeling a girl either does something about or lets needle her until she dies. And Gemma needs somewhere to stay. And from all Gemma's seen, Ava is generous, and Ava is kind.

The rideshare drops her off at First and Stephen. Gemma steps onto the shoulder, crunching on gravel, and then she leaves the road. A train's horn sounds in the east; there's a lull of cicadas. She ambles through still-wet prairie shortgrass with thin waves of skeeters rippling around her arms. The train's horn sounds again, farther away.

Gemma crosses South Railway and gazes up at the tower of Ava's building. When did they build this thing?

She enters to silence and cool air, waits between glass doors. The glass layers a faint triplicate of her image in front of her. She's in a belted black cloth coat with a red dress underneath. Her hair is in pigtail buns, her eyeliner heavy and winged. She turns with her hands in the pockets of her coat, examining herself from each angle. A flattening gust of wind passes the building outside. Thank God it stopped raining. The whole ride down, Gemma had worried she'd get soaked. She wants to look perfect; she wants Ava to open the door and see a dream of a woman looking back at her.

The elevator dings. There she is: fox-faced and gorgeous, standing three miles high in a cream scoop neck blouse and a pleather skirt with zippers. She strides through the lobby with a warm smile.

I forgot what you looked like, Gemma thinks idly. *I forgot the shape of your face.*

"You're here," Ava says. They hug, Gemma's face in her chest.

"Look at your fucking house!" says Gemma. Her voice is raspy and sweet. A thunderclap sounds outside. She really got lucky with the rain.

"It's bonkers, hey? Oh my *God*, you actually *made* it, you're *here*! Let's head up?"

"Nah, let's fuck here in the lobby."

"*Gemma!*"

"There's that cute little blush I remember." They get in the elevator. The doors close and Gemma tilts up her chin. "Hey."

Ava leans down and they kiss. Gemma lifts her hand to Ava's hair, gently wraps her fingers in it, then wrenches it back. "I missed you, you fucking slut."

Ava strains at her. "I—"

Gemma pulls harder. "Shut up."

Ava shakes and Gemma's clit pulses. Ava's brown eyes are convulsing pools. Gemma holds Ava like this for a long time. Ava lives on the thirty-eighth floor.

⌒

The building's hallway is musty and clean. Like a newly finished basement of a very old house. Ava beckons Gemma into her apartment. Gemma enters and removes her shoes; when she looks up, she finds herself facing a clacking curtain of red beads. Ava's body undulates on the other side.

Ava says, "Gemma? Baby?"

Baby.

"Come in," Ava adds. Her quiet, breathy voice drifts over Gemma, settles in her lungs, drips down the inside of her clothes. *I forgot what you sound like*, Gemma thinks. *I forgot that, too.*

The apartment is lit with floor lamps. Light rain patters on the floor-to-ceiling windows, and the shades are all lowered. Taped to the shades are pictures and postcards. In the centre of the room sit a corduroy recliner and a leather couch that is bottle green.

"Nice place," Gemma says absent-mindedly. "When was this built?"

"Hold on." Ava fiddles with some speakers, and then vocal music plays, dissonant and melodic at the same time. It sounds like liquid silver. It's beautiful.

Gemma folds her coat over the couch's back. "Pretty music."

"It's a choir in the city." Ava heads to the kitchen. "This piece is called 'A Boy and a Girl.'"

"A boy and a girl," Gemma echoes. Her red dress flutters around her knees. She takes in the apartment fully. It's cluttered but not dirty—books and spice bottles scattered on tables, a coat on the carpet. And on the other side of the room are three closed doors.

From the kitchen comes the sound of a cabinet opening, then Ava's voice. "Are you drinking right now?"

"I am," says Gemma. "Thanks for asking."

Ava returns with glasses and a half-empty bottle of red. She settles next to Gemma and pours. "How's that going?"

"It's fine," says Gemma. She sips and the blooming peace inside her magnifies. "It is what it is. You know?"

"Not really." Ava laughs. "I'd hear more about that if you wanted. Not that it's any of my business."

"Well"—Gemma shifts to face her—"how do I put this?"

Ava looks at her patiently. Gemma puts her glass on the table. She doesn't usually say this, but she sees so little point in lying.

Or, rather, she understands that coming here and lying will not get her what she wants.

"I'm an addict," Gemma says. "I understand that."

"Okay."

"And I could"—Gemma puts her hands up in a charming "who knows?" gesture—"I could pretend it was otherwise. But I've tried that. So I try to be safe. That's the best I can put it. Stopping again is always an option, and that keeps me sane. Just like when I'm not drinking, I know starting again is always an option, and that keeps me sane, too."

Ava looks very focused. She is focusing very intently on Gemma. "I think I understand."

"You don't have to." Gemma smiles. "It's okay not to understand."

"Can I tell you a story?" Ava says. "I hope it's appropriate. It might relate."

"Sure." Gemma leans back and puts her legs on Ava's lap.

"So my mom used to smoke a pack a day. My earliest memories, I was like, 'My mom's gonna die!' Those labels were scary, hey? I had dreams of her skin rotting off and her becoming a skeleton. But when I was in high school, she quit."

"Good for her," Gemma says. "How?"

"My dad turned forty. Story goes, Mom asked what he wanted for his birthday, and he said, 'I want a wife that doesn't smoke.' Mom goes, 'Gosh, better make sure that's me.'"

"That's cute," Gemma says kindly.

"She quit cold turkey. For ten years. Then she started again. Pack a day, picked it right back up."

"Fuck. What'd Dad say?" Gemma did this whenever someone talked about their family, adopted terms in conversations without possessive pronouns. (*Grandpa really did that? Oh no, Mom!*) Everyone liked it without noticing.

"Eh, they were already on the outs by then."

"Gotcha."

"When she started again," Ava continues, "I was pissed. Like, I was fucking *mad*." An ugly look momentarily appears on her face. "I just thought, 'Why? Why quit so long, then throw it away?' But, as maybe you'll understand better than me, that was the wrong idea. Because the right idea was: Mom got in a whole decade of no smoking. Wow. Good for her."

"Yeah," Gemma says. "You're not wrong. That is an appropriate story. You're not wrong at all."

Ava grins. Is it with shyness? Gemma can't tell. "Okay, great."

There is a silence, and then Gemma stretches a foot down and rubs Ava's leg. "So how's your life?"

Ava gestures around. "Can I complain?"

Gemma laughs, and then lowers her voice. "And how's stuff with your ex? ... Olive?"

"It's fine," Ava says. "It's weird, but. I don't know."

Gemma waits a beat, and then says, "Go on. If you want."

Ava rubs her eyes. "She's more a sister than an ex at this point. I don't mean 'sister' in some rah-rah trans Three Musketeers way. I mean like she's an *actual* sister. Some days I wish it were different. But that's how family works anyway, y'know?"

"I get that," Gemma says. "Generous of you to support her like that, though."

Ava shrugs. "Generous is for people with choices."

"Don't kid yourself. You've got choices."

Ava laughs. "Sure." She pours the rest of the wine into Gemma's glass. "Well, I dunno what you're doing next," says Ava, "and you don't need to tell me what's up with you. But you can stay here long as you need, hey?"

"Thank you," Gemma says. "I appreciate that. I do."

"Of course," Ava says placidly.

"This reminds me of church singing." Gemma gestures to the music. This town is heavy with Mennonites, this place where Gemma grew up. And Mennonites make up the family that Gemma comes from. "It's not the same. But a little."

Ava puts her head on Gemma's shoulder and their legs touch. The polyurethane of Ava's skirt is cool on Gemma's thigh. Ava traces a finger around the top of Gemma's hand. "I loved hearing you sing."

⌒

When they'd met that spring, it was at a party on Balmoral. Gemma'd been texting a friend, and then looked up to see Ava sitting next to her. They began talking and their hands and legs moved closer, the way they do when the bodies of women pull to each other without asking permission. They kissed quickly and inevitably; it was all so immediately obvious. They walked to Gemma's in the cool air and made love on her mattress, Gemma's palm on Ava's throat, Ava's body a ghostly cross-hatch below her, serrated by street light through the blinds.

They woke at ten the next day to an April prairie snow. Trudged over to the Nook in pyjamas for breakfast, back to Gemma's to spoon and fuck in front of the TV. Late in the evening, Gemma mentioned offhand that she'd grown up in choirs, and Ava asked if she could hear her sing. Gemma got bashful. *I can't do that.* Ava teased her. *Come on. For me?* And Gemma relented and sang "That Lonesome Road." She'd sung it in high school choir. But she had really learned to sing, Gemma said, in church. Not just at the church she attended with her dad but also with her Oma, who'd play an upright piano at her house in Mitchell, over round Steinbach area. She'd play through hymns on Sunday before services, and she taught Gemma how to sing. *You have a beautiful voice,* Ava said once Gemma had finished. *Thanks. I miss it sometimes,* Gemma said quietly. *That part of my life's gone now.* And Ava said, *I understand.* Gemma pulled up YouTube. *This is my favourite version of that song. A university choir, Wichita State. It gets done a lot, but it's always too clean. It's too calm. It's too sanitized. It's too joyous. It gets sung like a lullaby. It's not a lullaby.* Gemma got emotional, suddenly, saying that.

Next morning, Ava had to book it out early to make it back home for work. That's when Gemma learned she lived out here. *You're fuckin' kidding me!* she hooted. *That's where I grew up! That's my home-town! That is some janky shit.* Ava blushed and put on her clothes. At Gemma's front door, they kissed and kissed. Then Ava's face lit like a flame and she said, *Let's do this again sometime.* Then she left, and Gemma sat on the couch and the brain-pee deluge of dopamine drained away and regular life stepped back in front of her, a faceless shape in the doorway.

∽

"You're nice," Gemma says now. "Thank you."

Gemma puts her arm around the taller girl's body. Ava'd had ravaging acne as a teenager, and her back and shoulders are moon-gnarled with scars. There's something gorgeous and unfragile to how it makes Ava look, but Gemma keeps this thought to herself. "You're so warm."

"I'm always warm; I hate the heat."

"Oh no," Gemma clucks. "Don't tell me you thought it was hot today."

"I haven't been outside. My hands are always cold, though." Ava puts a palm on Gemma's cheek and she flinches. "See?"

"Damn."

"Bodies."

"Shit, speaking of bodies." Gemma picks up her phone. "I got blood work done the other day. Haven't had that in a dog's age."

"Ugh," says Ava. "I have it every six months, but there's no good reason."

"Well, apparently, I'm every six years. Let's see who lives longer."

"I'm serious! 'Less you have a condition to watch for. Do you?"

"No."

"Right!" says Ava. "It's only so they can, like, run up bills and feel like they have control when they don't have any more fucking clue what hormones do than we do! Hey?"

Gemma lowers her phone, bemused. "Well, colour me fooled, aren't you the angry little radical tran?"

"I'm getting my baeddel tattoo tomorrow."

"*Ha!*"

"Find out if you're dying yet?"

"The app hasn't updated." Gemma puts her phone away. "My blood's on an app. The future's fucked up."

Ava shifts her legs and the sound of her skirt puts electricity in Gemma's clit. "Do you have anything else?" Gemma nods to the empty bottle.

"Tequila. You're welcome to it," Ava says earnestly.

"Thanks. I kinda want beer, though." Gemma says, almost to herself. "There's a vendor at Trav's."

I think I'm comfortable with you, Gemma realizes. The easy feeling she has right now. It's exactly how Gemma remembered. She doesn't have to trust it to enjoy it. She realizes that in these last three months since they met, she's carried the memory of this feeling around with her, like a necklace beneath her skin. *I'm so comfortable with you.*

"I'd have a beer." Ava holds out her fob. "Mind going alone?" Gemma slings up her bag.

✑

Gemma crosses South Railway in the misty rain, up and over the tracks.

The Trav's building is right out of an Old West cartoon, like inside might be men in vests and handlebar moustaches. Gemma picks up king cans from a guy in a Timberwolves hat. When she comes out, the rain has stopped.

Most of her money is now gone.

She goes west down the alley, away from Ava's building. In the lightless alcove of the post office entrance, she sits and drains one of the king cans, hidden behind the wheelchair ramp. Gemma leans her head against the brick as restful calm wraps around her.

She emerges from the alley by the old library and the traffic light on Eighth Street. She's slick with humidity under her dress in the night. The light changes, but no cars go through.

Back at Ava's, they pop the beers and talk about a girl out east they both know ("She was in the psych ward, hey?" "She's better now. Wait, aren't you off the socials?" "I lurk; I have my secrets." "Bitch!"). Then Gemma says, "Come here," and there's a flurry of clothes and Ava's mouth becomes full with Gemma's tits and Ava wraps her legs around Gemma's back and Gemma can feel Ava's flesh fold into itself, condense, seek every opportunity to not be exposed to air. What Gemma feels is Ava feeling her own body.

They fuck against a window, Ava's skirt hastily flipped up, sweat matting the hair on her scarred back, their hands curled together on the rough fabric of the shade.

Afterward, they lie on the couch in each other's arms. One of the three doors on the other side of the room opens and a lone woman appears. She's slight and wearing a long slip. Her grey-speckled hair is frizzy with breakage, like marks on a cutting board. She looks older than Gemma or Ava. Late forties, maybe. "Baby," the woman says. "I'm going to sleep."

Olive, thinks Gemma. Ava walks over to her, still topless. They whisper in her doorway.

Gemma goes to the window facing west and raises a shade halfway. She can see down just enough to make out the traffic light on Eighth Street. Used to be the only stoplight out here between Winkler and … Lord, who knew how far west? The night sky is still clouds, and all she sees beyond town is a tinkle of farms and a sparse thread of cars on the number three highway. And the hamlets. Clusters of yellow, like fireflies in the night.

Hands come around Gemma's torso. Her neck warms with Ava's lips.

"What are you looking at?"

"Nothing."

Gemma gets another beer. Her red dress lies on the floor. "You work at eight tomorrow?"

"Yup. Shorter commute than last time, though."

"You don't say."

"Hey," Ava says. "There's a party tomorrow on the roof. For my work. Do you want to come with me?" She hesitates. "I promise it won't suck."

"Sure," Gemma says. "That'd be fun. Let's do that."

Palpable relief flushes through Ava. "Sweet."

Gemma's stomach turns velvet a bit, seeing Ava react this way. She has a growing feeling that Ava might like her, and it feels nice. Gemma winks. "I'm glad I came down."

"I didn't expect you to," Ava says. She's wide-eyed, looking into her beer. "I got nervous when you texted me. I thought, 'Jeez, there's no way this smoking hot girl would actually come down to Nowheresville, would she?'"

"Please, bitch"—Gemma's eyes twinkle—"I grew up in this town."

"Proving my point!" Ava says happily. "Why would you come down here, times infinity?"

"Because you're hot, you fucking slut."

Ava downs her beer and stands. "Gonna offer that tequila one last time."

They sit together on the couch with Gemma's fist on the bottle, cuddling and bullshitting. Like they've known each other forever. *Did you ever watch* The Cable Guy? *It's so weird; it was, like, dark and smart, but it wasn't meant to be.* Talk like that, stuff like that. Half an hour passes. Gemma is getting actually drunk now, the kind of drunk where her head feels like a machine. They kiss and Gemma puts her hand on Ava's skirt and strokes her clit and Ava's nails press into her skin; they leave body imprints of sweat on the couch when they go to the bedroom. The tequila comes with them. Ava unzips her skirt and Gemma lowers her body onto the carpet. Gemma sucks her and Ava takes Gemma's hair in her hands and undoes her pigtail buns and Gemma's brown hair falls down her back. She hears Ava take something from her nightstand. And then she feels something on her head. It's a brush. Ava brushes Gemma's hair as Gemma sucks Ava on her knees. "Good," Ava says quietly, her free hand resting on Gemma's head. "Good, good, good."

Eventually, they end up at the head of the bed with Gemma's fingers in Ava's mouth while Gemma jerks Ava off. Gemma reaches over once to take a long hit of the tequila. She doesn't spill. Gemma has always had an excellent sense of her body. Ava vibrates. Ava gasps. Ava knocks Gemma's hand away to take over, and then she is coming all over herself as she lies in Gemma's arms and Gemma kisses her, *God, this woman is truly fucking beautiful, she's so beautiful, she—*

2

Gemma wakes. It's morning. When had it become morning? She opens her eyes to see dawn through the shades and Ava snoring in a sleep mask, her feet hanging off the edge of the bed.

Gemma sits up. The clock reads 4:54. She is still drunk.

Ordinarily, Gemma would try to go back to sleep. But then she'd toss and turn; she might wake Ava.

She rises delicately, changes into her sleep clothes, and quietly moves into the living room, which is even more of a mess from last night.

She'll clean and make coffee. That's what she'll do. It is good to make herself useful.

Gemma bags cans. She returns pillows to the chair and couch. She returns her dress to her bag and hangs up her coat. She washes glasses. And she does it all very slowly. Her still-drunk is of a grade that makes it painful to move, everything happening three seconds behind itself. But this doesn't bother Gemma. She knows what's what.

After she is done, she raises a window shade and soon she is sitting on the couch, watching sun spill around the building and light up fields and sky. She holds an ultramarine mug and fuses her eyes with the view and drinks her coffee and Gemma ... well. Gemma hasn't felt so perfect in a long, long time.

As a kid visiting her Oma's house in Mitchell, Gemma could see the glow of city lights below the clouds at night. Even from forty miles away. Her Oma'd been the last generation in her Menno family to be taught that anyone who went to live in a city—well, they had no hope for salvation. Her grandmother had been a stern woman. But she had once told Gemma softly that as a little girl, on a farm not far from where they sat, she would watch that city glow with awe in the evenings. That could happen round Steinbach area. But you didn't see it out here. Not out here.

Gemma lies sideways on the couch with her eyes half-closed. She still feels perfect. She has a dream about a green stuffed triceratops she'd had in high school, given to her by a friend who'd fallen off the radar long ago. Gemma had named the dinosaur Carl. In the dream, Carl has blue hair. "Hey," Carl says, "Do you need—"

Gemma wakes to Ava rustling in the kitchen. "Hey." Gemma sits up and massages her face. "Hey, I made coffee."

"Did you," Ava says blankly.

Ava looks annoyed. She's wearing a long-sleeved cow-print dress and dangly earrings.

"Can I help with anything?" Gemma blurts. She feels sinkingly juvenile as she says this. She is absolutely still drunk.

"I don't think so." Ava shoulders a laptop case. She definitely seems annoyed. "I'll be back by five." She pecks Gemma on the forehead. "See you tonight." She travels through the curtain of red beads and out the door.

༄

Gemma has every reason to stay inside until Ava gets back. But Gemma's never been that kind of woman. That's just not in Gemma's DNA.

One of Gemma's favourite things, far back as she can remember, is showering at someone else's house. She's always loved trying every foam and liquid she doesn't recognize. (*The hell is body wash?!* was a puzzler as a kid.) Here at Ava's, she notices a container of Vagisil. So Olive has a pussy. How about that.

Gemma showers for a long time. When she was in high school, and it was winter, she would shave every part of her body, and then stand in the shower and hold her flesh with her eyes closed, and she would carry that peace forward into her day.

Gemma's never interacted much with trans teenagers. If she did, though, she'd talk about showering.

She gets out and Olive is sitting on the toilet. "Oh." Gemma fumbles for a towel. "Hi. Hi? I didn't know you were in here."

Olive doesn't look up. "Morning," she says. She's not unpleasant about it.

༄

Olive is eating soup on the bottle-green couch when Gemma emerges dressed from the bedroom. The door to Olive's room is open, but all Gemma can see from this angle is carpet. And a charcoal-grey wall.

Ava'd told her Olive was prone to freak-outs, though this was mostly when she'd lived alone, which had not been good for Olive. "She likes knowing other people are around her," Ava'd said.

"I'm Gemma." She sits in the corduroy recliner.

"I'm Olive."

"Cool."

"Sure."

"I'm probably going out for a bit," Gemma says carefully. "Does that make problems for you?"

Olive doesn't look up. "No, go crazy."

"Do you have a spare key ...?"

She shakes her head. "Inbox me."

Gemma adds her on Messenger. Then she sees her blood work's come in. Three results listed as ABNORMAL. Red blood cells low. Whatever. Vitamin B$_{12}$ low. Whatever. Ferritin high—

Wait, that was weird. *The hell is ferritin?* Gemma scans the reference range.

It was *way* high.

The fuck does this even mean?! She begins to google "high ferritin" and it auto-fills: "high ferritin levels and alcohol"—

"Ava tells me you're a Mennonite," Olive says.

"Huh?" Gemma looks up, dazed. She stows her phone. "My family is."

Gemma registers that though Olive is speaking to her in a friendly manner, she has a very intense face and very intense eyes. And she's wearing a satin nightgown with roses on it.

"You were raised that way?" Olive asks.

"I didn't—I didn't have a conservative upbringing." Gemma stands to leave. "My dad didn't raise me like he was raised. But I grew up here and I went to church, yeah."

"Tell me about that sometime."

"Uh, sure." Gemma picks up her bag. "I'll be back in a bit, 'kay?"

"Have fun." Olive gives a little wave.

A lot of people grow up in small towns because that's where their family's been for generations. Not Gemma. Her dad's from Steinbach, her mom Kitchener. They'd met at CMU back when it was Canadian Mennonite Bible College, then they came here for her mom's job at the research station. When they split up, her mom left and her dad stayed.

A lot of transsexual women gulp the lady pills, but people from past lives still see the same old face. Not Gemma. She hadn't been fishy pre-hormones; she was just a girl for whom estrogen had worked rare genuine magic. A deceitful face surgeon could've used her picture in ads—that's how extreme the dice had come up for Gemma. So that morning, she sits in Coffee Culture in black jean shorts and a ponytail through a ball cap, and no one looks at her askance.

And a lot of weirdos grow up in small towns, split once they can, and then go back for a visit to find the same old people doing the same damn shit. But not Gemma. She doesn't recognize a soul. Maybe, if she squints, that guy looks like Brandon Wiens, a kid in grade three who'd whaled on her balls with a hockey mini stick. Maybe, with some massaging of memory, that man looks like Mr Reimer, a principal who had been kind. But it's all just a guess. She leaves the café and walks down Stephen Street—everyone is a stranger. She puts her nose to the window of what was once d'8 Schtove Restaurant and is now the office of the Tory MLA. A staffer in shirt sleeves raises an eyebrow at her while Gemma imagines an elderly couple sharing Rollkuchen. She peers down Nelson Street, where she'd lived at the other end with her dad in a little bungalow. She walks to North Railway in the shimmering heat, laughs at the obvious Winklerites sneaking into the LC (what was the point of them finally getting one in their own damn town, huh?). She thinks about hoofing it out to Tasti's for a burger before remembering she's broke, and then remembering Tasti's has closed, too.

She's suddenly grateful, in a small way, that she only has five bucks left. She can't go to the LC and buy anything real. And for tonight there's still tequila left, plus whatever will be at the party—plus, she won't be alone. It'll all be fine.

She calls the clinic and makes an appointment to talk with the doctor in a couple days. At Coffee Culture, she'd tried looking up ferritin, but had *that* been an expedition gone tits up. High ferritin didn't seem good, but it could be related to a bunch of things for a bunch of reasons, and ferritin levels "differed by gender," so what the hell did that mean for Gemma anyway? Whatever. She's probably fine, but she'll be responsible; she'll talk to the doctor.

She peers into the old SAAN store, an empty building up for lease beside a spanking new Shoppers. Could she imagine having gone in there to try on, like, a skirt or something? *That would've been a hoot*, thinks Gemma. *That would've been just a hoot.*

Gemma is on the couch when Ava gets home. It's raining again. Gemma faces the window with the shade raised, idly on her phone in front of an ocean of water and clouds.

Ava bends forward over the couch's back and lets her hair fall down Gemma's shoulders. She kisses Gemma on the top of her head, holds her by her sunburned arms.

"Hi," Ava whispers.

Gemma leans back and closes her eyes. "Is the party still on?" she murmurs.

"The rain's supposed to let up."

It's nice that Ava's returned with warmth. Gemma hasn't welcomed a lover home from work in a long time. She'd forgotten she liked that feeling.

They make a box of KD and bring it to the bedroom. Ava lights a joint. The A/C has been shit today, and they sit and eat, sweaty in their underwear. Ava wears a heather-grey T-shirt, the saucepan resting on her stomach. They watch a comedy show about a team of caterers. This episode's plot turns on a failed sweet sixteen yacht party for the daughter of a famous film director played by J.K. Simmons.

Ava leans over to stub out the roach. "Do you remember the first party you ever went to? Like a real party."

Gemma'd been six. Her mom had just left. Her dad decided to go to a house party in the city. Gemma had to come with. Gemma's only memory was of lying on a blanket in a dark room while the party raged, and when she finally fell asleep, she dreamed of a man who came silently through the door. When she sat up and kneeled in fright, the man shot her in the head.

But Gemma knows that's not what Ava's asking. "I was in grade eight. These girls had a birthday party in their basement. Don't know why they invited me; they all had boyfriends. It was, like, seven people, but there was beer, music. I guess it was a party. One of the girls dyed her hair pink in the bathroom and one of the boys bragged he had Family Values Tour tickets. Maybe that gives you a picture."

Ava laughs. "Yeah, buddy." Ava's got a cute trace of a hoser accent, if you listen for it. "Did you have fun?"

"I did." Gemma can say this. "I sat in the corner. I did nothing. One of the girls, she asked if I wanted to stay the night. I didn't understand; they all had boyfriends." She glances up at Ava. "I think fondly about that now, for obvious reasons. I could've stayed if I wanted. My dad wouldn't have cared. But I was too scared. I liked being there, but I was too scared."

"You were scared?"

Gemma is silent. Had Gemma believed in God that year? That might have been part of it. But she can't remember. Her head is on Ava's shoulder and she can feel her hair soaking with sweat. She says, "I didn't see myself as a person in that room."

Ava kisses her head. "I understand."

"What about you?"

Ava pauses the TV. The faint sound of Olive in the kitchen comes through the door. She's listening to music Gemma can't place. Something new wavey? Is Olive singing along? That's cute.

"I was fourteen," Ava says. "My uncle, he liked the idea of ... taking me under his wing or something? I dunno. He took me to a wedding party, buddy of his. Rented a bunch of cabins out by a lake. Girls my age were there. And my uncle," Ava says darkly, "he said, 'See anything you like?' Wigs me out now, of course. But you know."

"I do."

"And I was already this tall back then, hey?" Ava says. "A girl sits beside me. She had a rumpled white button-up shirt—that's what all the girls my age wore. Her name was Charlie."

The tequila from last night is still beside the bed; Gemma drinks from it and sparkling lava drifts through her body. Gemma is the kind of addict who drinks when she feels awful and also when she feels very good. She puts her hand in Ava's. "I'm listening."

"At first, I didn't understand this girl was drunk," says Ava. "I'd only had a couple beers. She kept repeating, 'You're so nice! You're so nice!' Little later, she said, 'Why don't we lie down?'"

"We went to the cabin I was sleeping in with my uncle. We were alone. I thought she'd asked to lie down because she wasn't feeling well. She lay in bed. And I stood over her." Ava swallows. "She had the prettiest *body*. Like her torso. I just remember looking at her middle and thinking, 'You are perfect. You were made absolutely perfect.' Maybe you understand this." Ava bounces their interlaced hands. "She looked at me a certain way. It was then I realized, hey? Like, 'Guess what, dummy, she didn't say let's lie down because she was *tired.*'"

Ava stops talking. Eventually, Gemma elbows her. "So come on, you fuck her?"

Ava gives her a dirty look.

"Sorry."

"No," Ava says. "I brought her a glass of water. I said 'Are you okay?' in the most pathetic, squeaky-ass little voice."

"Heh," Gemma says. "Right. I see where this is going."

"I will never forget how hurt she looked." There is something desperate and haunted to Ava's tone. "When she understood that this boy was not going to touch her. What this boy would do was stand over her, frightened, gawking, like she was a helpless baby deer."

Ava swallows again. "I've never forgotten how hurt she looked, Gemma. And then she rolled to the other end of the bed and went to sleep. The next day," she says, "I woke up and she was gone. My uncle was on his bed, eating a Danish. He said, 'Get the fuck up. We have to go.' He was in his boxers and had fucking morning wood, too. Like his fucking cock was just—anyway, whatever. But he looked so disgusted talking to me, and he had this danger in his voice.

"This'll sound silly, hey?" Ava laughs nervously. "But like: I thought he was going to hit me. And on the drive back home he said, 'I woulda been all over her like a *pig in shit.*'"

There was a long silence. "I understand," says Gemma. They didn't speak for some time, so she adds, "How's your uncle these days?"

Ava unpauses the TV. "I don't know," she says quietly. The rain is still coming down, a staccato of car-wash sprays on glass. "I really don't know."

∽

The rain stops as they get ready for the party. The sky is the colour of bathwater. Ava puts on music and opens another red. Olive is finishing washing the dishes and she pours herself a glass. "Where are you going?"

"The roof!" Ava says. "Work party!"

"What are we listening to?"

"The internet."

"Har-dee-fucking-har." Olive falls into the corduroy recliner and swivels around.

"Can we put one of the shades up?" says Gemma.

"Sure."

"We live like vampiiiiiires," sings Olive as Gemma crosses to the window and sun floods the room.

"Megan Nash," Ava says, uncapping lip liner by the living room mirror, "is who we're listening to. She's from Saskatchewan."

"Pretty song," says Gemma.

Olive motions her thumb at Ava. "This bitch and her sad girls with guitars."

"Gotta be good at something." Ava smirks.

"Hey," says Olive, "are they fixing the A/C?"

"I've called a bunch."

"Philistines."

Gemma laughs. She's putting on a black tie-neck blouse over a green pencil skirt. "Even a place like this, landlord doesn't fix anything, eh?"

"You know it, girlfriend." Olive swivels again. It's kinda fun, Gemma thinks, seeing Olive lively in this way.

"Oh hey," Gemma remembers, "I saw a pair of ankle boots in the entranceway? Can I borrow them? The shoes I have don't go with this outfit."

"They're Olive's," Ava says. "Olive?"

"Sure, go crazy."

Gemma steps through the curtain of beads into the entryway. She tries on the boots—they fit, her feet clicking on the tile. The other two women laugh about something over the music. Through the curtain Gemma sees Ava standing in her bra and underwear, her hair shining in the sunlight. Gemma kneels to take the boots off.

The entryway floor tile is beige, and weathered, with a slight peel. Almost like it's been repurposed. Her Opa's place in Roland had tile like this. He lived there until he died. (The one apartment building in all of Roland.) Gemma'd stay nights with him often, when her dad was out doing ... well, who knew. Her Opa was a gentle man. Had been a pastor in Steinbach a long time ago, but by the time Gemma came along, he worked for Prairie Rose School Division and kept a crystal prism in the window that shined colours all over his apartment. And he would visit Gemma's Oma in Mitchell. His ex-wife, in a sense, though of course no one would've called her that. He'd fix up her house. Mow the lawn. Change the oil in her car. Sometimes those two would speak Plautdietsch to each other in passing, and once, her Oma threw her head back in laughter at the kitchen table ("Oh, *yo!*") as her grandfather tossed off a remark in his parka, shuffling out to shovel snow. Gemma never saw her Oma be expressive speaking any other language. Gemma'd never learned two words of Plautdietsch, but its cadence always brings her back to that kitchen, and whenever she hears it spoken now, it makes her want to cry.

Despite her Opa's visits, her grandmother never visited his place in Roland. Why the two of them separated in the first place, Gemma never found out. She'd asked, but—

"Baby? Baby, do they fit?"

Gemma looks up. She steps back through the curtain of beads. Ava's voice had come from the bedroom. Olive has disappeared.

For a second, Gemma is alone in the living room.

"They do," she calls out. She adds, raising her voice, "Thanks, Olive!"

"You got it, girlfriend!" Olive shouts from the bathroom.

Gemma goes into Ava's room and begins doing her hair, putting it up in pigtail buns again.

"There gonna be food at this thing?" Gemma asks.

"Probably. Do you need more dinner?" Ava's red mouth is a blade on her face.

"No," Gemma says. "I just like to know."

"Ah. Yeah, I get that, hey?" Ava steps into her dress, a grey and shoulderless heavy thing. She pulls it up onto her body and the fabric on her skin makes a sound that fills the room.

I might want to stay, Gemma understands as she watches her. It's right then that Gemma understands this. She'd come here because she hadn't known where else to go. And she had assumed she'd just crash until either she was told to leave or she figured out her next move. And now she thinks: *What if I wanted to stay?*

⌒

They go up in the elevator and emerge in a glass enclosure with a kitchen and a counter with platters of Chinese takeout. Gemma sees the bags and says, "Lucky's! Lucky's is still around?!" She says this mostly to herself. Beyond the enclosure is a wide-open roof with people and a firepit and sun through the clouds. Two men eating chicken balls stand across from them.

"It's like a devilled egg for your mouth," says one.

"Devilled eggs are also for your mouth," says the other.

"You homos!" says Ava. Everyone laughs. She whispers to Gemma as they walk out, "They might be microdosing?"

Gemma replies, "Hey, you know what they say on *Sense8*: 'Drugs are like shoes.'"

Ava chimes back with perfect timing, "'Everyone needs them, but they don't always fit.'"

A girl passes covered in navy blue sequins, peacock feathers sticking out from her back. In line at the bar, Gemma sees a girl with poofed-out eighties hair, wearing a big blue skirt decorated with clouds and a retro-style T-shirt that says, I JUST WANT TO BE GAY IN SPACE WITH YOU.

"Uh, babe," Gemma says to Ava, "is this, like—a costume party?"

Ava instantly laughs. "I'm so sorry!" she says. "I kept meaning to tell you, and then I just didn't ..."

She looks bashful, she does, that tall drink of water in red lip and a grey dress. Gemma smirks. "So you're cute when you're embarrassed. That's nice."

Ava puts a hand to her mouth and squeaks, "I hate costumes."

Gemma laughs and lifts her chin, her hands in the pockets of her black felt coat. "Hey," she says. "Do I look mad?" She swivels around. "Quite the co-workers you have here. This is the Big Tech lifestyle I'm missing, eh?"

"Shut uuuup!"

They get wine, and then a woman in a floofy grey wig pulls Ava aside. "One sec," Ava says apologetically. Gemma idly folds her coat by the firepit. The sun is lowering on a horizon that is miles and miles away. You can see the whole damn Pembina Valley from up here, and it's one of the most beautiful, unearthly sights Gemma has ever seen.

The girl with the eighties hair and the I JUST WANT TO BE GAY IN SPACE WITH YOU T-shirt taps her on the shoulder. "Hello friend, might you have a lighter?" The girl exudes delight. Gemma shakes her head, the wine spreading warm-cool through her system. The girl gets a lighter from a man in cat ears, and then she says, "You came with Ava, right?"

Gemma gets a little glow from hearing this as her eyes stray back to the horizon. (She had forgotten this, too, what that glow felt like.) "Yes," Gemma says. "I came with her."

"I'm Holly," says the girl. "Ava and I grew up together in St. Vital."

Gemma smiles. "No kiddin'."

Holly exhales smoke. "Here to help, not to hurt! I love that woman." She speaks with a sassy joyousness, like a bubbly kid who'll charm the adults but give them the gears the whole time.

"And you two ended up out here, eh?"

"Oh! Dude! Please!" Holly lifts a finger in glee. "I got her this job. Very proud, by the way, thank you tons, don't mention it."

What did Ava do before this? Gemma wonders. They are the same age: thirty-four. She knows Ava hasn't been here long. This causes a thought to kernel in her, honey warm and hopeful and exciting: *There is so much I don't know about her.*

"And you?"

"My name's Gemma," she says. "I'm visiting. I grew up here, though."

"Really!" Holly says. "Not a lot of townies at this shindig, I'll tell you."

Townies? Gemma laughs. "I could find you a few." This was a lie— Gemma'd kept in touch with literally no one. "Want to hear why it's evil to celebrate Halloween?" (This was also a lie. Plenty of religion in Gemma's town, sure, but they had Halloween; it's not like this was *Winkler* or anything.)

"It would be because of my heritage," Holly says dryly. "Are you Menno too, by any chance?"

"I'm a Friesen," Gemma says, her eyes drifting back to the landscape below. "You?"

"Holly Driedger's the full name, my mom's a Penner! My folks aren't super churchy or anything, though."

"Lucky you."

Holly blew smoke to her side. "I've said that to myself a couple times." Didn't miss a beat, this one.

The woman in the big grey wig walks past them. "Holly," Gemma says, "Is there a theme to this costume party?"

"That would be biophilia, madame!"

Gemma raises an eyebrow.

"Oh!" says Holly, again with the gleeful raised finger. "Funny you should ask! I, too, did not have that word in my immediate vocabulary." She pulls out her phone. "'Biophilia is the love of life or living systems.'" She puts her phone back in her bag. "True facts."

"What are you, then?"

"I"—Holly twirls in her skirt—"am the love of movement."

Gemma chuckles. "I like the clouds."

"Thanks, friend!"

"Hey," Gemma suddenly says, pointing down. "This building. Do you know when it was built?"

But Holly is now looking away from her, scanning the crowd, and if she has heard Gemma, she does not respond.

Then Ava walks toward them from the crowd like a mirage, her cheeks flushed under her red-black hair and her dress spotty with sweat. "The lady herself arrives," Gemma says to Holly, loud enough for Ava to hear.

"She's never been much for a bold entrance."

"Is that so?" says Ava, and then leans down to kiss Gemma on the lips.

"Looks like you lovebirds need more drinks!" Holly scampers away.

Gemma laughs. "Your friend's a trip."

Ava grins. "Yeah, hey? Holly's one of my favourite people."

Down on the ground, a firework goes off. Then three or four more in rapid succession. They're coming from the west, by the lake. It's hard to see with the sun. Ava looks confused. "Wonder what that's about."

"Probably just kids," Gemma says, more quietly than she intended. "Happens all the time."

When Gemma last visited town, in her early twenties, she'd come in boy mode. In winter, with her ex, to help her dad pack up the old bungalow on Nelson Street and move east. The ex had sat around while Gemma and her dad sweated in their snowsuits, but then at night she got restless, so Gemma said, "We could go to the lake." On the way down to the ice, they pushed each other into snowbanks.

That relationship hadn't exactly been good—her ex had been code-pendent, and Gemma'd been attempting to transition, and neither girl had known how to deal with herself, let alone each other. Those were years of Gemma's life buried in another person's mental anguish, years subsumed into one girl's poorly lit bedroom above Qu'Appelle Avenue. But that time on the lake was real nice. It'd been a postcard-classic Manitoba winter night: bright moon, still air, freezing but not that freezing. Even now, Gemma can perfectly picture her ex laughing, spinning on the ice, kicking up snow, construction-orange mittens on her hands.

Holly comes back with wine, and then the man with cat ears comes up to jaw at Ava and lead her away to some other circle. "Popular girl," Gemma remarks.

Holly giggles. "Yeah, dude, everyone at work loves her. Sometimes I'm like, 'Hello! Original Team Ava over here. A little appreciation?!'"

"Original, eh? Got any stories I should hear?" Gemma says it jok-ingly, but Holly's expression turns thoughtful. She lets a silence sit between them.

Then Holly says, "Here's one." She lights another smoke and sits by the firepit. Gemma follows suit.

"So it was almost Christmas," Holly says. "And we were chatting online. I was like, 'Whatcha doing for Santa Day?' and she said, 'Ordering pizza and watching every Teenage Mutant Ninja Turtles movie.' I thought she was joking. As you might guess, she wasn't. So I was like, 'Fuck it. Do you want to come to Alberta with me?' I was leaving the next day! But she rolled up to my apartment at six a.m. with a bag. And that girl *never* left her fuckin' house in those days." (*Mmm*, thought Gemma.) "We drove to my stepmom's in the mountains—"

"Wait, wait, wait"—Gemma laughs—"you're telling me you show up at your family's house in the wilds of Alberta with your transsexual buddy one night, like, 'Surprise!'?"

Melancholy crosses Holly's face. "My stepmom's house was like that," she says. "Everybody was always welcome in her home. It was one of those places. She had this big rambling log house ... It was just one of those places. I texted my dad I had a friend coming; I believe his response was 'Cool, we'll put a sleeping bag in your room, please tell me that unlike my crazy daughter she eats meat?'"

"Dad sounds all right." Gemma smiles.

"He is. They're not together anymore, which—anyway. But dude, Ava had such a good time. I'd almost never seen her that happy. She usually fucking hates Christmas ..."

Holly's eyes are suddenly glassy with emotion. This makes Gemma feel cold. Gemma feels a way about certain flavours of sympathy from cis women, cis women believing they'd witnessed something fragile and private, thinking they'd glimpsed trans pain or joy. Joy that wasn't fragile and often wasn't joy. Gemma can respect such good intentions. But she's not excited about them.

Holly blinks and she's bubbly again. "So we have a great Christmas, and then it's Boxing Day. Ava and I are both kitchen peons at shitty-ass restaurants and we've got work the next morning—"

"Hey homos!" yells Ava. "Can I introduce you to someone?"

Holly turns on a dime. "Shall I hold that thought? Allow me to hold that thought."

They go to Ava's circle—work talk that Gemma can't follow. She drinks another glass of wine. The sun begins to dip below the horizon, and she looks back to the lake. She can just make out some splashing. Almost certainly kids, all right. Bored teenagers. That whole thing.

Age she is, Gemma probably knows some of their parents. People have kids young around here.

Soon, the sun is completely down, and soon after, the party begins to filter away. Holly says, "You two wanna come back to my place? Olive could come too, if she wants." Ava pulls out her phone, and Gemma goes to the bathroom, where she finds and drains an abandoned glass of white.

∽

They go down to Holly's floor, but when they get off the elevator, Gemma doesn't pay attention to where she's going. She thought she was following the other two, but then suddenly, she finds herself facing a fire exit.

The red letters glowing under the bleary fluorescent light.

She takes a few steps back. Her boots are soundless on the carpeted floor.

Then Ava's behind her. She grabs Gemma's wrist. "Come on, you got lost!" Ava sounds impatient and happy at the same time. She pulls Gemma back down the hallway to Holly's place. Inside, Holly is slamming cabinets. "Do you want wine? I've got wine." Holly's shades are up, and the windows face south and are filled with dark and stars.

Gemma and Ava curl against each other on a couch, and Holly begins to spill about a boy back home in St. Vital. A boy who visits her plenty but just has so many fucking feelings! Gemma's thoughts begin to run just a little behind what Holly is saying. (That abandoned glass of white had been a choice.) But eventually, she says to Holly, "He's not an egg, is he?"

Ava laughs. "No. I mean, who knows? But he says he's not a lady!"

Holly cackles. "Oh buddy, she checked."

A cat noses around Gemma's legs. "Kitty!"

"That's Cinnamon Bun," says Ava. "She's cute, hey?"

Gemma scratches the cat's chin. "She is. Oh my God!" she blurts. "You should get a cat!"

She can hear the intimacy in her own voice as she says this, and it feels embarrassing in some way. But Ava just shakes her head. "I wish," Ava says. "But Olive won't hear of it."

Holly drops bags of crackers and chips on the table. Gemma remembers they were talking about Holly's boy. "So this boy," she says.

"This fuckin' *boy*," says Holly. She collapses on the opposite couch. "The real thing that bothers me?" She reaches for her wine. "It's embarrassing ..."

"Embarrassing's great!" says Gemma. Ava titters.

"Okay, okay. I don't mind him being emotional or whatever, and I don't even mind that I live far away." Holly turns red. "But for all his feelings and shit, like ... he won't call me his partner! He says he doesn't want to put 'labels' on things. It's so stupid to get hung up on! But I ..."

"I don't like him," Ava says to Gemma brusquely.

"I know you don't," says Holly. "I get it."

"Holly," Ava leans forward. "It isn't stupid. Labels aren't stupider than anything else. If he doesn't want to call your relationship that, that's fine for him. But he has emotions about it, just like you. It's not as if *you're* being emotional and he's *not*, you know?"

"Don't kid yourself," Gemma says out of nowhere.

"I know, I know ..."

"Words mean something, or they don't," says Ava. "If 'labels' shouldn't mean anything, then saying 'I love you' shouldn't mean anything."

Holly gathers her knees to herself and sighs with her whole body. There's an awkward silence, and Gemma looks at Ava with a kind of intrigue. She has to ask. In a calm, measured tone, she says, "Do you have labels you have feelings about?" There's more silence. "I mean, maybe you don't have any," she clarifies. "But I'm feeling what you're saying." Gemma manages to say all this pleasantly and normally. Sometimes Gemma is drunk without anyone noticing.

Ava hesitates. Holly perks back up. "She's gonna give you the partner rant, buddy."

"*What?*"

"No!" Holly laughs. "Sorry. What I meant is that she hates the word 'partner.'"

"I *hate* it so much!" bursts Ava.

"Why?" Gemma says. "I'm actually curious."

"I don't care if anybody else uses it!" Ava stresses. (Holly raises a hand. "Thanks, bud.") "But I'd *never* want someone to call me their 'partner.' Or their 'person,' either. That's up there, too."

"Really?"

"Yeah, it's just"—Ava rotates her wineglass—"I didn't get a sex change for someone to call me 'person.'"

"I get that," Gemma says instantly.

"If I'm in a relationship, an actual committed relationship, to me, that's being a—"

She hesitates for an imperceptible second before saying the last word—"girlfriend. Or a wife. That is just how I feel. With 'partner' or 'person,' I just *feel* myself disintegrating into the wall or something!"

"'Sex change.'" Gemma says, in a delayed reaction. "That one needs to make a comeback."

"Sex changes for all," Ava agrees.

The door opens and Olive rolls in. "Dudes!"

"Olive!" says Holly.

She gets up for another bottle of wine. Olive intently beelines for Ava and begins jabbering about an appointment she has forgotten. Gemma doesn't like this. "I'll just see if Holly needs help in the kitchen." Ava nods and Gemma rises.

The kitchen is strangely dark and shadowed, the light coming in sideways from the living room. "I was actually gonna cut up this fruit," Holly says. "I'm trying to eat more fruit." She gestures drunkenly to an array of apples surrounding a cantaloupe. "Can you cut up this fruit?" Her skirt of clouds billows around her body as she moves.

"Sure." Gemma gets herself set up chopping apples as music and Olive's continued jabbering come from the living room. Gemma realizes she might not be as drunk as she thought.

Holly opens the fridge, then visibly has a thought and wheels to face Gemma, her skirt whirling with her. "So your family's from here?"

"Huh? No. They're more … Steinbach area."

"Steinbach land!" Holly shrieks. "That's where my *mom*'s from! Blumenort?"

Gemma's tickled at this. "Close. My grandparents grew up on farms around there. Why, you wanna check if we're relate—"

"*Oh no, don't you try that Mennonite Game horseshit with me, missy!*"

Gemma laughs. "I know. '*Everyone's related!*' Who cares."

"I *know!*" says Holly. She retrieves two bottles of white wine from the open fridge. "My grandparents were second cousins. Who gives a shit? It's not special! Okay, look," she says. "Do you call yourself a Mennonite?"

"I don't … I don't know?" says Gemma. "I guess so, but I can't remember the last time I actually said that to someone. It never comes up. "

"Hm," Holly says. She pours herself a glass, then hands Gemma one of the whole bottles.

Gemma takes the bottle and stares at it, then looks up at Holly. "Why do you ask?"

Holly sips, then begins to slice the cantaloupe. The music coming from the living room is soft and melodic. Gemma can hear that Olive is still talking fast. And Ava is speaking to her in hushed tones.

"I think my parents are ashamed of it," Holly finally says.

"Ashamed?" Gemma repeats.

Holly's arm moves methodically in the shadowed light. "Yes."

"Ashamed how?" Gemma asks. She drinks from the bottle she's been given. A few more of her sensory handles slip away. Her stomach is complaining, she realizes latently. She is in some degree of pain.

"Sometimes it's politics," Holly replies. "Something racist or homophobic happens out here and they're embarrassed. Fucking Bill 18, that kind of shit," she says. She stops slicing and looks at Gemma. "But that's not what I'm thinking about. See, they were raised to be ashamed to take pleasure in anything. They were raised in a way that taught them almost everything they wanted to do was selfish, that so much pleasure was untoward, a sin. And sometimes, I think," Holly says, reaching for her glass, "as a reaction to this, they learned some ... wrong lessons."

"What makes you say that?"

An ugly look moves around Holly's face. "Pleasure is important to them. They taught me it was okay to take things. They were very concerned, when I was growing up, that I wouldn't take things if I wanted them."

Gemma can't relate, but it's not the time to say that. "And this is because they're ashamed of the church or such?"

"I don't know what they went through." Holly says abruptly. She resumes chopping.

Gemma takes another drink from the bottle in her hand. She turns back to her apples. Gemma realizes that Holly is not exactly sober herself, and perhaps it's indeed best if the conversation doesn't continue. Though she does wonder why Holly handed her a full bottle of wine. *Mennonite women notice things.* Her dad had said that once.

It occurs to Gemma that Holly has perhaps drunk-talked herself into a mood. Gemma can relate to that. She changes the subject. "Weren't you telling me a Christmas story earlier?"

"Right!" says Holly. She waves the knife over the cantaloupe in a manner that would be hilarious in a movie but is terrifying right now. "So we're driving back from Alberta. It's winter and shitty as hell and we get a late start. We stop in Regina for dinner and, like, it's already late in the evening, the wind is Salad Shooting air blades at my skin, we still have hoooooours left to drive, and me, genius that I am, I leave my phone on top of the car outside a Wendy's. By the time we realize, the phone's already long gone. Ava calls it a bunch, and after, like, the tenth call, it starts going straight to voice mail. Ava knows how to track it, but I don't. She finds out it's at an apartment building. I'm ready to write it off, y'know? I'm embarrassed. I do *not* want to try to bust into this fucking building where God knows *who* is in there. But Ava's like, no, we're getting your phone back. And dude, like I said, she never left her fucking house in those days. She was such a recluse, such a shut-in. I was worried about her those years."

Holly's eyes falter a bit again. This time, Gemma's heart is less hardened.

Holly continues, "But she goes into this strange-ass building in Regina, and she's calling my phone, which is now ringing again, and she knocks on *every single fucking door* until this old woman opens her front door and gives my phone back! Like what were the fucking odds, right? She stammers that her grandson found it, she was gonna give it to the cops tomorrow morning, and we're like, yeah, yeah whatever, thanks for giving it back, let's go." Holly takes all the fruit they've cut and piles it into bowls. "I just remember Ava was so determined, like she was on a *mission*. It, like, wasn't a question. There's a loyalty to her, I guess is what I'm trying to say," concludes Holly. "At the time I would've said it was out of character for her, but now I realize it wasn't. I don't know if that makes any sense."

"It does," says Gemma, scooping the last of her apple slices into a bowl. (In no life would Gemma have gone on such an adventure over a fucking phone. But Gemma gets what Holly's trying to say.)

"Well, anyway. Funny postscript to that story? I'd forgotten that as a joke I'd labelled Ava's number in my phone as 'Some Slut.'"

"Oh my God. So when she was blowing up your phone, and the old woman was seeing it ring—"

"Poor her."

They serve the fruit and sit back down. Gemma has drunk much of the bottle of wine. She slouches her body into Ava's, wrapping herself in the girl's heat. Gemma's satin blouse makes a scratchy sound against the heavy fabric of Ava's dress. Gemma realizes her apple slices are mutilated to shit and look terrible, but who cares. Ava strokes Gemma's hair, puts a long arm around her waist. Lets her fingers drift toward Gemma's ass. From this angle, Gemma faces the night of the open window. There really is very little to the south of here. A few winking lights of houses. One hamlet over the border. Olive continues talking very fast, excitedly. She has one of those perfect stealth voices. Olive's voice rolls over Gemma. If Gemma'd called her on the phone, she'd assume she was cis. Olive needs Ava to drive her to the hospital tomorrow for her appointment. Olive has repeated this fact a few times and Ava says calmly, "Of course, of course." Olive keeps chattering about how her doctors are psychos, and could Ava please, please come with her, please. She sounds energetic and excited. Ava says, "Of course," over and over, in that same robotic, calm voice. Gemma hopes this doesn't disrupt Ava's day too much tomorrow. Did Holly scream? Was that screaming, what Holly was doing? No, she is laughing—at what, Gemma cannot tell. If the old hospital were still open, it'd be a block away and Ava wouldn't need to drive Olive at all, but ugh, when they built the new hospital, they just had to fucking share it with *Winkler*, so now it's all the way out at the fucking mid-point on the highway. Funny that the old hospital is a massage centre now. And the back of it is a gym. Food has now somehow spilled and Holly is rising to clean it up. Gemma is more or less lying on Ava and can feel Ava's clit hardening beneath her dress. Olive is speaking very, very fast and Gemma just cannot make out her words anymore; she is having enormous difficulty focusing. Her fingers are dry and her chest is so sweaty. There is a wall on the bathroom (how did she get into the bathroom?) and someone is yelling. The porcelain of the bathtub is cooler on her skin than the plastic of the toilet seat, and this makes no sense. A fluorescent light is buzzing and flickering and it is cooler now, it's mustier. There is a voice from the music and it is a girl singing very high and she sounds very beautiful, but Gemma can't make it out, though maybe it was gone now it was coming from—

Gemma wakes while it's still dark out.

Instantly, she is hit with an ugly feeling, an intractable knowledge teleported into her body: something bad happened in the night.

She is still in her clothes and in Ava's bed. The A/C is still broken, and every part of her skin is sticky. Her mouth feels like bugs. In the moonlight through the shades, she can see Ava in her sleep mask under the covers, snoring quietly, her hair snarled. She looks gorgeous like that.

What happened? What happened? Gemma can't remember. Her body hurts, and she can already tell she will be very shaky if she stands up. Her back ... her back has a burning sensation? That's weird. She remembers very little after they left Holly's place. Could she remember anything? Anything? She'd been on a toilet and it was too warm. There was a buzzing fluorescent light; it reminded her of a basement back in the city ... She couldn't remember anything else.

Hey! Hey. Whatever happened, there's nothing you can do about it right now. Take a shower. Take a shower and change into your sleep clothes. And you can lie back down next to this girl you like and you'll wake back up sprightly, smelling good in the morning, and you can figure out everything from there.

Gemma rises, but she has not truly reckoned with the requirements of standing at the moment, and so she sinks onto all fours on the carpet.

There on the floor, she removes her blouse and then her skirt.

She scrabbles around and finds her sleep clothes and her phone. In the process, she discovers the tequila bottle, now empty. *Heh*, she thinks.

Silently, she rises again and exits the room. Slowly, shaking as if she's just come inside from extreme cold. She nearly crashes full force into the bathroom door but steadies herself last minute. *Oh boy.*

Inside the windowless room, she turns on the light, and then a stabbing cramp hits her out of nowhere. She doubles over and sits naked on the toilet. It's an intense cramp.

Oh fuck, like a *bad* one. Shit, *shit*, like *shit*, this *hurts!!!* Gemma clutches herself. Her eyes water. She waits for the pain to fade. It doesn't fade.

It continues to not fade.

It keeps not fading. It's excruciating, what Gemma's experiencing, and it's not stopping.

Her eyes stream as she's bent over in the searing light.

She breathes, and breathes again, and breathes again, and breathes again. Eventually, the pain leaves.

"Fuck," she whispers to herself. She's been cramping more lately in the last few months, sure, but that was ... awful.

Sweaty in the baking room, she drinks cold water from the tap. (She notices she has an apple piece stuck in her teeth. Good times.)

She lets the hot shower sauna her body. She washes every part of herself and holds her torso and closes her eyes.

There.

There.

Did something happen last night? She was usually well behaved in blackouts, but.

What if she'd really done something bad this time?

(Or had something happened with Olive? The lady had seemed kinda in a state.)

Stop, Gemma thinks. *It's all probably fine.* Her instincts are telling her differently—but Gemma knows better. She has woken up enough times after blackouts with alarm bells crying wolf in her gut. She is aware that sometimes your instincts do not help you. She'll check her phone for any clues, and if that reveals nothing, she'll leave it be. She does wish she'd taken pictures, though. Stupid world she lives in. She has a device that takes limitless free photographs and she never uses it. When she was a kid, grade five maybe, her dad gave her a pocket camera for Christmas, and it felt like a magic wand that made her life beautiful. It had died a year later during recess, slapped out of her hands and into the snow. She'd been particular about what she snapped pictures of, in a very ten-year-old kind of way. Dishes in the sink. Her Opa's record player in Roland, holding a still Burl Ives LP. The sapling planted years ago by the owners of the house on Nelson Street. Her father's bedroom window and, beyond it, the sky.

She should've taken pictures last night. Oh well. Gemma towels off and changes into sleep clothes. She checks her phone for messages, calls, even her steps ... nothing out of the ordinary. *Everything's fine*, she soothes herself. *Go back to bed.* She opens the door and Ava is standing there, glaring in the dark.

"The fuck are you doing?" Ava says, pushing past her to the toilet.

Gemma stammers. Her arm prickles where Ava made contact. Eventually, she echoes, "What am I do—"

"What?" Ava interrupts. She smiles mockingly with her mouth open.

"I wanted to shower," Gemma says in a small voice.

Ava laughs, high-pitched and cold.

"Are you okay? Is everything okay?" Gemma says, her voice smaller still.

Ava leans forward on the toilet. Her hair obscures her face. She has not looked at Gemma since she sat down. Finally, she says, "I'd like you to close the door, please."

Gemma shuts the door. She looks at the dark living room. She feels like her throat is closing. She goes back to the bedroom and gets into bed with the covers unfolded above her knees, lying there like an open sandwich. She begins to hyperventilate. Which is bad. She knows she has to calm down. Only bad things will happen if she does not calm down.

Fortunately, Gemma is still nicely drunk. And so, she becomes calm soon.

Pictures. Minutes ago, she was thinking about pictures. She picks up her phone. What's the last picture she took in the first place—

Wait.

Gemma focuses. What *is* this picture?

It appears to be of a hallway in the building. Aimed at a corner. The picture is filled with beige walls, plain white moulding at the bottom, the perspective as if she'd taken it sitting or lying on the floor.

She scrolls. Another one of ... a ceiling? And a shape that looks like a limb on the right side of the screen.

The carpet, she realizes. *That's why my back hurts.* The pain in her back is like a rash.

Above both images:

Today 12:31 AM

She puts her phone down and lies still, facing the wall. Ava enters the room and gets into bed as Gemma lies there with her eyes open in the night.

∽

Gemma wakes to full daylight and the sound of Ava in the shower.

A weightlessness floats up from her ribs, rising through her, a vessel of resigned shame: *All right, then. Did you fuck it up? You fucked it up. It's ruined! Hope you're happy! What'd you do? Does it even matter?*

Almost instantly, this is followed by a second weightlessness, jumpy and cloying, breathing through her windpipe with not shame but fear: *Why was Ava like that last night? She seemed ... mean. And she was acting weird yesterday morning, too. Shit, what did* she *do last night that you can't remember?! Is this place actually safe—*

Stop, thinks Gemma. *Stop.* None of these questions are helpful. But they stay, drifting and settling around her like poison gas.

An actual hangover for the ages is kicking in, too, though that is not the biggest item on her problem list.

She checks the time; Ava's going to work soon. *Get up.* She lifts her head. Okay. *Move.* She gulps six T1s and changes back into her red dress and puts all her shit in her bag. She puts up her hair and brushes her teeth and shaves over the kitchen sink and sips carefully at a glass of water. Coffee? None has been made. (People who didn't drink coffee first thing in the morning ... Why even have a machine on the counter? To Gemma this made as much sense as keeping shampoo in the back of the closet.) She's still sweating from the broken A/C, but she gets a pot going. She does her makeup in the living room mirror.

Soon, Gemma's on the couch with her bag by her feet, sipping from the ultramarine mug. She hears the bathroom door open. Gemma freezes at first, staring at the blank shade. She hears Ava's footsteps. But before she can turn to face her, she hears Ava's bedroom door close.

Gemma stands and raises a window shade and looks at the morning landscape.

She can wait.

This was the last town Mennonites really got claws into, this far into the province. Even here, they didn't dominate; they were only, like ... half the population, she'd guess? Not like Winkler or anything. Sure, immediately west was a Hutterite colony, some Holdeman out-posts. A church in Manitou here, one south of Crystal City there. But this town, that's mostly where they'd stopped.

Olive comes out of her room and waves to Gemma, her demeanour pleasant. She knocks on Ava's door, and then enters without a sound. Gemma looks at the red curtain of beads by the entryway.

Last night. The parts she can remember: Gemma had dreamed of that kind of life. When she was younger, she'd dreamed of that kind of life. A life where she woke next to a good woman and they went peaceably about their days and the evening spread wide between them and friends, sweet and trusted friends. Gemma'd never had that. But it was all she'd ever really wanted.

After she and that ex had split up, Gemma finally came out socially, in her early twenties. (The ex had been fine with Gemma going on hormones, but in public—yeah. It'd been a whole thing.) Gemma lost her job, and then she started camgirling. Then it occurred to her better money was available in person. Sick of the prairies, she hoofed out to Toronto to crash with a girl she knew; they slept together and worked together for a few months and it was nice, but then they had a fight. She went out to Nova Scotia to visit her dad, but he'd thrown in his lot with his new wife and her church, and the new wife and Gemma didn't get along, which birthed the current relationship Gemma has with her dad, where she sees him once every couple years and they talk mostly on Christmas and birthdays; it's all pleasant, but the sporadicity of the contact is what keeps it pleasant. Gemma's come to terms with this, but back then ... It was a head-spinning time.

In the decade since, she'd pieced together an existence through different cities and houses and lovers, few of which ever lasted. She was always short of money, but she always got by; it was a stressful life, but it was a life. Somewhere early along the way, evenings became permanently linked with alcohol. And it was such that this life of Gemma's was also a life of peace. Since she was small, living had been a trial, and when she was drinking, it was not. She'd read tearful stories of alcoholics whispering, "I don't even like it anymore," and Gemma just couldn't identify less. Yeah, she'd go on the wagon now and then, but mostly that just confirmed that life continued to be intolerable sober. *Do I want to quit? Let's give this a whirl. Nope, still sucks.* She hadn't lied when she told Ava it kept her sane to know stopping was an option. She knows it's an option, and she doesn't want to, and there's a certain clarity to those twin understandings. (Though this ferritin bullshit—well, she'll see what the doctor says.) Sure, Gemma feels more energetic when she's sober, more attuned to life, but that's not a plus. Drinking, for her, turns violent despair into garden-variety sadness. If it works that way, she'll take it.

(One thing Gemma does notice when she's on the wagon. Sober people say their appearance changes when they stop drinking—shrunken booze bellies, unmottled skin. None of that stuff's ever happened to Gemma, with the exception of her eyes. Normally, the bags under Gemma's eyes are deep, numerous, and tinged with sickly yellow-green. Except during her bouts with sobriety, when they instantly go away.

They always come back so quick.)

Articles come across her socials that relate addiction to trauma. Years before, the articles related addiction to illness, a disease like any other. Before that, she'd hear it emphasized as something that ran in a family, a risk to watch out for like cancer. And before that, she'd hear it was the Devil, and a solution might be prayer. Gemma always feels detached from these explanations. Sure, they all make some sense, but like ... put it this way: if you ever asked Gemma to put an origin story on her alcoholism, she would not invoke predictive trauma or inevitable disease or unholy evil—she would simply say she had loved booze from her very first drink, and she knew from the start it was a dangerous love, and there was a point in her young life when the rationales and faith required to not nurture that love—they just all fell away. Sure. Maybe it would've shaken out differently in another kind of life. Gemma just isn't sure that matters.

What Gemma thinks matters: she is an addict, and there are things addicts do. She'd seen it enough growing up. There was Tamara, who summer after grad tried to drink herself to death and was now lucky to be alive. There was Andrew from choir, who came to every practice blitzed, who turned up in the city years later on Portage guzzling God knows what, who didn't even recognize Gemma once she explained who she used to be. There was a friend of her Opa's, a sweet grade four teacher, who snapped when Gemma was in high school and now lived in his son's basement, alternating between AA and boxes of wine. Some people might say it was Menno shit, or small-town shit, but Gemma knows better. None of it's special. There's a line in a book by Miriam Toews herself: "It's just something that happens sometimes, a story as old as time, and this time it happened to me."

Gemma accepted this about herself long ago. She is who she is. And Ava knows who she is. If Gemma's fucked it up already, so be it.

What Gemma will not do is listen to the whispering weightlessness telling her dark and awful things. She will wait here and talk to Ava and see it through.

Though ... the way Ava had pushed past her last night. There'd been something mean about it, something mean in the way she'd touched her. There had been, she isn't imagining that. (She's not, right?)

It's not like you actually know this girl that well.

Gemma can hear terse whispering now behind Ava's bedroom door and it's starting to wig her out. Her brain is beginning to play last night in the bathroom over and over and she has Ava's face in her mind laughing at her and she knows that kind of laugh and she knows what that kind of meanness looks like. Gemma is very familiar with what that looks like and she sees the curtain of red beads and she sees herself hoisting her bag and walking out the door right now, she could do it if she wants to, she could just do it right now and indeed that is part of what her instincts are telling her, gas inside her ribs telling her to get out get out get out you know you won't have the courage to do it when she's back—

Stop it, Gemma thinks desperately. Gemma knows she runs away easily. Her flight mechanism is primed from many angles. Chalk it up to childhood bullshit, crap with her ex, close calls in T-girl Hookerland, a blacked-out brain that has long mixed the fragile watercolours of memory and nightmare—Gemma lost interest in divining whys long ago, but sometimes panic ripples up in her brain, and it is doing so right now as Ava's mean, high-pitched laughing face from the bathroom last night is staring at her and circling her mind—

Stop it! Gemma pleads with herself. She is not going to leave. She felt something deep with Ava last night, and regardless of what else happened, she is going to stay right here and when Ava comes out of that room she is going to talk to her.

It becomes one of the hardest things Gemma's done in her life, these few minutes, resisting.

The T1s kick in. The interlocking pains in her back and muscles and head all fade slightly. She draws an invisible blanket around herself. *Not yet.* A voice appears inside Gemma to affirm her on this. *No, no, don't leave yet.*

She turns to the window. It's a sunny morning here in the Pembina Valley, and the number three highway is moving across the plains.

Olive emerges, and then goes into her room. Ava comes out in a blue maxi dress. "Hey."

Gemma gazes up at Ava, a cobalt obelisk standing above her. God, this lady is such a fucking knockout. If it doesn't work out between them, Gemma might dye her hair like Ava's. That red-black thing could work for Gemma.

"Hey," she echoes. "Going to work?"

"Soon."

Ava joins her on the couch. Gemma places her hands on top of hers. In real time, Gemma sees Ava's body untense itself into something gentler. Ava strokes Gemma's palm with one finger and the touch moves like a wind through Gemma's body.

Ava looks down.

"I'm sorry I was weird last night," says Ava.

"It's okay," Gemma says. "But thanks, thanks for saying that." She pauses and considers how to articulate. "Your demeanour did catch me off guard."

"Yeah." Ava sucks in air. "Yeah, I was upset. I'm sorry."

"It's okay."

Ava continues to look down, moving her finger around Gemma's hand like she's drawing.

"Ava, I'm gonna be honest with you." Ava looks up. "I don't remember everything about last night. After we left Holly's. Did anything happen I should know about?"

"Oh." Ava exhales. "No. You were really drunk, though. You had trouble walking? You disappeared into the bathroom for a while and Olive found you sleeping on the toilet. It freaked her out. She was convinced you needed a hospital? She can get like that. Anyway, it was a whole thing. We tried to carry you home, but Olive's not that strong ... so I had to like. Half drag you, sorta."

"That explains why my back hurts," Gemma says dryly.

"Heh," Ava says. She puts a hand to her face. "Yeah, your shirt rode up a lot."

"Sorry about that."

Ava shrugs and looks down again.

"Did that make you upset?" Gemma asks plainly.

Ava scrunches her eyes. "A little."

"I understand. It's okay to be upset about something like that." Gemma feels very calm saying this. She has learned this too, about addiction. Running at the truth was the only debt-free way to modulate its destruction. "I'm sorry you had to take care of me in that way."

"It's okay."

Ava goes back to tracing her finger around Gemma's palm. "I think I like you more than I understand."

"I like you a lot, too. Maybe you know this by now."

Ava breathes out.

Tell her you feel something for her. Tell her you want to see this out. Tell her. Gemma opens her mouth as Ava says, "I don't think you can stay here much longer. Do you have somewhere else you can go?"

∽

Fuck.

∽

"Yes," Gemma lies.

"Cool," Ava says, visibly relieved.

Gemma gazes at Ava with a face of glass. "Mind if I head out tomorrow?" she asks.

"Of course," Ava says quickly. "One more night is fine." They're silent for a minute. "But tonight, uh, should we get up to something?"

"I could make dinner." Gemma says this without thinking.

Ava breaks into a wide smile. "That'd be cool. What'll you make?"

"I could do a Menno supper." The T1s have definitely kicked in. Gemma's brain is a smooth lake. "Wareniki and Foamavorscht."

"Uh—"

"That's Plautdietsch for perogies and sausage," Gemma says. "But better."

"Oh, I've had that stuff! Holly took me to the Don once."

"Gotta love the Don," Gemma says coolly.

Ava gets up. "Sweet. Been a while since we cooked anything real in here." She gestures to the kitchen. "Use whatever you need."

"Okay." Gemma looks out the window as she hears the clack of the beads.

∽

Alas, Gemma now has a new problem: she has no money for the groceries to make this meal.

Yes, she could've asked Ava. She could've asked for $50, and Ava probably would've immediately e-transferred her $100 with an insufferably sympathetic look on her face, and frankly, Gemma would rather get run over by a truck.

She resurrects an ad and posts her location. *Yes I am actually here!* ☺ *One day only.* She doesn't actually expect to snag a boy, but. You know. A smart girl at least casts a line out.

She flits through her socials, and it is then that a veil of heaviness descends upon her. She's leaving tomorrow. And she really has tapped out all the favours she can call on. Even if she can hitch back to the city, where is she gonna go? (She has no booze for tonight either, *fuuuck*.)

It's so stupid. Gemma grew *up* in this town! Yet she'd had so few friends, and now, no family. Even the people who would've been nice to her—she just hadn't stayed in touch, hadn't wanted to, and now she recognizes no one; there's no one …

Her phone dings. *Hey babe you're really here?*

࿉

Minutes later, she's plodding down Mountain Street in her black cloth coat, her body still woozy and achy. It's too warm for the coat, really, but she disappears easy in it and that feels best right now.

The guy'd said to meet him round back of the old video store. One of her old haunts, actually. Had a pool table and arcade games. In theory, doing a call there should be weird, but in practice, Gemma's bar for weirdness was obliterated long ago. She rounds the building, crunching on shale gravel, and sees him waiting, a stocky white guy in jeans and a tan jacket. Thousands of this guy in a town of thousands.

Down a flight of stairs there's an office crammed with movie posters, a fantastically old computer, a cot in the corner, a small window with a little curtain.

The man puts $200 in her hand and a cloudburst of serotonin crackles through her brain. She does the call with pleasant mindlessness. The guy sucks her for forever, and then she blows him as he stands against the door.

Afterward, he falls on the cot, still naked. Gemma realizes he's younger than she thought; he has a beard and is balding early, but shit, it's possible that she, like, went to high school with him? Who knows?

"How you like our town?" he says.

Gemma zips up her dress. Her body has severely amped up its complaining. "It's great."

He snorts. "Great. Sure." He leans over and opens a mini fridge. "*Great*. You want a beer?"

It's eleven in the morning, and her stomach is roiling from the T1s (plus, like, she'd swallowed ...). But still, she says yes, and then they're drinking as he sits on the cot. Gemma sips gingerly and immediately she's dizzy. Funny life it is. Funny life.

"Sorry," she says, sliding down to the ground against the door. "I need—I need to sit down."

The guy laughs. "One beer drops you, huh?" It's the thoughtless laugh of someone who's not a bully but not exactly the nicest, either.

Gemma smiles tightly. "It's a long story." The cool concrete is nice on her legs. She feels for the bills inside her bag, and the solidity of the polymer is electric on her fingertips. She tilts her head back against the door, looking up at the joists in the ceiling.

For a few seconds, she's a teenager drinking in a small-town basement again.

(Hell, for all she knows, she's done exactly that with this very dude.)

"You want to hang out for a bit?" he says. "I got time."

There's that wide-eyed, casual loneliness in his eyes, the volatile loneliness of men's eyes. Her stomach is a nest of hornets, and even through the T1 numbness, her head pulses like a swelling bruise. Her body is telling her she needs to rest. Puke first, actually, then rest. Her body is a workhorse going on strike; it is very sorry, it is telling her, but there is no way she is rising from her place on the floor; that is just not happening.

But Gemma learned long ago that dissociation did not come without silver linings, that she is able to pull back her body's automatic overrides, to manually guide her physical being forward to wherever it needs to be, like a lone man rising from a snowbank in nighttime winter cold. She stands and slugs the whole beer in two series of voracious gulps. "Nah, I gotta go."

"Damn, you can suck, eh?" He snickers to himself.

Gemma winks and thinks, *This fuckin' guy*. She tamps down a burp and shrugs on her coat. Her head and her stomach are exploding. Can she reach the doorknob and turn it? Yes, yes, she can. None of this matters. She is walking out the door to make a good meal for a beautiful girl, who's real, who's here, who's no memory or mirage, who Gemma likes so, so much, and they will have one more night together and she will cherish and delight in it, and then she will leave. In this, there is dignity. *Do not worry about tomorrow, for tomorrow will worry about itself. Each day has enough trouble of its own.* She opens the door and looks back at the guy, and this time she flashes a genuine smile. "See ya around."

⌒

Gemma pounds up the steps aaaaaand pukes on the shale pretty much immediately. Whatever! Pouring beer on a T1 haze—she had it coming, and she almost immediately feels better. The fresh air feels good on her cheeks. She takes mints out of her bag and walks on—boom— good as new. She crosses the tracks and strolls down Stephen Street. In front of the Chicken Chef, an old man tips his cap (John Deere, natch).

She stops at the LC for a handle of vodka, and then heads over to the IGA—bah, right, it's a Giant Tiger now.

Flour, butter, heavy cream. Cottage cheese, kernel corn, and— holy shit, by some heavenly fuckin' miracle there is farmer sausage at the fucking Giant Tiger! Gemma remarks on this to the cashier, an old woman with an old-school accent who says, "Oh yah, you're lucky now. We dohn't get the Foamavorscht in that much." Then a pale blond teenage boy wearing no uniform asks the woman something in Plautdietsch. The woman turns to Gemma. "Would you like help carrying this to your car?"

Gemma's eyes have filled with tears at these sounds. She is embarrassed. But she's embarrassed with the fullest of hearts. She only wishes she had a way to respond. She wishes she had a way to communicate to the woman what she understands, but all she can do is shake her head no. The woman turns back to the boy, as if he has not also been watching Gemma. "*Nee*, Alvino," she says quietly. "*Dank*."

On the way out, Gemma finds it in her to whisper, "Thank you" to the boy as she moves past, and when she does this, the boy's eyes grow wide.

Gemma exits and hauls the bags over to South Railway, up and over the tracks. A cold front's come in while she's been out, blowing the belt of her coat around her. Times like this, when the wind comes down from the north, you can feel the spectre of winter, even this time of year. You can smell the thirty-below waiting, breathing inside the breeze.

She reaches Ava's building. A train's horn sounds from the east. The groceries were only thirty and change, so Gemma's still got a hundred bucks left. If she can hitch into the city tomorrow, she can get a room for the night. Snag a couple boys to buy a few more days and figure out the rest from there. Maybe it's time to skip town for real. She knows a girl in Montreal who once told Gemma to visit. Maybe. Fuck, they shut the buses down, though ... And the train is always booked up in summer. And even if she could rustle up flight money, she'd need to get an ID ... Ach, whatever, that's tomorrow's fire! In the meantime, she has one more night to spend with Ava, and Gemma wants it to be beautiful.

She enters the building and Olive lets her into the apartment. "I'm good," Olive says happily, though Gemma has not asked her a thing. Olive is watching TV on her phone. "You want a beer?" she asks, and Gemma tells her no, thank you, she's not feeling particularly well, and she thinks she needs to lie down.

Gemma half wakes in the early afternoon to brilliant sun coming through the shades. Sounds of movement come from the living room. It must be Olive and Ava, getting ready to leave for Olive's appointment.

It comes to Gemma one final time, behind lidded eyes, floating on the border between sleep and consciousness, that what she wants in this exact moment, more than anything, is for Ava to open the door and kneel by the bed and put a hand on her back and say something like, "Shhh. Hey. I know sometimes I get weird. I'm sorry. I want you to stay. For a little while longer, anyway. If you want to stay, I want you to stay." Gemma knew last night these were the contours of what she wanted, and now she knows it again one final time. She dreams of Ava opening that door and appearing behind her in this room.

So, when an hour later Gemma's phone alarm goes off, she sits up in an empty apartment and puts her head in her hands. *Okay, love. Okay. Okay. You had a good feeling about this girl and you came here to check it out and you had a place to stay for a few days. And now you know. And you'll go on. As you do.*

The way you made Wareniki was simple. Gemma's dad had once taught her how. "Shame you couldn't learn from my mum; she was the best. My brothers didn't care about cooking. I always did ..." He'd stared off. "But hey, imagine coming home to this after a full day working on the farm." That's where their history came from, of course. The farm. Though her Opa'd been a teacher, and same with all his kids. No farmers left in the family by the time Gemma came along. Heh, and now you can go to MJ's Kafé in Steinbach and buy a T-shirt that says GOT SCHMAUNTFAT? and that book *Mennonite Girls Can Cook* was a bestseller. Of course the cooking was by women. Her dad a beautiful anomaly in that way, Mennonite men and cooking an oxymoron even when Gemma was growing up. Those nights she'd stayed with her Opa in Roland, his way of making Gemma lunch for school was ordering an extra burger at Dairy Queen the night before and putting it in the fridge overnight. Gemma didn't mind. She'd liked her grandfather. He'd fall asleep to a giant radio while Gemma lay awake on the other side of the bed, listening to a lull of talk on frequency bands she then didn't understand and now couldn't remember.

But Gemma's dad, he'd taught her how to make Wareniki, though Gemma's fucked it up a couple times since. Once, in Toronto, Gemma'd promised to make that roommate/lover a big pan of them. But she bought pastry flour not knowing the difference and ended up with a huge flavourless pile of dough holding tiny circles of filling. She'd felt so stupid and lonely, lifting those heaving mounds out of the oven in that shitty East End apartment. It was a silly thing to be upset about. But Gemma had been so fucking sad.

First, you make the perogy dough. Just use flour and water to make a bunch of it (a bit of salt and baking powder, if you want). Make sure it's not sticky. Chill it in the fridge for an hour.

After that, you make the filling. There are lots of options, but you grew up with cottage cheese, and that's what you are going to make. You take two big containers of the stuff and put it in a bowl. Stir in a few healthy dabs of salt and an egg, and then *lots* of pepper. You want enough pepper that the top is nearly solid black before you start mixing it in.

Next, preheat the oven to 350, and then roll out your dough. Make it thin. Use a glass on a cutting board to cut out individual Wareniki and put the cottage cheese filling in the centre. Make sure you don't put too much; you want to be able to pinch it off clean when you close the dough. There, you have your first one. Repeat until you have enough to fill a baking pan.

Now you're ready to bake. Some people boil, and some pan-fry, but your father baked Wareniki when he showed you how, and so you are going to bake. Take out your vodka, pour two shots into a pint glass, then fill the glass halfway with water and shoot it back, the liquid drawing bulky fingers through your throat, falling in glittering trails down your insides. Melt a stick of butter, and then pour it into the baking pan. Put in the Wareniki, melt another stick of butter, and pour it over top. You're ready to put them in the oven now. Set the timer for twenty minutes. Believe it or not, you're mostly done. You only have to cook the meat and make the sauce and heat up some vegetables and set the table, just in time for your hungry family to come inside and sit down.

⌘

The front door opens. Ava and Olive enter through the beads. Gemma is frying sausage in the kitchen. She has on a black polyester dress with a pattern of purple waves. Olive goes to her room and Ava carries a bottle of wine. She puts an arm around Gemma's stomach from behind. "That smells good."

Gemma tilts her head back into Ava's neck. "Gonna taste good, baby."

"Should I open this wine?"

"What's the opposite of no?"

Ava kisses her. "I'm just gonna change."

When the sausage is done, you'll need another pan, one you can cover. Transfer the meat to it and keep it warm. Take out the pint of heavy cream and pour it into the first pan with the drippings. Yup, the whole thing. Oh, is that ever a brilliant sound, a brilliant little flat volcano, calmly roaring in every part of the pan. Stir; admire this.

Gradually whisk in a few tablespoons of flour until it's the thickness you like. Add a few dashes of salt and pepper, and then do a taste test. It should be more savoury and creamy than anything you've ever tasted in your life. If it's not, you have options. A favourite choice of

Gemma's father's was to fry up some bacon and pour in the grease, but however you like to fatten a sauce, whether with more butter or perhaps sour cream, that's up to you. The English term for this is cream gravy, and the Plautdietsch term is Schmauntfat.

Let the gravy simmer. Set the table. Put out salt and pepper, as well as a container of sugar. Clean everything up and take one more shot of vodka; put the handle away in your bag. A melting evening stretches before you in its goodness. Heat up the corn, which is going to taste wonderful with the gravy. When the oven timer dings, put the Foamavorscht and the Schmauntfat and the corn and the Wareniki into their serving dishes and call everyone to the table. It's okay if Olive comes too, and it's okay if she doesn't, though she will. This makes you happy. You have never wanted to cook a meal without a household in mind. And so, for nearly all your adult life, cook a meal without a household you have not. You have spent much of your adult life alone, not cooking meals. Olive and Ava come to the table, and you sit down and explain what you have made. You ladle gravy onto your plate and sprinkle sugar on top of the Wareniki—not too much. Traditional Russian Mennonite food is all grease and cream, you explain. It might seem counterintuitive to put a little bit of sugar onto this, you say. But bear with; it'll be tasty. And it is.

$\sim$

It occurs to Gemma halfway through the meal. "We should've invited Holly. Inconsiderate of me."

"That's okay," says Ava.

"I could bring her leftovers. Maybe later I'll put some in a Tupperware and go up."

"Oh, she and I are having lunch tomorrow," says Ava. "I'll do it. This keeps well, doesn't it?"

"Yes, very well," says Gemma. "In fact, it makes for a good cold lunch."

"Perfect!" says Olive immediately.

Gemma realizes it's possible Ava's really saying that Gemma going up to Holly's isn't the best idea. But Gemma can understand that. "I hope Holly didn't find me too embarrassing last night," she says.

"Oh no"—Ava smiles—"not at all."

"Phew."

Olive and Ava exchange looks. They could be humouring her, or perhaps what they are *really* trying to do is prevent Gemma from wandering around the building in any respect. (Gemma can understand both those things as well.) In any case, it doesn't matter. They are tucking into a nice meal, and Olive is already reaching for seconds. "This tastes so *good*."

"I am certainly glad you're enjoying it," Gemma says, seated at the head of the kitchen table, wineglass in hand, sitting back in her chair. She is enjoying watching Olive and Ava eat. "Go to Kopper Kettle if you ever want this on your own. Kopper Kettle's still around, eh? Certainly don't need me here."

There's an awkward silence after that, and then Olive says, "Holly's Mennonite too, right?"

"Yeah," says Ava. "I mean, she's not—Like, her parents aren't ..." Ava looks to Gemma.

"You are trying to say she was not raised in bonnets and buggies," Gemma says, a soft tease in her voice.

Ava blushes and nods. She's wearing a red flared skirt and her hair is in a high pony.

"Were you?" asks Olive.

"No," Gemma says quietly. "I went to a church that met in a house. It was liberal, comparatively. We met in people's houses all around this area. My father and I. He wasn't even that religious then. He is now; his new wife's Baptist. Anyway. Back then, around here, he was looked on suspiciously enough as a single father, and he was a teacher; he had a position in the community. Way he saw it, he needed to be at a church. And with me ... I'm not sure he even would've known how a kid gets raised without one." Ava nods. "I wonder sometimes if it was hard for him. He had to leave his church after university."

"Why did that happen?" asks Olive.

Gemma gazes at her. This might be the first time she's witnessed Olive be interested in something. Gemma does not enjoy the sensation of being interesting. But she will go with it. "He told his minister he did not understand why the fact that someone did not believe in Jesus Christ meant that they should go to hell. And the minister did not have an answer."

"Gotcha."

"So when I came along, we went to the church that met in houses," Gemma continues. "Any member with a living room big enough to fit, they'd host. Which was not my dad and I. Though, certainly, I've been to traditional churches lots. When I visited my Oma out in Mitchell. Or when I stayed with my Opa in Roland. But out here, we went to houses."

"Did your dad grow up with bonnets and buggies?" says Olive.

"No, he was Steinbach in the seventies. He grew up with record purgings and *Hymn Sing*."

"What?"

"Never mind. He grew up conservative, yes. Sin and you go to hell, that stuff. But that didn't mean the plain dress or the buggies or all that. It's never that simple. Even the Hutterites, you know—we went out there for a meal once—they wear plain dress, and the family dining room was the sparest big room I ever saw. But still, they tooled around their colony in a four-wheeler. This old woman whipped me around in one and I was terrified. That would be to the west of here"— Gemma gestures with her head to the window—"in the valley, where you start to have hills."

"That's funny," says Olive.

At first, Gemma does not respond. A world has begun to form in Gemma's third eye as she has been talking about this. Then she says, "Funny. I suppose. All of those people, where they truly went wrong was in wishing to remove themselves from the world. 'The world and its desires pass away, but whoever does the will of God lives forever.' It seems charming, in its own way, doesn't it? They wanted to just be left alone. But on the scale of an entire life, or an entire community, that is a childish desire. Not to mention an impossible one."

"What do you mean?" Olive's really focused on Gemma now.

Gemma puts down her cutlery. It has been a long time since she has heard her grandparents speak, but there is little of their sonority she does not remember. "The temptation to remove oneself from the world does not lack for appeal," she says. "The idea does not need a Scriptural mandate to accrue power. Anybody who doesn't feel accepted within the world—which is most people, regardless of whether it's actually true—can be excited by this desire." She drains her glass. "The idea of forming a little pocket universe where everyone already believes the truths you hold, where you can build a family according to those truths, and where you make a promise to yourself and everybody else in that

universe that you're going to do right by them. And all the cruelty of
the world, the ugliness, the bullheadedness—you and a few other people could just band together and make a bulwark against these things,
couldn't you? Put it that way, it sounds beautiful, no?"

"I see where you're going with this," Olive says calmly.

"Who would *want* to leave that? But the promise never, ever works
that way. I still believe in God"—in her peripheral vision, Gemma
sees Ava turn her head, stunned, to face her—"whether I want to or
not. But isolation, walling off from the world with no expiration date,
that I'll never believe in. Isolation corrodes. Makes your mind do bad
things. It narrows your trust to a tiny circle, and then it narrows it a
little more."

Ava reaches across the table and takes Gemma's hand as Gemma
pours herself more wine. Ava massages Gemma's knuckles.

"Removing yourself from the world isn't actually an option,"
Gemma says. "My ancestors on my father's side believed they were
running off to the middle of nowhere to live peaceably. They wanted
less possessions, less worldliness, they thought everyone was getting
too extravagant and ungodly back in Russia. They were also the first
settlers here after Treaty 1. There's no such thing as opting out of
your life's worldly consequences. Thinking otherwise is just fooling
yourself."

"I see what you're saying," says Olive. "But wait, your father's side?
I thought both your parents were Mennonite?"

"Yes, but my mom's family came over in the twenties. To Ontario.
They were called Russländers, back then."

"Does your mom meet in a house?" asked Olive.

Old Mennonite churches had no decoration or ornamentation,
still didn't in many ways. Gemma would walk into those churches and

they were the sparest large rooms. Another way meeting in the houses had been different; those had been as stuffed and lively as any other country house with a big family.

"No, she does not meet in a house."

Gemma's drunk for real now. She continues, "To cut yourself off from the world. It makes you resistant to outside forces, yes. But narrowly. Not in a way that is strong. Like a tree that grows only upwards, never outwards. Is a poplar not easier to fell than an oak?"

Gemma pauses, refocusing on the two women in front of her, returning a bit to Earth. Gemma realizes she could've said a lot of other things. She could've relayed the story she once heard from her Russländer grandmother in Kitchener, a story *her* mother had told to her, about soldiers who swept through what was then southern Russia during the Revolution and rolled up pages of the family Bible for cigarettes, soldiers who ate all their food and left them to starve, and starve some of them did, yet the story was always framed as how lucky they were, that it could've been so much worse. One only needed, Gemma surmised later, to hear one story about a different family who, say, had their heads cut off and placed around the dinner table. One likely only needed to hear that story once. (This same grandmother had showed Gemma that documentary *And When They Shall Ask* when she was in frickin' grade two. There was a joke in that decision somewhere.)

But the story her Russländer grandmother relayed: That *her* grandmother, Gemma's great-great-grandmother, had noticed the soldiers itching; their coats appeared to be moving. She realized the coats were infested with insects, but the soldiers did not see this. So, Gemma's great-great-grandmother took the coats and put them in the oven to kill the bugs. This did not change how the soldiers treated them, yet when Gemma's grandmother told this story eighty years later in a Kitchener living room, her eyes were enchanted and alive. "The soldiers were confused! They would think, well, why is she being kind to us? They were confused!" She became serious. "You understand what I'm saying. There is a reason she survived. My grandmother believed in Jesus."

The point of that story was not that it represented the unvarnished truth of the Mennonites during the Revolution. Gemma's also heard the stories of Mennonites who took up guns and were slaughtered, of Mennonites who outfoxed and killed their share of soldiers, of Mennonites who were as courteous as could be to the soldiers and were raped and murdered for their efforts, of Mennonites who had become wealthy landowners by the time the Revolution came knocking and who perhaps were not completely innocent in the eyes of certain impoverished locals. Gemma's no historian, but she guesses that time in her people's lives was probably just as chaotic and complicated and horrifying as that of any community who found themselves tangled up in war. But of her grandmother's story, the point to Gemma was this: Once they were over here, kindly taking the soldiers coats were the tales her people chose to tell. They had a smorgasbord of narratives available. That was the one everyone wanted.

The day Gemma came out to her dad, he lowered his head and said, "When they hear about you, everyone back home will finally know that I am garbage."

When Gemma's Oma in Mitchell died, Gemma discovered an old church charter in her things, from the late 1800s. It said evangelizing was unbecoming of a Christian, and it said the same about laughter.

Gemma is acutely aware, now, of the silence she has created. She has been thinking silently for some time. Olive had really seemed fascinated by the meeting-in-houses thing, so Gemma says, "'For where two or three gather in my name, there am I with them.'"

"Christ said that," she adds eventually.

Olive and Ava look at her. At that moment, Gemma remembers the trick from earlier, in the old video store basement. She *did* meet him in high school. She'd been at a house party and a guy was making himself a very complicated fajita in the kitchen. And he was also telling a story to some guys about his girlfriend, about how the girl really didn't want to do anal, and he was like, "Holes are holes," and that made everyone laugh, including Gemma. That was the same guy from earlier today. The guy had gotten on Facebook years back and was excited to announce he was having a kid and—

"It's from Matthew," Gemma says, desperately now.

"I'll do the dishes later." Ava puts on music and opens another bottle of wine. "Let's go sit."

Olive sits on the corduroy recliner, Ava and Gemma on the bottle-green couch. Gemma rests her head on Ava's shoulder, Ava's body furnace-like as ever. "They ever fixing the A/C?" Gemma says absent-mindedly.

"Someone's coming tomorrow," says Ava.

"Seems like this place'd be okay to ride out winter," Gemma says. She is so tired. She is so very, very tired. But she very much loves the feeling of sitting here next to Ava's body, and she is grateful for the rest.

"The heat's good," says Olive. "Thank Christ. I'm not bad with winter, but I get mad depressed if my place is cold."

"Yeah?"

"Yeah. I once had this basement apartment. I lived there alone after my boyfriend left. I was working two jobs, burning the candle at both ends, and in winter I would go crazy. I mean, like actually crazy. Like I'm not being ableist; I'm actually crazy. It was so bad for my brain."

"How long you do that for?" asks Gemma.

"Years," says Olive, clearly travelling back to that time in her mind. "I would get up, and I'd never feel rested. I would shiver over to the shower, and no matter when I left the house, it seemed like it was always nighttime, or about to be nighttime. And I could never get warm. And I was always so, so tired."

"I understand," says Gemma.

Ava kisses Gemma on top of her head. "I guess I should at least put that food away. You sit here and visit."

Visit. That was the word her grandparents had always used. "I'm so glad you could come over to visit," her Oma would say as Gemma and her Opa rolled into the Mitchell house on weekends, her Oma slowly getting up in her study and easing her way into the living room. It was unusual, Gemma learned later, for a Mennonite woman of that time and place to have a study with books. Suspiciously unusual.

Her grandparents had always looked so excited to see each other. Gemma had taken a picture of them once, sitting together in her Oma's living room. And she had taken a picture of her Oma's bedroom, a small rectangle of dark blue linoleum with a small bed against a wall. She had tried taking a picture of her Oma's pill bottles too, as there were so many of them, neatly arranged in lines on top of her dresser, but her Opa had passed by then, grimaced faintly, and said, "No, no." Gemma wishes she still had all those pictures. She doesn't know how long she can continue trusting her memory.

The clink of plates and the rush of tap water come from the kitchen. "Where you going after this, Gemma?" says Olive.

"Eh, I dunno." Gemma smiles. "Back to the city tomorrow. Then maybe east. I'll figure it out." She says this sincerely, even though it'd occurred to her earlier: she can't get a room for the night without an ID either. But she's got some dough; she'll figure it out. She always has.

Ava returns to the living room as Olive makes a disgusted snort and tosses her phone on the table. "Oh no," says Ava. "Is there discourse?"

"There's discourse," says Olive. "Yes, it's trans discourse. It is the worst. Don't you miss the socials?"

"See," says Gemma, "to me, social media is for, like, making jokes and making sure my friends are still alive."

"I don't miss the socials even a little bit," says Ava.

"So what's the trans community saying now?" mumbles Gemma, reshaping her body around Ava's. Gemma feels incredibly warm and peaceful, as if she is wrapped in something like grace.

"Age bullshit," says Olive. "You know that stuff about 'trans time'?"

"Oh," says Gemma. "Like that whole thing about how our age is also how long we've been out or on hormones or whatever."

"Yeah," Olive says seriously. "I mean, it's all true. Time's weird for us. But also like: it's *so* complicated. I've been a gay weirdo for over two decades. I'm not even sure I know what age *means* anymore."

"The 'trans community,'" Ava suddenly says gently. "I wish we didn't use that term."

"Oh?" says Gemma sleepily.

Ava hesitates. "Like what Olive said about age—I don't know anymore what that word *means*. Way we use it, anyway. Seems like it means whatever someone wants it to mean that day. Like, I think of a community as a group of people who have to spend time around each other whether they want to or not. A job where you see the same twenty people every day? That's a community. A town like this? It's a community. Though I guess I haven't done much to be part of it."

"You're saying"—this just occurs to Gemma, rising through her tiredness—"that we use 'community' to mean this dramatic thing, whether it's nice or horrible, when it's just this really mundane thing dictated by these mundane circumstances."

"Maybe," says Ava.

"It is weird when people talk like we're one big group," Olive said, frowning at her phone, talking as people do sometimes when they've just looked at their phone. "We're as divided as society itself, right? By if you went to college. Class. Race. Religion."

"Yeah," says Ava. "It all makes me think, like, is 'community' even a thing at all? I guess it probably is, even if I can't put my fingers around it. I just think, like: I have friends. A few close, dear friends who are also trans, and I can count them on one hand. They've altered the course of my life, and I might not be alive without them. That's true, yes. But where that intersects with the idea of community, I don't know. I'm not even saying it's bad. I see fundraisers go by and I give money to people who need it and I don't know them. Is that community? Probably. Is that good? I feel glad I can do it. But I still can't help but think that term the 'trans community' can mean whatever I want it to mean in that moment. And that isn't true about my friends."

Olive nods and raps her knuckles on the coffee table.

"That's nice, Ava," says Gemma.

Ava parts her lips for a very small, bare-teeth grin. "Get me a 'them' op-ed, stat."

"Only if you do the next one about your baeddel tattoo."

"*Ha!*"

"It's funny, though," says Gemma. "You said a town like this was a community. But when I was growing up, I could tell you every way from Sunday who wouldn't talk to who. And I could drill down for you and tell you who hated who and who'd be there for who. This is maybe like Olive's point, I guess. Anything you want to call a community, there's fractures all the way down, no matter how small. Isn't there?"

There was one more story about Gemma's family. In the fifties, her great-uncle was excommunicated. This happened because he stood up in the congregation one Sunday and had the temerity to say he *knew* he would receive salvation, that he was a faithful servant of the Lord Jesus Christ, and he had no doubt that upon death he'd receive admittance into heaven. The church didn't agree. Gemma knew this story thanks to her Opa, telling her this at the Dairy Queen one day when she was in high school. See, Gemma's Opa, he didn't like that his brother had been so caustic in referring to this experience. "They booted me out," the brother had said. Gemma's grandfather took exception to that term. "Booted." It was a harsh term, he said. Though he soon was joking again, with an easy smile. "See, Mennonites are like good wood," he counselled. "Easily split." Her Opa was rarely so chatty. Her Opa was a private man. Gemma never did find out why he and her Oma had separated. All her dad, or her Opa himself, would ever say was that they decided they no longer wanted to live together. She'd pushed her Opa on this exactly once, and he'd snapped, "There is simply nothing more to it." Was that true? She'd never know. Perhaps she might not want to. *Be careful not to practice your righteous acts before men to be seen by them. If you do, you will have no reward from your Father in heaven.* Mennonite secrets often covered for cruelty and evils banal. But sometimes, every now and then, they could contain an intentional kindness.

She'd never thought to ask her Oma about the whole thing. Gemma had always been too scared of irritating her, that steely-eyed woman who always moved with an immense tiredness. There was an ocean of something visible in that woman as she walked across a room. And then, one day, she got a blood clot and she was gone.

When Gemma was a child, she barely even knew what the term "Mennonite" meant. She thought it was just a random word she didn't understand, like "Lutheran" or "Anglican" or whatever. Different churches had different names—who cares? All she knew was Jesus Christ and peace and faith and crowded Sunday couches and an old man and an old woman who spent nights alone in silent bedrooms. Facts that she now understood were freighted but at the same time unremarkable and immediate and total as thirty-below air. *Whatever you have learned or received or heard from me, or seen in me—put it into practice. And the God of peace will be with you.* One of those evenings staying with her grandpa, they'd been in Winkler having dinner, and a bad storm was coming in. Gemma was worried about the drive back to Roland, and she begged for them to stay at a friend's place. But her grandfather wouldn't hear of it. "No," he said, with a wavering shake of his head. It took them two hours to make it twenty klicks. He drove with a flashlight out the truck's window to see the lines on the road, Gemma huddled and freezing on the other side of the cab. There's nothing but farmhouses and granaries on that drive between Winkler and Roland. It's a beautiful drive even in winter, so long as the weather's good. When the sun sets, and bursts of colour fan out in rays over miles of fields, a panorama of oranges and reds and purples over wizened patterns of white-blue, the snowdrifts shining like fossilized waves. But on that trip it was storming, and the sun was already down. Gemma could see nothing; nor could she hear anything over the wind. Gemma was unspeakably scared. But her Opa always knew himself. Her Opa had always known what he could do, and what he couldn't.

A bolt of pain hits Gemma's stomach hard. Well. The meal they'd eaten certainly wasn't easy on the system. She is very sleepy, but she does not want to go to bed just yet. She slinks into the kitchen and quietly pours herself another hammer of vodka and swallows it down.

She sits back down, and Ava kisses her. Her hands go up the polyester of Gemma's dress.

Olive goes into her room.

Ava stands. "Get on the floor."

Gemma gapes up at her. She lies down.

"Close your eyes," says Ava. Gemma closes her eyes. "I want you to jerk off. Keep your dress on."

Gemma moves her hand beneath her dress and begins to stroke herself.

"Good."

Gemma hears Ava move around the apartment and turn off all the lamps. She feels the presence of Ava kneeling on the carpet beside her. Ava takes Gemma's free hand. "Shhh," says Ava. "Don't stop." Gemma doesn't stop. She feels Ava's tongue cover the palm and fingers of her hand, and then Ava dips Gemma's hand into—what is this? It's the sugar bowl. Ava dips Gemma's hand in the sugar and brings it to Gemma's mouth and Gemma opens willingly. "Eat," says Ava. Gemma sucks her crusted fingers and the taste of the sugar pops in her mind's eye like fireworks.

"Eat," Ava says softly.

When Gemma has finished sucking the sugar a second time, Ava says, "Open your eyes."

Gemma opens. Ava stands over her without underwear in her flared red skirt. "Don't stop," Ava says. She lowers herself. Her skirt closes over Gemma's head and immerses Gemma back into darkness. She feels Ava's clit enter her lips. Slowly, slowly, Ava fucks her tender sugar-stained throat. "Don't finish yet," Ava whispers. She makes the smallest of sounds, she does, coming in Gemma's mouth.

4

Gemma wakes to still-sticky air. It's not as hot this morning, though her throat is a desert and her stomach churns. Ava's stirring. The sun is up. At first Gemma worries, *Is Ava late for work?* But then she remembers it's Saturday. And it's also time for her to leave.

Plan for today: She'll get herself together and go down to Pharmasave. Get something for her stomach, and then hitch into the city. Try snagging a rideshare if that doesn't work out. Figure out her next move once she's on the road.

Back in the day, she used to love getting a big carton of orange juice after a night of real drinking. Her system probably couldn't handle that anymore, though. That was kind of sad.

Ava rolls over and spoons her. "You're still here," she says dreamily from beneath her sleep mask.

"Yup."

Ava plants a long kiss on Gemma's neck. "It's nice to wake up to you, lover."

Gemma sighs with her whole body. It's lovely to hear this. She brings Ava's hand up to her mouth and kisses it.

They stay like this for some time.

Then Ava gets up and Gemma hears the shower.

Lordy, this is a comfortable bed. Gemma splays on it like a star. Soon, soon, she'll get up soon.

When Ava comes back, she says, "I have to pop into work for a minute. Bullshit. You know. I'll take those leftovers for Holly."

Gemma nods into the sheets. "Mmm."

Ava goes about her morning as Gemma dozes.

Then Ava puts a hand on the back of Gemma's head. She leans down and kisses her. She says, "If the A/C guy comes, let him in, hey?"

"Okay."

There are footsteps, the clack of the beads, and the sound of the front door, and Ava is gone.

Gemma sits up.

Don't wait for her to get back. Don't hang around. Don't make it weird. It's easier this way. Leave a nice note. Or don't. Or something. Whatever. She showers and puts on her black dress with purple waves and brushes out her hair and puts it up in pigtail buns. Makes a pot of coffee and raises the shade to look out the window one last time. Nice day by the looks of it. No clouds.

She takes a few pictures of the view for keepsakes. It has been good for Gemma's heart to see this, these wide fields, and the number three running through them.

Gemma realizes she didn't take any pictures of Ava.

Who, of course, is not on socials.

She will have no way to access a reminder of what Ava looks like.

Gemma feels the tiredness in her body. Not mentally, though of course she is tired in that way too, but the undying fog-behind-the-eyes physical fatigue that she is never not experiencing. When was her last real REM-filled sleep? Must've been when she last went on the wagon, which—well, hell, Gemma can't remember the last time she did that. It's been a while. Intellectually, she knows her sleep is ersatz, but now and then she really feels it.

Gemma doesn't hate herself. She used to, of course, but she came up against the hard limits of that hatred's usefulness over the years, bumped along its ceiling like an aquatic creature in a tank, and somewhere in the sea of sweaty, trembling mornings, that hatred faded. Gemma's not a happy person, but she doesn't hate herself.

She is, however, unable to truly understand what she looks like. When she is moving her body, when she is running down a sidewalk or closing a bathroom door, she is unable to conceive of a real picture of her likeness. The woman the rest of the world sees does not live inside Gemma's mind. The woman is external, and to Gemma she has always been this way, and probably always will be. Her inner conception of her appearance is amorphous and difficult to describe, but if she had to try, she might say it is of something masculine without a face, a muscular crush of feathers travelling through a room.

∽

She washes out her cup and lowers the shade. She finds a pen and paper and doesn't overthink it for a second. She writes:

Ava,

Thank you for a lovely few days. I'll come back anytime you want me. Don't be a stranger or a lurker—I love every second I spend with you.

Yours,
Gemma

Some things aren't complicated. So hey, there she be. She goes into Ava's room and leaves the note on the bed.

And then she exits the room and she is going. There is the curtain of red beads; she has to go through it and be done, and then she will move on. She's only been in Ava's presence less than a full week, combined. Strange, isn't it, how nevertheless she would've stayed? Her dad said something once, when he remarried so quickly after meeting his new wife: "At a certain age, you understand yourself enough to know when you don't need more time." Was that true? Gemma doesn't like the woman he married, but Gemma also knows, far as she can glean, that her dad is happy.

Gemma really would've stayed here. The joke about lesbian U-Hauling isn't a fucking joke to her. But neither is moving on, and she is good at moving on. She walks soundlessly into the curtain.

"You're leaving?"

She turns with a start. Olive is wearing that long slip of hers that nearly touches the floor.

"Good morning!" says Gemma. "Yeah, it's about that time. Bye. It was nice meeting you and all."

Olive's face crumples. "Are you fucking serious?"

"Huh? Yes. I mean. Why wouldn't I be? I told you yesterday, remember?"

"What do you mean *yesterday*?"

Gemma is at a loss. She stares at Olive for a second, and then blurts, "Are you mad at me?"

Olive does not reply at first, but then she repeats, "You're *serious*? You're *leaving*?"

Gemma is getting absolutely wigged out. Involuntarily, her eyes shut. "Ava told me yesterday morning that I needed to leave, and this made me sad, but that is fine, and so now I'm leaving, even though that feels like a bummer! You seem very upset! Please tell me why you are upset?!"

"Oh."

Olive says nothing else. Gemma opens her eyes and Olive is ... smiling?! This is all making Gemma feel like she's about to *lose her fucking mind*, and she is just about to turn tail and bounce without another word when Olive says, "You don't remember what happened last night after you two were done fucking, do you?"

Gemma stands there speechless as there's a knock on the door.

"Hold on," says Olive.

She opens the door and a man with a tool box sweeps in. "Vent problems with your cooling, hey?"

Olive nods and shows him in, then she says to Gemma, "Let's talk in my room." The guy eyeballs Gemma as they go.

⌒

The charcoal-grey walls in Olive's bedroom are undecorated. She has a small TV and stacks of DVDs. A dresser beside the bed, on top of which are picture frames, envelopes from a provincial agency, an electric kettle, and a glass container filled with tea. All her window shades are open and the room faces north. In the foreground, Gemma can see the big trees in the old part of town, and then beyond, the rec centre and the point where houses dissolve into bright yellow canola.

Olive turns on the kettle. Gemma sits on the carpet against the door and bends her knees. Finally, she says, "No, I don't remember what happened last night."

"You were messed up, girl."

"I'm sorry."

"Don't be sorry," Olive says. "I heard you two go to bed. Then I heard Ava crying. And then I heard—maybe you don't know this, but Ava punches herself in the face when she gets stressed."

"No," Gemma says after a silence. "I didn't know that."

"I came in. You looked real frightened when you saw me. Sorry about that. I get"—Olive pauses—"a bit mama bear about that woman. Now, is any of this jogging your memory?"

"No," Gemma whispers.

The kettle boils and Olive makes tea. She offers a cup to Gemma and Gemma shakes her head. "What happened after?"

"You were both a little hard to understand. It's probably better if you ask her," Olive says, looking Gemma in the eye. "And you should probably tell her you blacked out again."

Gemma nods, a lump in her throat.

"What I do know," Olive continues, "you said you liked her more than anybody else. 'Anybody else on this shit-ass fuckwatered planet' were your exact words, I believe. It broke the tension; we laughed. You're funny when you're hammered, by the way. But Ava was shocked by this, Gemma. She had no idea you wanted anything more than a place to crash and a good time before flouncing off."

"That's not it," says Gemma. "She told me she wanted me to leave. It hurt, but she told me that very clearly." *Didn't she? It seemed really obvious—*

Olive sighs, and Gemma realizes that Olive looks absolutely exhausted. "That girl." She dunks her tea bag. "You should talk straight with her about this, in a state where you can remember it all. I know she likes you. And sometimes she says dumb shit when she's scared. But last night, she said she'd love you to stay here a while. She said that to you directly, to your face."

"Oh my Lord," says Gemma. "Yes, of course I will."

"You said you would," Olive says plainly. "You're telling me the truth? You're sure?"

"Yes."

"Good," Olive says. "I need you to not hurt her, Gemma."

"I won't. Promise."

"I need you to keep that promise."

"Okay." Gemma feels like a stern gentleness in the universe has lit a match for her. They are silent for a while. Gemma's eyes drift to a picture frame on Olive's dresser, and she sees what looks like a younger Olive with a girl covered in tattoos. In the picture, Olive's laughing with her eyes shut, an arm around the tattooed girl. The girl has her hands up in a goofy "Who, me?" gesture.

"Is that you?" Gemma points.

"Yeah. Me and my friend Tracy."

"Where's she?"

"She's no longer alive," Olive says. "But she moved out west decades ago."

"I'm sorry," Gemma says. "I hate losing people."

"I don't even know anybody who knew her anymore," Olive says. "I'm the only one. Sometimes it breaks my heart so hard I can't even think about it."

Gemma is beginning to understand her place in this apartment, where she might fit, the three of them. Not completely, but some blanks are getting filled in.

With this also comes a latent understanding, something Gemma has subconsciously already known: if she ever wanted to quit drinking, and quit for good, she might be able to do that here. If she wanted to, she could do it here. With these two women, she could ask for their help and she could try.

Gemma has never felt that to be a real possibility with another soul. It feels nice.

"What was Tracy like?" Gemma asks.

Olive looks out the window, like she is deciding whether to answer. "She had a gorgeous voice. She was a beautiful singer. Legit talented. She was the kind of friend you could've seen actually making it, y'know?"

"Oh, wow."

"Yeah. I miss her. Always do I miss her. Only one other person I've been that close to besides Ava. Well—"

A strange light, gleeful and mournful, suddenly flickers in Olive's eyes.

"'Person.' Not always the right term, is it? But yeah, Tracy was something else. She helped me transition. And straight people didn't do that in my day. I changed my name again after she died, actually. Being Adrienne—that was my first name—it was too tied to her. I dunno. I couldn't deal with it."

"Damn."

Olive shrugs and sips her tea. She leans back against her headboard, settling. "So you're gonna hang out in this town you grew up in. What's that like?"

"Oh, shit. I don't know. It's been so long. Stuff's different. Small towns aren't supposed to change, but mine did. It's grown, too; it was smaller when I was a kid." Though as Gemma says this, she remembers the trick from yesterday, like a figure rising out of TV static.

Olive laughs and pulls up her blankets. "Give it time." Gemma remembers, too, her thought on the roof seeing Ava walk toward her, and then the morning after as she waited for Ava to come out of her room: *There is so very little I truly know about her.* She feels this truth now, in its iron mesh of beauty and warning.

"I do have to go out for a bit." Gemma stands. "Anything else we should talk about right now?"

"I don't think so. Inbox me when you're back. We'll get you a key on Monday."

"Cool." Gemma opens the door and Olive says, "Oh. Gemma?"

"Hm?"

Olive's face is turned to the window now, only her trails of grey-speckled hair visible over the covers as she speaks. "Waking up alone makes her sad."

$\backsim$

Gemma pops out onto South Railway in the sun. The skeeters aren't that bad as she crosses through the grass, up and over the tracks. She picks up Pepto and ginger chews at Pharmasave, and then walks up to the road that leads to the highway. She leans against the railing of the MTS building as a prairie breeze ripples around her shoulders.

Looking south, she can see their building from here, dwarfing all in town. When *had* they built that thing?

The doctor rings right on time, and they say pleasant hellos. "They have you workin' on a weekend, eh?" Gemma says.

"Yes." The doctor chuckles. "Saturday clinic. Five-day workweek's not what it used to be, that's for sure. I guess that's just our times now."

Gemma thinks about the A/C guy still in the apartment. Everything here used to shut down on Friday at six. Even on top of the old Sunday laws. (Though she guesses life is still like that in, you know, *Winkler*.) Gemma has a memory of her dad speeding to the IGA to make it before closing on a winter night.

Gemma bears no grudge against her father. He'd done what he needed to do in his life. And in that way, he'd given Gemma a gift, for Gemma has taken her cue from him and done the same.

"I see you want to discuss your blood work?" says the doctor. "Let's take a look here."

Centuries pass as the doctor's keyboard clacks.

"Your vitamin B_{12}'s a little low. You might want to take a supplement. Your estrogen levels look good. You had questions?"

Gemma shuts her eyes. *Just say it.* "My ferritin looked pretty high?" she says rapidly. "Should I be concerned about that?"

"Hmm."

She stares east down the highway. Across the road, a car door slams and shoes crunch on gravel.

"No, no, I don't think so." The doctor suddenly sounds irritable. "Ferritin can bump for a number of reasons. You're at three hundred and twenty micrograms per millilitre; I wouldn't be concerned about any level lower than four hundred."

Oh, thank God. "Is that so?"

"Yes. As far as I can see, you're healthy! Young and healthy and living your truth." (The doctor no longer sounds irritable.) "Anything else you'd like to talk about today? It doesn't have to be related to your blood work."

Got away with it again. Gemma grins to herself. *Another pass.*

Then: *One day, those passes will run out.*

She stands up in the wind. The breeze has picked up. She can feel the glint of rain in it. She should have brought her coat. "No. Thank you, doctor. Have a nice weekend. I hope it's sunny where you are."

She texts Ava and Olive, asks them if they need anything from the store. She wonders what they'll do for dinner—there are still plenty of leftovers, and she hopes that will be okay. Sometime in the next week, though, she'll suggest to Ava they get Marathon Pizza. Maybe invite Holly? Marathon's still around, bless them. Is Trav's open this early? It must be. She feels like sitting in Trav's for a minute. Ava texts back: *Can you get seltzer? I like raspberry.* Olive texts, too: *We're out of soap.* Gemma will swing by Giant Tiger. Cats. Gemma does wish they could get a cat, but hey—if Olive won't hear of it, then Olive won't hear of it.

Walking down Seventh Street, she sees a man in a tan jacket enter the old movie theatre. Looks like they use it for dance lessons now. Funny. Guess if you want to see a movie these days, you have to go to Winkler. It all jogs her memory of a boy from her past, a boy who'd played video games with her in middle school, a boy who tolerated her presence and in whom Gemma'd taken comfort. Few years before that, he and some other boys had said they'd show her something funny behind the school, and then suddenly she was on the ground with a shoe on her forehead. Grade four or something. Whatever. That was all such a long time ago. Who knows where that boy is now?

The door to the theatre swings back and forth. Gemma walks on and hits Stephen Street with a laugh. Who's going to complain? Not Gemma. Gemma doesn't complain.

$\backsim$

Well. That about brings us up to now. It's around noon and Ava's not home yet and Gemma is sitting on the bottle-green couch with the shade raised in front of the number three highway, a thin slice of grey under after-rain clouds, carrying this corner of the world through green and yellow and light. She's a little buzzed off two beers from Trav's and Olive is in her room. Gemma knows she has something special, a pass she cannot waste. Peace fills every pore of her at once, as if she'd stepped out the window to walk on the sky and a wind of stardust had swirled through her body and shot her higher, like she was nothing, nothing, nothing.

Blackouts are gun-toting enemies fused to one's back, pale, disinterested monsters impassive to the ruin of ricochet. Can they ever surprise with unintentional kindness? Make sufficient the evil of the day? A gift untraceable to either heaven or hell, a glowing orb that can't be trusted, but neither can it be refused? Gemma feels like maybe she can trust these two. She'll find out if that's the case. She'll figure it out. She is a woman about to attempt to be alive for the millionth fucking time.

Gemma presses her nose to the window while Olive blinks in and out of sleep while Ava and Holly laugh at a workstation while a pocket universe unspools. Gemma had that only partway right. It begins as a universe as hopeful and possible as any other. It will quietly weave its own fence posts, it will discover its rhythm and order.

FLOODWAY

I was out front of the Toad after closing time with a bunch of other weirdos. I started talking with this short guy with curly hair. "You want to get a king can?" he said. His name was Owen. "I'm not from here," he kept saying. "I grew up in a small town." Owen was from Île-des-Chênes. He was pretty, and he was nice without being attentive, and I liked that about him.

We were drinking our last one in the parking lot when Owen's friends drove by. "We're going to see the meteor shower! Out by the floodway, wanna come?"

In 1950, the Red River catastrophically overflowed. It destroyed four of Winnipeg's bridges, blanketing the valley to the south. In the years after, they built the floodway: a long, giant drainage culvert dug into the side of the prairie. It sends the river away from the city when it floods. They called it Duff's Ditch after Duff Roblin, the premier, and my dad always said they voted him out ASAP because of how much money it cost. My dad loved to say that, but I looked it up and it wasn't true. The guy was re-elected twice.

To answer Owen's friends, I did want to go to the floodway, yes. "I can get my dad's car. I've got keys," I said to Owen. "We can follow them."

I went to pick up the car and drove back and got Owen and added Amy, a quiet punk with a black hoodie and no makeup and a backpack.

We stopped at Mac's for smokes, and I pissed in the alley. This was back when I lived on Spence.

Out by the floodway, we lay on blankets and someone produced beers. We tried to watch the meteor shower, but mostly the sky was blank—occasional traces of falling dots you strained to see, the opposite of a spectacle, the city lights still too bright out here.

But the guys were clowning around, and the sky was still beautiful, and I drank my beer lying on the blanket, looking up. "Josh on his way?" "He's twelve miles past Beausejour." "Twelve Miles Past Beausejour is the name of my new Nickelback cover band." And I said nothing, and it was so nice to just be and not need or be needed.

Then Owen's friends said they were going farther out, to really see the shower. We were totally in, and we got back in the car and followed them. They drove west for a while, and then turned south onto the number seventy-five highway.

We drove for a while. Then another while. The city was long behind us. Owen's phone was dead, so we couldn't call his friends.

I started to get worried.

Amy said, "Does anyone mind if I open a beer?"

We didn't. But Owen's friends kept fucking driving! All the way to fucking Morris! The only stop between the city and the border, the only place for miles in the country with a gas station open at night.

They stopped at that gas station and we got out. We said, "What the fuck?" But they were just as surprised. "You drove all this way? Why didn't you turn around?! We were just out of gas." It struck me, later, how there's a divide in the expectation of whether someone will be concerned for you, or not, and how sometimes that divide falls along gendered lines (and sometimes not).

It was past four a.m. and we were zonked. We turned around to drive home. And then, as dawn filtered into the sky, Owen's friends pulled over and jumped out of the car.

There's a singular tree off the number seventy-five at that point just north of Morris. The boys ran across the road toward it, through the field, gradually lit by the slow prairie light. Owen and I sat on the hood of the car with a blanket wrapped around us and watched his friends climb in the sunrise. They looked beautiful.

Did we kiss then? You know, I don't remember. I only remember how his body felt against mine under the blanket, how his friends looked like ants on the horizon, bathed in yellow and orange.

Back in Winnipeg, we dropped Amy off, and then went to Owen's place in South Osborne. Inside were empty beer bottles and a room-mate freshly home from work, a guy with a mean look to him, that look certain young men have that says they're fucking their lives up now, and maybe they'll be doing the same in two decades, or maybe they'll own a house with a pool and shithead kids.

By then it was full daylight. Owen led me into his room: a single mattress and scattered piles of crap on the carpet. We lay on the mattress and made out. I told him I was trans, but it seemed like he'd guessed that. He asked some stupid questions, and then he stopped. I started jerking him off, said I wanted him to fuck me. He stopped moving and stared at the ceiling.

I can take a hint, you know? I got up and walked out the door so I could give the car back and sleep a few hours before my shift. I never saw Owen again, but one evening, a month later, I woke up to a sunset and I remembered when the sun had risen over the tree with his body next to mine under the blanket, and a softness in my heart awakened and said, *What if you hadn't run away?* That night, I went to the beer vendor and asked after him, as one of his friends from that night worked there. The friend was the guy who said we should leave the floodway.

The friend was heartened that I'd asked after Owen. He gave me his number, said, "You should get in touch with him." The friend looked hopeful as he said it. I wonder if I could've communicated to him. How as soon I took the number down, I knew. I knew I would be too chickenshit, too courageless to crack the door on even the chance of a good outcome. I didn't have the courage. That was a long time ago, and I lost the number, but I still remember the feeling.

Acknowledgments

The stories in this book were written across many Canadian provinces and US states. I've called a lot of places home, but nowhere more than the prairies of Treaty 1 territory, homeland of the Metis Nation. I am grateful to be from there.

Friends who read these stories first—I couldn't have written this without you, thank you: Jeanne Thornton, Meredith Russo, Cat Fitzpatrick, Daniel Shank Cruz, Calvin Gimpelevich, Alison Pick, Kai Taddei, Alex Leslie, Kyle Lukoff, Nathan Dueck, Grace Kehler, Lindsay Wong, Hazel Jane Plante, Mapes Thorson, Patty Yumi Cottrell, Torrey Peters, Jessica Westhead, Alexis N. Wright. Particular thanks to Michael Hingston for his work on "Hazel & Christopher," and enormous gratitude to the best writing group: Rebecca Novack, Megan Milks, Craig Willse, Ayeh Bandeh-Ahmadi, Raechel Anne Jolie, and Svetlana Kitto. Finally, an overwhelming thank-you to Shirarose Wilensky. You're a stellar editor, and this book and I have been fortunate to have you.

A big thanks to all the sweet, hard-working souls at Arsenal Pulp—Brian Lam, Robert Ballantyne, Cynara Geissler, Jazmin Welch, Jaiden Dembo, you're true publishing angels, all!

Thank you to the Canada Council for the Arts and Princeton's Hodder Fellowship for invaluable financial support. Thank you to MacDowell and PLAYA for providing residency space and quiet, and thank you to my cohorts at both for your friendship and kinship

(and dance parties, croquet showdowns, the Democracy Express, the Paisley Saloon ...)

Thanks to Sybil Lamb and Carly Bodnar for teaming up to art battle on a gorgeous fucking cover. Thanks to Kate Friggle for the joke about hormones being bullshit. Thanks to Imogen Binnie for the phrasing of starting as one cis person and ending up another. Thanks to Erika Lopez for that hairbrush idea, *Flaming Iguanas* forever. Thanks to Jeff Randall for saying in a key moment, "You give so much and you get so little." Thanks to Cat Fitzpatrick once more, as we pondered a memory, and you gave me the phrase "excitement and embattlement." Thanks to loveandcrossbones's Threadless for an excellent I JUST WANT TO BE GAY IN SPACE WITH YOU T-shirt that I still wear. Thanks to the crew at Biblioasis, who understood I had to go. And thanks to Joni Pedersen for the Biophilia Party—there was no better way to be unknowingly sent off into quarantine.

In "Enough Trouble," the Miriam Toews quote is from *Swing Low*: "It's just something that happens sometimes, a story as old as time, and this time it happened to me." The Megan Nash song they all listen to is "Summer"; it's Prairie Voices singing Eric Whitacre's "A Boy and a Girl." And the show they're watching is *Party Down*—big ups to Kellen Cozzens and Dillon Flynn for turning me on to that one. Thanks, too, to Sherri Klassen for your essay "Four Mennonite Morality Tales and a Revolution in Russia."

I must obviously beg apologies from the Winklerites—if you made it this far, you know I write with love! And thanks to my mom, my dad, and Harold, three very different people who all never cease to ask nor answer questions.

To the Oregon crew of Olde, how could I even begin ... you were all my first adopted home. If I even tried to name you all, I'd run out of page space so fast. So I'll just say: Sarah, I love you, I miss you. Shads, Eric, Russell, Em, I love you all always. Tara and Glo, 2009 changed my life and I'll never forget it. Ashley and Jess, let's bathe in a fountain sometime. Everyone else, you know who you are <3.

Shout-out to the hilarious, caring, wild, beautiful, dreamy denizens of Instar Books Radio. I'm so glad I didn't have to experience pandemic life without you.

And thanks once more to the housemates who put up with me. Gwen, Kiki, Sybil, the results are in and the House of Lamb Sandwich will live forever. As for everyone else, if you're ever rolling through Windsor, stop at Villains for karaoke and the DH for a meal. Get the Wake Up! burger.

CASEY PLETT is the author of the novel *Little Fish* and the short story collection *A Safe Girl to Love*. She is the winner of the Amazon Canada First Novel Award, the Firecracker Award for Fiction, and two-time winner of the Lambda Literary Award for Transgender Fiction. She co-edited (with Cat Fitzpatrick) *Meanwhile, Elsewhere: Science Fiction and Fantasy from Transgender Writers*, which won the ALA Stonewall Book Award-Barbara Gittings Literature Award, and she has written for the *New York Times*, *McSweeney's Internet Tendency*, *Maclean's*, and *them*, among others.